BREAKING POINT

Chris Colt tried to walk a tightrope between divided loyalties. Nephew of the gunmaker Samuel Colt, and Chief of Scouts in the U.S. Cavalry, he could not betray his flag. But as a blood brother of Chief Crazy Horse and trusted friend of the Indians, he could not aid the army's treaty-shredding onslaught against the Nez Perce in their fight through Montana t...

...Cavalry on foot, a ... ... into the In-... village. Col... ... large sergeant viciously swing his rifle up, the butt smashing a woman under the jaw. Her baby fell on the ground and the NCO's size-twelve boot smashed the toddler's head.

Colt screamed, *"No!"* His hands flashed down to his pistols and came up, the right gun bucking in Chris's palm. A big spot of red spread on the sergeant's chest. Colt wheeled around to face the swarm of other murderously marauding troopers. He yelled, "Try me, I'm not a woman."

Chris Colt's tightrope had snapped. . . .

HORSE SOLDIERS

HORSE SOLDIERS

by
Don Bendell

Chief of Scouts,
Volume 2

A SIGNET BOOK

SIGNET
Published by the Penguin Group
Penguin Books USA Inc., 375 Hudson Street,
New York, New York 10014, U.S.A.
Penguin Books Ltd, 27 Wrights Lane,
London W8 5TZ, England
Penguin Books Australia Ltd, Ringwood,
Victoria, Australia
Penguin Books Canada Ltd, 10 Alcorn Avenue,
Toronto, Ontario, Canada M4V 3B2
Penguin Books (N.Z.) Ltd, 182–190 Wairau Road,
Auckland 10, New Zealand

Penguin Books Ltd, Registered Offices:
Harmondsworth, Middlesex, England

First published by Signet, an imprint of Dutton Signet,
a division of Penguin Books USA Inc.

First Printing, December, 1993
10 9 8 7 6 5 4 3 2 1

Cover illustration by Ron Lesser.

REGISTERED TRADEMARK—MARCA REGISTRADA

Printed in the United States of America

Believe it or not, this book is dedicated to a horse, but he was also more than a horse: he was my friend. With his bloodline dating all the way back to Chief Joseph's brilliant animal husbandry program and development of the Appaloosa breed, Hawk was a true Appaloosa and was very tall, jet-black with a white rump and black spots on it. He saved my life several times, won me some blue ribbons in gymkhanas, a trophy for "All-Around Cowboy" at a ranch rodeo, and several stake races. He loved herding cattle, and we chased bears, mountain lions, deer, elk, and sometimes the rainbow, on almost every peak in Colorado's Sangre de Cristo mountain range. The poem about Hawk is based on a true story and tells what he was all about.

—Don Bendell

HAWK

Hawk's air-spring muscles helped him glide
So swiftly down the mountainside.
With sinew-bulging spotted rump
He vaulted o'er a rocky hump.

Descendant of Chief Joseph's herd,
Hawk's canter was like flying bird.
Swollen streams couldn't break his stride,
His head held high with Nez Perce pride.

I rode that steed with fleeting speed,
His strong legs breaking through high weed.
Hailstones splattered, horseshoes clattered,
And a flock of sage grouse scattered.

On shale slid Hawk tripped and stumbled.
Down the slope we flipped and tumbled.
Then snowflakes started swirling down.
As I lay hurt on rocky ground.

I was dazed, my body aching,
Dizzy, sore, and both legs shaking.
We both felt pain from heads to toes,
Yet hurt, Hawk raised me with his nose.

I wrapped my wounds and, mounting, moaned,
Said, "Come on, Hawk, now take us home."

Around his neck my arms were tied.
He started down the mountainside.

I dreamed of being safe and warm,
As Hawk plowed through that raging storm,
And somewhere on that awful trek,
I slumped across that great arched neck.

Then thoughts came flooding in my head.
My wife sat crying by my bed.
I won't forget those words she said.
"He brought you home . . . but Hawk is dead.

"For three full days you've been asleep.
The snow outside is five feet deep.
Once you were home and safe and sound
Hawk whinnied once, then dead fell down."

She said, "He brought you here on will
And fell while coming down that hill.
His legs were gone, but he still came,
And when he stopped, you breathed his name."

"Oh, no! My God, it just can't be!"
The screams were coming out of me.
"Oh, please don't tell me Hawk has died!"
Then my wife held me while I cried.

I know he wasn't man, of course,
But just a big old spotted horse.
So tell me, should I miss him so?
A friend who took me through the snow.

—Don Bendell
from *Songs of the Warrior*

"Hear me, my chiefs! I am tired. My heart is sick and sad. From where the sun now stands I will fight no more, forever."

—Chief Joseph of the Nez Perce nation
October 5, 1877, Snake Creek, Montana

But on our trail, horse-soldiers in darkness came,
With hope to surprise us. Fools—
With gear jangles and horse fart! Though we needed not that.
At the heart of the night we heard what we heard—
The wailful howl of the sad coyote.
But no coyote! It was our scout.
He lay there in the darkness, owl-eyed, deer-eared.
At dawn they came to surprise us.
Surprise! It was theirs.

From "Chief Joseph of the Nez Perce"
by Robert Penn Warren

Chapter 1

>>>>>>>>>>>>>>>>>>>>

The Scout

The rifle shot echoed off the black rock canyon walls and bounced upstream. The battle was fierce, and the lone rider tried to identify the weapons by the sound of the gunfire. He was careful as he walked his big black and white paint down the fast-running whitewater stream. He had been following the tracks for several hours, simply because this was some of the wildest country in the American West, and he needed to know who was near him.

He had rendezvoused a few days earlier with his blood brother Crazy Horse in the Yellowstone and killed Will Sawyer—a giant of a man who was very much in need of killing. The rider was traveling west, but he had cut down through the Grand Tetons, deciding to take the easier route to Oregon along the Snake River. His destination was Fort Lapwai, where he was to report to old "One-Arm" himself, Brigadier General Otis Owen Howard, whom the soliders called "the Bible-reading general."

He had left the woman he loved, Shirley Ebert, at her restaurant in Bismarck, North Dakota Territory.

But she vowed that she would be there for him when he returned.

The stream he now rode was teeming with brook trout, rainbows, and cutthroat and had provided him with some good eating for breakfast. If he had known how the day was going to turn out, maybe he would have stayed upstream and fished all day.

The sounds of gunfire kept getting louder and the echoes were now passing beyond him going up the vertical canyon walls. The mountains all around were majestic and unforgiving. These were not gentle, easy, sloping mountains, but harsh, black granite sentinels to the Far West. Snowcapped and treeless halfway up, they went straight up to the clouds, and the Creator didn't stop to worry about travelers' ease and comfort when he created them. He did, however, think about something to rest your eyes on and take your breath away when you've had a hard day of pushing cows, hunting buffalo, or riding on patrol.

The tall man knew that the gunfire was now coming from just around the bend in the canyon wall. Movement. Two bald eagles came up the canyon, apparently spooked by the gunfire. They flew overhead, and the man couldn't help but think about what a good totem that was for most Indian nations.

He pulled his Henry rifle out and jacked a round in the chamber, eased the hammer off, and held it across the swells of his saddle. His sixteen-hands-tall horse knew that something was amiss, and it seemed to pick its steps more carefully. Nostrils flaring, its ears pricked forward trying to home in on any sound, no matter how slight.

The man whispered to his horse, "What do you think, War Bonnet, will they notice us?"

He laughed at his own joke. War Bonnet had been a gift to him from Crazy Horse, and ever since, he kept the Indian's accoutrements on the mount—three red coup stripes around each foreleg, a red handprint on each rump, and several eagle feathers attached to his mane and tail. Whoever was in the battle around the bend would certainly notice him.

The man himself would be hard to miss, as well. He looked like the type that men would want to have as their commander in combat, that women would want to have beside them in bed, and citizens would want as their town marshal. He wore yellow-striped cavalry pants, cowboy boots and spurs, a floppy leather scout's hat with a beaded hatband, a fringed elkskin Lakotah (Sioux) war shirt with colorful porcupine quillwork on it, and a worn but well-maintained gunbelt and a quick-draw holster with a pearl-handled Colt .44 revolver. He also had, on the other hip, a large Bowie knife in a fringed and colorfully beaded sheath.

The man stood a bit higher than six feet and had a ruggedly handsome face, which looked like he had spent more nights under the stars than indoors. His hazel eyes normally went to green, and his dark brown hair lent a sharp contrast to them when the light hit them just right. They also had little smile creases in the corners that made them look like he had a secret joke he was sharing with someone.

The man eased his course around the bend following the numerous unshod and five sets of shod hoofprints. He knew exactly how many people were there, their sexes, and their nationality, because he was an excellent tracker and scout. In fact, he was a sought-after chief of scouts for the U.S. Cavalry. His exploits were fast becoming legendary. He could read a track and figure out an entire story from it.

By studying the tracks for a number of miles, he had seen that five white men were pushing a herd of unshod horses. Not only that, he knew that the horses were spotted. He knew they were spotted because the herd climbed over and around rocks without slips or falls, where other breeds of horses would have balked at even crossing that rough terrain. The horses were Appaloosas, the spotted breed of mountain horses developed by the Nez Perce nation of American Indians. He also was able to tell that two more unshod horses were following the herd and these two had riders, both young, both Nez Perce. The occasional moccasin tracks were similar to those of the Lakotah (Sioux) or Chyela (Cheyenne), except that the braves in those two tribes walked more pigeon-toed, but the Nez Perce walked with their feet pointed straight ahead. Also, because of walking more in mountainous country the Nez Perce walked with the heel first and toe second, but the Sioux and Cheyenne walked just the opposite when stalking an enemy.

These two young people were stalking the white men. The rider saw several places where one of them would leave the trail, ride to higher ground, hide his horse, and sneak to a vantage point to watch the white quarry they were following. The tracker assumed they were young because of the lightness of their bodies and small size of their tracks. He figured one was around twelve years old and the other around ten. He knew they were boys and not girls because of some of the stalking techniques they had employed that would have been taught to young boys by older warriors. They followed the herd without walking over the tracks to keep from spoiling any possible clues hidden in the trail and to help avoid being discovered by someone checking their back trail.

The gunfire stopped, and the tracker heard the sound of voices and laughter. A few minutes later he rounded the corner and stopped his big paint. The gorge widened out into a small bowl, and a herd of spotted horses milled around.

Two young Indian boys were in the midst of five very rough-looking characters. Three of the men were bearded, one was baby-faced, one was Latin in appearance with a long black mustache down to his jawline. Two of the bearded men were black. All five wore dirty clothing and wore guns in holsters that had been well used. The Mexican was short and wiry, while the other four looked like they had easily pulled stumps out of the ground many times.

One of the black hombres held the older youth and laughed with the others as the baby-faced man held the ten-year-old by the throat and punched him repeatedly in the stomach. The boy's body was limp and lifeless, blood pouring from his mouth, nose, and right ear. He grabbed the boy by the legs and held him high overhead ready to toss him against the rocks.

The tracker fired a bullet into the man's chest, and he fell dead, the boy landing on top of his bloody body.

The other four stared at him as he rode slowly forward, his Henry trained on the group. They thought about going for their guns, but to a man they realized this was no dude. They raised their arms; and when they did, the twelve-year-old spun, yanking the knife out of the belt of the man who held him, and rammed it to the hilt into the man's midsection. The black cowboy's eyes opened wide in horror, and he stood straight up on his toes, a long low howl coming from his mouth. His mouth suddenly twisted into fury and he took two steps forward, his arms outstretched, ready to squeeze the life out of the boy, while his own drained out of his body. The boy stood his ground and spit at the outlaw, but the dying man kept coming forward. The tracker fired a shot at the feet of the outlaw, but he ignored it and grabbed the boy.

The tracker shot him through the head, and the rest made sure their hands were high in the air.

The Nez Perce boy kicked the dead bodies of both men, then checked the heartbeat of his little partner. He looked sad. His eyes met the tracker's, and he shook his head no. The buckskin-clad man felt a fury inside that was hard to control.

The boy walked over to the tracker and, turning, stared at the remaining men with deep hatred in his gaze.

Until now, nobody had spoken, but finally one of the

men, the white bearded one said, "Yer damned sure biting off one hell of a hunk a tough jerky here, mister. What's yer name?"

The tracker said, "Colt. Christopher Columbus Colt. But my friends call me Chris. You can call me Mr. Colt. Drop your gunbelts."

The men all got a surprised look on their faces when he said his name. This man was famous on the frontier already, and he was still relatively young.

He signed to the young man, "Go-get-weapons-bring-to-me."

The Nez Perce boy scurried to each man and picked up their variety of weapons, belts, and holsters. He brought them to Colt and dropped them at the feet of the big paint, War Bonnet.

Colt looked at the Mexican and said, "Okay, amigo, what's the story?"

The man said, "We were hired to, Colt."

Colt said, "I told you gentlemen that you can call me Mr. Colt."

The Mexican sneered and said, "Like I say, Colt, we were—"

Boom!

The Mexican fell on the ground screaming, blood running out around the sides of his hands and between his fingers, while he grasped what was left of his right ear. He stood up again, pulling his kerchief off with his left hand and pushing it against the bleeding ear.

Colt was a tough man. You had to be tough to accomplish what he had, and he knew men like this. He had dealt with these types before, so he knew that he had to get and maintain the upper hand. If he showed any sign or indication of weakness at all, he and the Nez Perce boy were dead. These men were like buzzards, or more like a pack of coyotes.

Since they recognized his name when he mentioned it, he knew that his reputation probably would help intimidate them, too.

Colt had been born and raised in northeastern Ohio, Cuyahoga Falls, near Akron. His father and his father's brother were estranged, but his parents did let him visit his uncle on occasion. His uncle was the famous Colonel Samuel Colt, the founder and owner of Colt Firearms. Young Chris learned from the Colt gunsmiths—many of them former shootists, or gunfighters—just about everything he would ever need to know about firearms.

He left home as a youngster, lied about his age, and joined the 171st Regiment of the Ohio National Guard, fighting for the Union in the Civil War. Colt ended up scouting and running clandestine operations deep into Confederate territory, reporting directly to the regimental commander. Not only was this very dangerous but incredible as well, in that Chris Colt was the youngest man—boy, actually—in the entire regiment. After the war, he went west for adventure and excitement and new places to see. He didn't really care about fortune.

He had spent time as a lawman, cattle driver, stagecoach driver, and guard, but most of his time had been spent as a scout and tracker for the U.S. Cavalry. He was so good with a gun that he could have been a famous shootist, but that was the last thing he wanted.

Chris Colt wanted his life to stand for something, to mean something important. He did not like the regimentation of army life, so he worked as a civilian contractor as a scout and later chief of scouts.

Marrying a beautiful young woman of the Minniconjou tribal circle of the Lakotah nation named Chantapeta, Chris was very happy and became very close to the Lakotah, the Sioux. They had a little girl, whom they named Winona, which meant "First Born." A raiding war party of Crows, however, raped and murdered his wife and daughter. Colt didn't hate the Crow over it. He understood how it was, with the war between the red men and the white men, and between the red nations.

He had, in fact, just worked alongside Crows and Arikaras when he was chief of scouts for the recently deceased General George Armstrong Custer of the Seventh Cavalry. Having become good friends with Crazy Horse, Colt had first gotten in trouble with Custer and was arrested because he wanted to save his new love, the beautiful Shirley Ebert of Bismarck, North Dakota Territory, who had been kidnapped. Chris escaped, then was captured and held by Crazy Horse and witnessed the death of Custer and his command at the Battle of the Greasy Grass. Colt had decided never to tell that he witnessed Custer's fall, or the military might question his loyalty. In actuality, he had been prepared to fight against Crazy Horse or anyone else, alongside Custer, the man he hated and despised.

Because he had gone after Shirley and returned with her after she was kidnapped and traded to the Sioux, he was an even bigger hero in the white community. When he and Crazy Horse met, Colt had had his horse shot out from under him by Crazy Horse's warriors and was very courageous in facing the many braves. His courage impressed Crazy Horse, the famous Oglala war hero, so much that the warrior gave Colt his own prized horse.

He was in love with Shirley Ebert, and she with him. She, however, understood that his work would take him far away, for long stretches of time. She told him that he could see other women as long as he didn't fall in love with them. Colt knew that he couldn't love other women. His heart belonged to Shirley.

The young Nez Perce boy knew that he had to help this big warrior fight their enemies, so he would mourn over the death of his younger brother later when it was safer.

Colt said, "What is your name, boy?"

The boy said, "I am called in your language Ezekiel. In my language my name means Boy Who Bites the Badger."

Chris said, "You speak English good. Learn from missionaries."

"Yes, Catholic," Ezekiel replied.

"Okay, Ezekiel," Chris went on, "how about grabbing their ropes off their saddles and we'll fix these gents up."

The surviving men were not in a mood to argue, or even chance blinking their eyes. Colt had made believers of the men.

"What is your nation?" Colt asked, already knowing the answer.

Ezekiel replied, "I am Nez Perce with the band of Hin-Ma-Too-Yah-Lat-Kekht."

The white man said, "Who the hell is that?"

Chris laughed. He didn't speak the tongue of the Pierced Noses, but he knew that name.

He replied, "Thunder Traveling to Loftier Mountain Heights."

"What the hay?"

Colt laughed and said, "White people know him as Chief Joseph."

Chris looked down at Ezekiel who had gathered the ropes by now and said, "I am on my way to where your band lives."

"You go to work for the bluecoat father who has one arm."

Colt grinned and said, "How do you know I'm going to work for General Howard?"

Ezekiel laughed. "You said your name is Colt. All know the name of the great scout Colt. Joseph said you are like the strawberry that has been covered with snow."

Colt, surprised that Joseph had heard of him, said, "Why did he say that?"

"He said that because you are white on the outside but red on the inside."

Chris laughed and climbed down from his horse, which stood still, ground-reined. The Lakotah used to put a very long lead line on a horse that was a herd leader, usually a mare. Whenever they had to gather a herd quickly, they simply went out and caught that one and the others would follow. Chris Colt taught his horse how to ground rein shortly after he got him from Crazy Horse. He simply buried a log under the ground and had a piece of rope with a snap coming up from the ground. He would ride the horse up to that spot and get off, dropping the reins on the ground. While the horse really didn't understand what was going on, he hooked the buried line to the chin strap at the bottom of the horse's bridle. Every time the horse tried to move, he would tug at the line and was unable to budge. It didn't take long before War Bonnet would stand perfectly still until his master came to him, gathered up his reins, and mounted.

Within ten minutes Colt had tied each of the men backward in his saddle. Hands tied behind them, the men had their hands tied to their saddle horns. They also were bound around the arms with numerous wraps, and each man had his feet tied into the stirrups and the rope was run under the horse's chest.

The Mexican protested, "I weel bleed to death, señor! Please?"

Colt laughed and said, "No, I believe you're going to die of hemp fever. You quit bleeding several minutes ago."

The white man said, "Hemp fever! You're gonna lynch us?"

"No, but I'm sure the law will."

The black one said, "For what, killin' injuns?"

"No, I didn't even ask Ezekiel here, but I guarantee you stole this herd of Appaloosas from the Nez Perce.

Now, if you want, I'll take you to Chief Joseph instead of the nearest law."

"I'll take chances with the law, uh, Mr. Colt," said the white one.

"Fine," Chris said. "I'm sure they'll be happy with you characters doing what you can to start a war with the Nez Perce."

The black one spoke. "What if our horse bolts while we're tied like this, or our horse falls?"

"Then you might die. Should have thought of that before riding the owl hoot trail, mister. Honest men might not make big cash sums, but they usually don't have to worry about being tied backward on their horse, either."

Ezekiel said, "My brother Little Red Crow and I guard the herd. These men take. We follow. I must take ponies back."

Chris gave the youngster an appraising glance. "You followed these crooks all these hundreds of miles. Did the camp know you followed them?"

"Yes," Ezekiel said. "I told them that it was my job to do. My brother followed. Can we bury him first?"

"There is water, shelter, firewood, and graze. We will make camp in this place," Chris said. "Then we will make your brother ready for his spirit journey."

Ezekiel choked back his emotions. "It is a good thing."

Later, Colt untied the three men and let them bury their partners. He also let the black one bandage the ear of the Mexican. Chris then went through their saddlebags, taking what ammunition he needed, and took their food out to use. The three men were tied to trees and a campfire was built. Colt wrapped the men in sitting positions with their blankets.

The white one said, "Mr. Colt, are we ta sleep this way?"

"Yep," Colt said.

The black one asked, "Are we gonna git fed?"

"Nope."

The Mexican started to say something, but when Chris turned his head to listen, the man shut up quickly, thinking about his partially amputated ear.

Colt fixed a meal of beans, coffee, bacon, and biscuits. Afterward, he allowed the boy and himself a cigarette. He didn't smoke much, preferring cigars when he did, but occasionally the scout would roll a cigarette and enjoy it. With the Indians, tobacco was a real luxury and used in conjunction with spiritual ceremonies, along with relaxation.

The next day they departed after daybreak, leaving behind a small valley containing the bodies of two greedy men and one small boy. The slate-gray cliffs shot straight up toward the heavens, standing guard over the burial sites.

Chris reflected on that as they left the gorge. He thought about the many piles of bones he had seen, over the years, in the desert, out on the prairie, and up in the mountains. So many men, like himself, had left home at a young age and wandered toward the horizon where they had been watching the sun set every night. Colt wondered how many of those lost souls had wandered into a Comanche hunting party that didn't care for white-skinned intruders, how many had been struck by lightning out on the wide flat prairie, or how many had tumbled off a cliff into some lonesome gulch. The scout pictured families sitting at home, for years, wondering about the fate of a sister or brother with wanderlust who hadn't answered any letters for several years. He wondered if he might become one of those unnamed skeletons someday. Colt also wondered how many people would miss him if he disappeared.

They pushed farther down the canyon, their minds set on the Snake River. Colt studied the young Nez Perce lad out of the corner of his eye. The boy sat his Appaloosa proudly, eyes straight ahead and back very erect. His young copper body blended into the rhythm of the spotted horse's movements, one with the pony.

The boy noticed Chris looking his way and gave the big scout a quizzical look.

"Quite an equestrian aren't you, young man?" Colt chuckled.

"Huh?" the little warrior said.

"Never mind."

They came down out of the rough rocks around noon and passed into a large valley choked with hardwoods and evergreens. Several ice-cold streams cascaded down canyon walls and cut swaths through the forested gorge.

Chris Colt loved the smell and sound as they rode through the stately pines and firs. He heard Ezekiel chuckling now and turned his head toward him.

The young warrior said, "I see it on your face, Colt.

You are like the Nez Perce. You hear brother wind singing a song in the big trees and like his words. There, hear it? That way, the *wapiti* calls far off. He wants to fight another, for he is truly a powerful warrior. Up there, listen to it, Great Scout, do you hear it?"

"A red-tailed hawk."

"He cries out to the rabbits down here," Ezekiel said. " 'Watch out! I am up here, and I am looking for you.' "

Chris said, "How do you know that he is not saying, 'Please don't attack me, rabbits. I want to land down there, but I am afraid of you.' "

Ezekiel laughed loudly. "He would never say that. For he is the hunter, and they are the prey. That would be like the great Wamble Uncha telling these bad white-eyes that he is afraid of them and wants them to leave him alone."

The three men looked over at the boy, then the man. All three of them shook their heads, as if they had planned it like a synchronized cavalry troop movement.

Colt said, "Do you smell the bear, little one?"

"Yes, his smell is on the wind which runs into our faces," Ezekiel replied.

Colt reined his horse and those of the other three. The boy stopped next to him and looked at his eyes scanning like a Nez Perce warrior's. His eyes panned the ground immediately to their front going left to right, then viewed a few yards farther out and scanned back to the left. He then viewed even farther out, his eyes going left to right again, checking every little piece of foliage and terrain, looking for a telltale patch of fur. The herd acted nervous.

"Señor," the Mexican bandit whispered, "what is it you look for? Ees it Indios?"

"Better hope not," Colt replied quietly without looking. "Now keep quiet."

His nostrils flared in and out slightly as he sniffed the air. He looked to Ezekiel like a mighty bear himself testing the wind.

The scout said, "He is between us and the ponies. See how they're moving forward fast now? They are beyond the smell and just want to get away. If he makes a charge, you take the horses and these critters, and I'll get between you and him and shoot him. No matter what, keep going."

Colt thought back to his first grizzly bear. He had been out with his father-in-law on a scout looking for a bison herd. On the way back to the camp circle they made camp in a stand of cottonwoods next to a creek. The two men were sent up a tree for two hours by a very angry sow grizzly, which wandered along the creek bed with her two cubs. They could have shot her, but not with cubs.

Chris felt the bear's presence, and it scared the heck out of him. It was close, but he couldn't pick up any sign of it.

Suddenly, with a tremendous roar and a rush, a giant silvertip grizzly came from the thicket on the uphill side of the trail. This monster stood over eight feet tall on its hind legs, and looked to weigh well over a ton and a half.

A grizzly bear, on level ground, could outrun a race-horse in a short distance, and this big boar was no exception. He closed the distance between the thicket and Colt in seconds and the scout barely had time to spin and fire from the hip, his bullet taking the bruin in the front of the left shoulder with little or no effect.

The bear slammed against the rib cage of War Bonnet, its teeth popping and a roar emanating from deep in its chest that reverberated through the canyon like a mighty avalanche. Colt flew sideways and the horse rolled once and bolted toward the herd and fleeing men in front of him. The bear stopped and stood on its hind legs, nose testing the wind, while it swung its watermelon-sized head from side to side.

Ezekiel hesitated. Colt yelled, "Go! Save the horses!"

The bear dropped to all fours and faced the intruder again. Colt raised his pistol, aiming at the bear's face. The bruin charged and Chris fired, the bullet glancing off the bear's skull, creating a crease along its head. The bear slammed into Colt and only the pistol saved Chris from the mighty teeth and jaws, as the bear bit down on the gun, mangling it.

The grizzly took a quick swipe at a sapling. The tree splintered in half. Colt pulled his horn-handled Bowie knife from the beaded sheath on his left hip and switched it to his right hand, facing the shaggy killer. The bear stared at Colt through little pig eyes. Heavy breaths poured out between spike-sized teeth.

Colf felt no fear. He was conditioned not to feel fear until the combat was over. Much like many of the cavalry troopers he scouted for and American Indian warriors he fought against, he would feel great fear when the danger was past, but right now his head was clear. His nerves were steady. His adrenaline coursed through his body and he was prepared to match his wits and strength against this superior foe. He knew the odds, but he felt that he could not be defeated.

With a roar like Satan unchained, the bear charged. Colt stood his ground and the big furry body slammed into Chris with tremendous force, but Colt fell backward and let the big body pass over him, striking upward full power and thrusting the big Bowie into the buggy-sized chest just behind the left front leg.

With agility that seemed incredible for its size, the grizzly jumped in the air with a loud roar and twisted its body at the same time, biting at the knife that was buried to the hilt behind the joint. It rolled beyond Chris Colt who lay unconscious on the ground, his head having slammed into a flat rock when the bear crashed into him.

Chantapeta, Chris Colt's wife, wore a soft buckskin dress as she tiptoed into the tepee and wakened him with a large apple pie. Colt smiled and looked at the steam coming off the apple pie and thought about how good it would taste. Then he frowned while lying on his buffalo blanket. How could a Lakotah woman make an apple pie, in a pie pan, in the middle of a Minniconjou village? He couldn't figure it out, and it made his head hurt. He looked from the pie to her and she had changed into the woman he loved, Shirley Ebert. Long, naturally curly auburn hair hanging down well below her shoulders, she had a smile that looked like it had been stolen off the face of a cherub. Chris felt better now. Shirley's pies were the best anywhere. He was no longer frustrated, so he could just curl up on his buffalo robe and let his mind slip into the comfortable blackness again.

War Bonnet rode across the plains and Chris admired the long flowing white mane and tail, eagle feathers floating out with the wind, muscles and sinew working all over his black and white body. Head swinging proudly, the big horse jumped over a clump of mesquite and playfully kicked with his hind legs in midair. He slowed down as he got closer, and he started walking slowly toward his master. The intelligent steed sniffed Colt's face, and Chris wondered how he got on his back suddenly. When he was watching his horse galloping toward him he had been standing up straight and now he was on his back. He closed his eyes to sleep, but War Bonnet stuck his nose under Chris's torso and prodded him, trying to lift him off the ground.

Colt opened his eyes and sat straight up. His head swam and he looked up at his horse. War Bonnet stood over him, and he was in a wooded valley with steep sides. The back of his head ached.

The grizzly bear! Colt reached quickly for his pistol and his holster was empty. His hand went for his Bowie knife and it was gone, too. Colt felt the back of his head and there was a lump there. He looked back and saw the rock he had hit it on.

Realization started flooding into Chris's mind. He

had been attacked by a big cinnamon-colored boar, silver-tipped guard hairs on its neck and shoulders. Colt had shot it twice and stabbed it with his Bowie knife. He looked around and saw the bear lying about ten feet beyond him. Colt made himself get to his feet, head pounding, and he ran to War Bonnet, vaulting onto the paint's back. He rode the horse about ten feet and spun him around. The griz didn't move.

Chris rode slowly forward and dismounted about twenty feet from the bruin. He picked up a large rock and mounted up again. Colt threw the rock at the big animal and it hit its side with a loud thump. The bear didn't move.

It suddenly dawned on Chris that his horse had come back to him and tried to lift him up with his nose. That's what awakened him from his state of unconsciousness. War Bonnet pranced and snorted nervously as Chris rode him closer to the grizzly. He dismounted and moved slowly forward until he saw the handle of his knife sticking out of the bear's chest, just below the left front leg. The handle did not move. The bear was dead.

Colt admired the big creature as he walked up to it. The ground all around it was torn up and totally defoliated where the grizzly had thrashed around in its death throes, tearing up everything within reach of those mighty paws.

The scout pulled his knife out of the big torso and felt the bear's body. A shiver ran through Chris Colt. The body of the bear was cold to the touch. It had been dead a long time. Almost in a panic, Chris ran over to where he had last seen Ezekiel and the prisoners. He found their hoofprints. The edges were not sharp but slightly rounded and looked like they had been wetted down, then dried out. He knew what this meant, but still Chris couldn't believe it. He stuck his nose down into several of the tracks and sniffed.

He got up and shook his head again, as he quickly got light-headed. Colt walked over to War Bonnet and smiled at the big horse, patting him on the neck.

Chris said, "It's a good thing you came back for me, pal. I can't believe I was knocked out for a full day."

Chris felt a rumbling in his stomach, and he immediately reached down and grabbed some tinder and dried sticks. He found a couple of small pieces of log and quickly built a fire just a few feet from the big bear. Going into his saddlebags, he got out the Colt Navy .36-caliber revolver he carried with him as a backup gun. He checked the action and holstered it, pulling out a box of bullets, and started replacing some of the .44 rounds in his belt with .36s. Next, he looked for his Henry repeater and found it near where the bear had slammed into War Bonnet's side. Colt had been holding the rifle across his saddle, but the attack was so quick, the scout instinctively drew his six-gun and fired, after hour upon hour of practice and experience. He checked his Henry and made sure the action was okay and the barrel was free of dirt or obstructions.

Next, he made coffee, biscuits, and even pulled out a tin of peaches he had been saving. Chris felt he deserved it after what he had been through. Besides that, he had gotten a bump on the head and needed some nutrition before trying to take off at a fast pace to catch up with Ezekiel. The young Nez Perce boy was not a match for the three desperadoes with him, but Colt couldn't travel at breakneck speed with a concussion, lacking food or water.

He gutted the giant bear and cut some meat off the rump. Colt then spent several minutes trying to trim as much fat as possible off of the greasy meat. He put the meat in the pan and started cooking it slowly over some embers at one end of the fire. Chris was not familiar with the term trichinosis, but he knew that, like pork you had to cook bear meat thoroughly or run a high risk of getting sick. While the meat cooked, he cut the long nonretractable claws from the four plate-sized paws. Colt put the claws in his saddlebags.

After eating, he removed the saddle from his horse and let the mount roll and shake. Chris then resaddled him. He felt sorry for War Bonnet, the paint having worn the saddle and bridle all day and the previous night and day. Next he used a short braided rawhide rope he carried in his saddlebags and made a war bridle like the Indians used, Going around his horse's nose and along his head, it would give the steed's mouth a few hours of comfort from wearing the leather bridle and bit in his mouth. Colt would stop then, let War Bonnet take a blow, and put the Army-issue bridle back in place. He didn't like the Army's McLellan saddle, preferring to have a saddle horn to dally a rope around when he needed to and to have something to hang things on such as his canteen or a pair of binoculars.

Chris finished eating, extinguished his fire, mounted

his horse, and headed in the direction of the Pacific Ocean without a look back at the behemoth that almost took his life. He would canter and trot, alternating between the two paces, and take a short break during the night. Colt would do this until he reached the boy and the brave young warrior's tremendous load of responsibility.

Colt headed down the canyon and hoped that the herd would move slowly and keep the Indian occupied chasing them into the gather. The going was very rough as the valley narrowed into another rocky gorge after just ten miles. Chris found where the herd of horses had to carefully pick their way through the rocks. He again respected Ezekiel for protecting the herd to save it for his tribe.

He kept pushing both himself and his horse but Chris was careful to watch warning signs with War Bonnet. He thought back to the horse he killed on his way home from the Civil War. He vowed then to always treat his horse as if it were the King of England. He had pushed the horse to a lather and beyond for many miles, too many miles when the young veteran came to the Tuscarawas River in southeastern Ohio. He and the horse started to swim the river when the exhausted animal's intestines twisted and he died before making it across. The young Union scout and soldier sat down on the northern bank and wept, feeling more shame than ever before in his life.

War Bonnet was drenched with sweat as he labored across the countryside, and he would kill himself if his master drove him to it. There was no danger of that, though. Colt had been checking the trail carefully and figured he was about four hours behind them when he stopped for the night. He would sleep for three or four hours where War Bonnet would have good graze and water and a chance to rest for a bit. Hours before the scout had found the place where the group had spent the night, so he knew it wouldn't be too hard to over- take them the following day.

Checking where they moved from their campsite, Chris was impressed with Ezekiel once more. Instead of worrying about pushing the herd and keeping them gathered, he had roped the lead mare of the Appaloosa herd. Ezekiel led the horse and the herd followed. Horses were very much herd animals and these spotted steeds were no exception. In fact, they had all been together since the birth of each, because of the culling and selective breeding of the Nez Perce who developed this special tough breed of mountain horse. The entire herd had followed Ezekiel and the lead mare.

Colt also knew that Ezekiel would have to move very slowly, because he was also leading three men tied to their horses.

The scout gave his horse as much rest as possible while he got several hours sleep. Before daybreak, the scout broke camp after a quick breakfast and coffee. He started his fast pace again and traveled like that for two hours before stopping again.

Chris found another spot where the group stopped, and he halted to inspect the sign. Colt got very con- cerned now, as he saw where the lad had apparently, for convenience's sake, untied the black rustler and let him lead the other two.

The three men were just too worldly, evil, and clever for the young boy to let any of them have any freedom whatsoever. Chris felt real panic now, but he also knew he must pursue, yet be sensible about how hard he pushed his horse. Colt felt thankful that Crazy Horse had preferred large horses instead of the little wiry mustang ponies preferred by most Indians. War Bonnet's long-legged stride ate up the miles as they continued after the young brave man and his vicious prisoners.

It was close to noon when Colt finally caught sight of the group. He topped out on a big rise and saw the men and herd in a grove of aspens down below him. The gorge had again opened out into a small mountain valley and Chris could clearly see beaver dams and ponds in the wooded bowl below.

The three men were loose and had a fire built. The young boy, Ezekiel, was tied to a small aspen, and they appeared to be burning him with flaming sticks from the fire. Chris could hear them laughing, but he could not hear the boy yell out in pain, at all. Even at that distance he could see the bright red blood on the boy's chest and on the light-colored dirt around him.

It was combat again. Colt felt nothing but fury. Three grown vicious killers were torturing a small Indian boy. For what reason? He could not figure it out. He didn't want to. Colt wanted to just make them believers. He wanted them to know clearly that this young Nez Perce boy was a friend of his, and you do not hurt a friend of Christopher Columbus Colt's unless you are totally prepared to go to war, full-scale war.

Colt swung the paint off the trail to his right and into the aspens that ran up over the ridge line and went on for a full mile. As he headed downhill paralleling the trail, he pulled his Cheyenne bow and quiver of arrows from his bedroll. He stopped and quickly dismounted, strung the bow, then swung back up into the saddle. When Chris reached the bottom of the hill, he angled to his left and dodged in and out between trees until he saw the smoke from the cooking fire.

Colt dismounted and weaved through the trees. He got behind a large aspen and fired an arrow, watching until he saw it find its mark. The arrow took the black bandit through both upper arms and his upper torso, with just the last half of it still remaining in his body. He screamed so loudly and horribly it made Colt think of the cry of a dying catamount. Eyes bulging and looking down at his paralyzed upper body, he stood up on his tiptoes, twisted, and fell face forward in the fire. His body convulsed in further pain, then suddenly stopped moving. The others stared in abject horror.

The white man screamed, eyes wide open, and the other dived for cover. The white one tripped, falling across the black one's body, burning his right forearm in the flames.

Colt laughed as he heard their screams: "Injuns! Injuns! Take cover!"

Colt ran downhill, quickly darting from tree to tree, and dived headlong onto his belly, immediately scrambling forward on hands and knees. He made his way to an area opposite from the fire and looked more closely at the brave young Indian lad. He had a bloody knife wound in his chest and burns on several places of his body, but he looked like a young man playing tag and taunting someone to touch him. His lips were closed together tightly and his chin stuck out defiantly.

Chris moved expertly along on his elbows, hands, and knees toward the end of a depression where he saw the Mexican disappear. He crawled into the furrow in the earth and faced the upper part of it toward the campfire. Within seconds, the Latin rustler crawled around the bend of the draw and came face-to-face with Christopher Columbus Colt. He never said a word. His hand just streaked down for his gun and Colt released the arrow, which crashed into and through the man's forehead.

Colt got to one knee and looked around at ground level. Nothing moved. Nothing stirred. He heard a sound off to his left and immediately recognized it as a fox squirrel. His eyes kept straying to a large clump of brush to his right front. His mind automatically catalogued the area he saw the white man disappear into and this clump of thick brush was the closest and thickest cover.

Chris raised up on one knee and fired an arrow into the middle of the clump and listened. While up, he spotted the horses of the men and that was what would help him. He looked at the three horses the bad men had ridden and saw the horses all staring at a second clump of brush a little beyond the first. Their ears were all directed forward toward the brush, as well. Without hesitation Colt stood and drew his Colt Navy .36. He fired into the middle of the brush and the man stood holding a large red splotch of blood on his lower right side. He raised his gun with his left hand and tried to aim at Colt, but Chris's gun blossomed flame again and again and two more spots of red appeared in the middle of the man's chest. The .36 didn't have the knockdown power of Colt's mangled .44 but it definitely could kill.

Chris ran to the boy, reloading his pistol on the run. His scalpel-sharp knife was out in a flash and cut through the young Nez Perce warrior's bonds like they were butter. All the while Colt never said a word but kept his eyes on the fallen white man. He moved to him, the Indian following.

The man was in obvious pain and shock and was trying to scream but couldn't.

He looked up at Chris and weakly said, "Shoot me, please?"

Colt grinned and said, "It appears that I already have."

The man looked at Colt with deep hatred and his eyes slowly closed. A wet spot appeared at his crotch. His entire body convulsed once and suddenly went limp.

Ezekiel looked up at Colt and smiled. His left eye was puffed up and blood was finally clotting from the wound. Chris led him back to the fire and had him sit down. The scout grabbed the dead bandit, still burning in the fire, and dragged his body off away from the fire and downwind from the duo. He had to block his mind out from the stench of the man's burning flesh. It was a hideous smell that Colt hated, but this was certainly not the first time he had smelled it.

Chris added some small logs to the fire and broke out his coffeepot. He also retrieved the bone-handled knife the boy wore. It had been removed and stuck in a nearby log. Colt wiped the blade carefully on his pants and stuck the end of the blade in the fire.

Ezekiel's eyes opened wide looking at his knife, but he checked himself.

He said, "Great Scout, why do you put my blade in the fire?"

Chris grinned and said, " 'Cause I don't want to chance ruining the temper of my own blade."

As was the custom with most tribes, Ezekiel didn't thank Chris for saving his life, but it was understood between the two.

Chirs poured out two cups of coffee, after a few minutes, and gave Ezekiel one with lots of sugar in it. He checked the end of Ezekiel's knife and saw that it was red-hot.

Chris said, "I have to cauterize that knife wound in your chest, boy. That means—"

Ezekiel interrupted, "I do not understand big word, but I know what must be done."

"Want me to make you sleep?" Colt asked.

The boy said, "No, I am Nez Perce. Do what must be done."

Without further comment Chris moved the blade up to the stab wound and burned all the sides and edges of flesh and muscle that were exposed. Ezekiel stared straight ahead and didn't wince or make any change in his expression, but he was drenched with sweat in less than a minute. When Chris set the knife down, Ezekiel nonchalantly picked up his cup and took a swallow of the steaming hot coffee.

"Coffee good," he said.

Chris smiled and said, "You know how I make coffee?"

Ezekiel shook his head no.

"I make it as strong as I can and then add more powerful medicine to make it stronger. I know it is strong enough when I drop a bullet on it, and the bullet bounces off."

Chris held a bullet from his belt while he explained and shared a laugh with the Indian boy afterward.

"Ezekiel, we will camp here for a couple of days," Chris said, "then take these Appaloosas back to Chief Joseph."

"Young Joseph will be surprised," Ezekiel said. "These days he is not used to white men giving things to him. They only want to take."

Chris said, "I have heard this."

Colt looked at the Nez Perce boy and smiled. Ezekiel had fainted. Chris elevated his feet and splashed cold water on his face. Ezekiel came around and stared at the muscular white scout. Chris covered him with a blanket, and threw some more logs on the fire. Colt picked up his Cheyenne bow and quiver of arrows.

Chris said, "You sleep, young one. I'm going hunting up on the ridge."

Tossing Ezekiel the Navy .36, Colt said, "You fire that if you need help. Cock that hammer on top. Pull it back, then pull the trigger, like a rifle."

Ezekiel nodded and set the gun near his head. He closed his eyes and went to sleep.

Chris disappeared into the quaking aspens.

A half hour later found Chris high up above the campsite. Here on a windswept ridge, he looked out at the valley that would lead them into the valley of the Snake River. In some places he had heard the valley would be wide and easy travel and in some places there would be untraversable white-water gorges. Colt decided they would take the journey one leg at a time, one day at a time, one event at a time. He would not and could not afford to worry about what might or might not be. That attitude had kept Chris Colt alive many times and always made him come out on top, no matter the challenge.

He dropped down off the ridge line traversing the paint horse back and forth across a treeless avalanche slide. The scout dropped down two hundred feet into the black timber in a bowl surrounded by three towering peaks of black granite. He dismounted and dropped the reins to War Bonnet and the big mount ground-reined where he stood. Colt weaved in and out through the trees, his eyes automatically shooting back and forth in front of him in a fan pattern looking for sign. He saw plenty. This deep black timber was protected from wind and predators by steep terrain and was usually a favorite bedding area for harems of elk.

Colt found fresh droppings, hoofprints, and rubs

where bulls had torn up small bushes and sparred with saplings, rubbing the bark off and leaving bare patches around the thin trunks.

In less than a minute after spotting a pile of dark brown, round pellet-looking droppings with steam coming off them, Chris quietly dropped to all fours and crawled slowly forward, up a small rise only five feet in height. Twenty feet away lay a sable-colored bull elk with antlers sporting twelve tines over one foot in length. The bull was nervous and his nostrils flared hysterically, his muscles bunching as if he was readying himself to bound from his bed. His ears twisted this way and that and Colt decided to instantaneously loose an arrow. The mighty bull was ready to leap away into the thick stand of evergreens.

The bull moved quickly as Colt raised, drew, and released his arrow. It sliced into the left rib cage of the stag as it tried to speed away, breaking one rib as it cut through the left lung, the aorta, and the left ventricle of the heart. Colt watched as the bull kept on by instinct and adrenaline and ran out of sight, his mighty antlers twisting this way and that through the many thick branches in the forest.

Chris rolled a cigarette and sat down leaning against a tree. He lit the smoke and removed his floppy leather hat, looking up at the sky, so close he felt he could stick his hand straight up and touch it. The scout would wait and let the elk bed down and bleed to death. He was positive that it was lung and probably heart hit, but Colt had followed enough blood trails to know how many times a shot had been misjudged.

Arrows never, in Colt's experience, made instant kills on animals. Unlike bullets, they killed by hemorrhaging, not shock. The elk would soon lie or fall down and get weaker as its life's blood drained out, finally closing its eyes and falling asleep, never to awaken.

He looked around the woods and his thoughts drifted back to a hunt with his former father-in-law, a Minniconjou Lakotah (Sioux) warrior of great repute by the name of Kicks the Bear. Chris's wife, Chantapeta, was with the women at their lodges on the Rosebud and his daughter Winona had yet to be born.

The two men had spotted a harem of elk in a high country meadow. It was shortly after daybreak and the elk were grazing on tall gamma grasses growing wild in the meadow. There were about thirty head of cows, several satellite bulls and spikes that stayed around the outside of the herd, and the majestic old herd bull—a dark brown old man bearing scars from many battles. While the two warriors listened to bugling and grunting, they watched two big bulls come crashing out of the north and south end of the meadow to challenge the big monarch for his harem.

Wearing the hides of two cow elks, the two men crawled down to the meadow. Checking carefully to insure that they were downwind from each of the challenger bulls, they crawled closer and closer to the fight scene. The larger of the two challengers was almost the same size as the sable bull Colt had just shot. It was closest to the scout and had a dark mahogany-colored coat. The other bull, near Kicks the Bear, was almost blond and had a twisted tine on its antlers growing down in front of its forehead. Chris even spooked one of the satellite bulls with his scent, and it ran up the hillside behind him, but the three were so angry and intent on fighting each other they didn't notice the fleeing young stag. The blond bull had pieces of leaves and twigs hanging from its rack, as it had beat up the ground with its long tines, and downed a small tree, while the two others pawed the ground and made bluff charges toward each other.

The hunt was exciting for the adventurous young man who had grown up in the relatively tame woods and cornfields of northeastern Ohio.

He and his father-in-law quietly observed the fight, as the old herd bull quickly pushed one of the two into retreat, then charged the other. Less than five minutes of clanging antlers caused the second challenger, the blond one, to take off into the deep timber, huffing and panting. Colt and the old man crawled away not wanting to snuff the life out of the majestic elk. They felt that blood such as his should keep running through the veins of many more animals.

They were happy to down a spike bull they found an hour later, a mile away.

Chris took a long drag on his cigarette and blew the smoke out and watched it be carried off on the breeze. He suddenly felt a sharp pain where the grizzly had smacked into his head and his eyesight got blurry. He shook his head and his eyesight cleared, but he still had a monster headache. This hadn't been the first time that had happened to Colt.

Chris put out the cigarette on the ground. He then

stripped it apart, rolled the paper into a tiny ball, and flipped it into the undergrowth, after letting the wind carry the tiny pieces of tobacco away.

He walked to the spot where the arrow hit the bull and immediately spotted the arrow shaft, covered with blood lying on the ground twenty feet beyond. He inspected it and saw it was covered with bright red blood. He saw bright red splotches of blood on the ground leading off where the bull had bounded away. It had been hard hit.

He found the dead elk lying fifty paces farther. He found the damage done by the arrow. Chris's head pounded like a miner's doubletree while he deftly gutted and quartered the giant stag. Colt carried part of one rump over his sinewy shoulder while he moved toward the spot where he had left his magnificent stallion ground-reined. When he got close enough, he gave the whistle of a red-tailed hawk, and the big paint headed toward him with his head twisted slightly to the side so he wouldn't step on the dropped reins. It only took War Bonnet having his head quickly jerked toward the ground one time to learn that behavior.

When Chris got the two-hundred-pound chunk of meat loaded on the heavy-boned horse, he suddenly felt another sharp pain in his head that dropped him to his knees. He shook his head and started seeing things with double vision. Grabbing his canteen, he poured some of the cold liquid on his head while he shook his head from side to side. His vision finally cleared by the time Colt finished tying a diamond hitch with his leather braided riata, his Mexican lariat. The headache started to subside a little bit and Colt turned the horse, leading him back after some more of the meat.

An hour later the cavalry scout stepped back from the horse and grabbed the lead line, after tying even more meat on the big mount. It was a lot of extra weight but War Bonnet was a very strong horse. It was enough to take back to the camp where the boy needed nourishment badly.

The ruggedly handsome scout was only able to take three steps when it happened. His world went suddenly black. With Chris's second step he could see clearly all about him. With his third step touching the ground, he went completely blind. The suddenness of the malady caused Colt to trip and fall headlong over a log across the path. His hands went out and broke his fall. He rolled onto his back and automatically clutched at his eyes, which he started blinking over and over again. Everything was pitch-black.

The scout felt sheer panic, and he heard a sob escape his lips. That little noise snapped him back to reality and put him into his survival thinking. Chris Colt loved the mountains much more than the desert or the prairie, but he knew better than most that the Rockies were absolutely unforgiving. A person with sight and *all* their faculties could be easily killed by the unpredictable mountains if he did not work with them, and not against them. In the Rockies, a storm, even a blizzard, could appear from nowhere in the late spring, early fall, or summertime. A flash flood from a storm at higher ground could send a killing wall of water roaring down a steep-sided gulch sweeping anything in its path toward rocky cliffs and boulders down below. On high ground a lightning-caused forest fire could suddenly appear from below a cliff lip and sweep over a hapless traveler who is unaware.

Colt knew that he had to avoid the luxury of feeling sorry for himself or worrying whether he were permanently blind. He had a courageous, gravely wounded young Indian brave counting on him to keep him alive. He also had a woman he loved back in Bismarck in the Dakota Territories expecting him to stay alive, no matter what. On top of that, he had, in himself, an innate survival instinct that made him feel that he was always vulnerable but incapable of being actually killed by any circumstance. His instinctive give-it-all-you've-got attitude had enabled him to live through many dangerous situations that would have killed a normal man.

Cole stood and threw his shoulders back. He carefully turned and reached back for his companion and was shocked to feel the paint's nose as War Bonnet stretched his neck forward knowing Colt was hurt. Colt moved forward and wrapped his arms around the steed's neck and hugged him hard. He thought for a minute and decided what he must do.

Number one, he had to get the elk meat down to the campsite so he and Ezekiel could survive. Number two, he could not—he would not—kill his horse in the process, so he would have to lead War Bonnet back to the camp miles away and thousands of feet farther down the mountain. He knew that he might have been able to climb up on the horse even with all the weight on War Bonnet's muscular legs, and he knew that the paint might have been able to home in on the campsite because they had stopped there, but Chris could not take that chance. The horse might head back to the previous stopping place or catch a scent of some wild horses on the wind and head that way.

Colt tied the lead line around the neck of his horse. He dropped down on his hands and knees and felt for War Bonnet's hoofprints heading back down the mountain. He felt the edge of one with his left hand, so he reached forward with his right and found another a little farther on. Colt's knee and hands moved forward and the other knee glided across the ground. This would be how Chris would make it back down to the campsite to the sleeping Nez Perce boy.

Many of the penny novels about the Old West glorified the cowboy, scout, cavalry trooper, mountain man, and so on. They also glorified the horse, with wonderful spellbinding tales of heroic deeds in service and loyalty to their masters. In actuality, however, horses are not really very smart animals. In fact, Chris Colt would never consider owning a horse that was *too* smart. They were easy to tell. The big-brained horses had large lobes over each eye. Those were also the horses that always seemed to try to brush a man off on a hardwood tree trunk or boulder, long after the horse was broken to ride. Those were the horses that would try to throw themselves on their back unexpectedly while their rider was in the saddle. Nevertheless, every once in a while a horse like War Bonnet came along with maybe more than his share of common sense, instinct, and loyalty toward his master.

This was clearly exhibited when, an hour later, Chris Colt, with sore knees and bleeding hands, was knocked forward onto his face by a strong nudge from War Bonnet. The horse reached down with his teeth and grabbed Colt by the shirt and helped raise him off the ground. Knowing the horse was trying to communicate somehow, the scout stood erect, the backs of his knees and calf muscles cramping and locking up painfully. He shook it off.

The horse walked by him and swished his tail across Colt's arm as he passed by. Chris grabbed the tail and held on, as War Bonnet carefully picked his way down the mountain trail. Colt pictured steep cliffs and drop-offs with every step, but he held his friend's tail as the horse gingerly and slowly worked his way down the mountainside. Chris tripped and fell once after that but was unhurt and arrived back at the campfire, an hour later, still unable to see but very thankful for an Oglala war hero and good friend by the name of Crazy Horse. The man who gave him the horse had probably saved his life and that of the young Indian. There was no telling how long it would have taken Colt to make it back to camp feeling for tracks on his hands and knees. He had accidentally gone off, at one point for fifteen minutes, following the tracks of a large bull elk that went down the trail briefly. He finally got to drier mud and felt the tracks in the middle made by the beast's split hooves. Colt had had to backtrack to the original horse's trail.

When they arrived at the camp, Chris first heard the fire cracking and popping and a smile crossed his windburned face. He let go of the horse's tail and moved toward the fire, holding his palms outward and using them to let the warmth guide him closer and closer. He called out Ezekiel's name and heard only the soft, steady breathing of the boy.

Using his hands as eyes, he stuck some new logs in the fire, then led War Bonnet to a large limb he had already picked out for hanging meat. After ten tries, he finally flipped a lasso over the limb and was able to begin hoisting the elk meat aloft. He cut off several steaks and felt his way back to the fire. Colt tied a string of rawhide to the handle of his frying pan and ran it to his hand while the steaks sizzled and biscuits cooked over the hot fire. As he checked the progress of the cooking elk he ran his hand along the string to the handle of the pan, not worrying about getting accidentally burned.

"The *wapiti* has given up the ghost so we can continue our journey." Ezekiel's voice pierced through the blackness of Colt's mid-afternoon.

"He wants Ezekiel to become strong quickly in case he must soon become a chief."

Ezekiel's voice had a puzzled note as he replied, "Why would a mighty chief and warrior say such a thing?"

Colt said, "Never know what can happen in life, son. How you feeling?"

Ezekiel said, "I am stronger, but a big bear has ripped my chest out and left just the skin, I think."

Colt laughed.

Chris heard no more noises, no further words from Ezekiel for a couple of minutes. Using the rawhide thong he reached down for the handle on the pan again.

Ezekiel spoke, "What has happened?"

"A bear hit me on my head and knocked out my brains."

Ezekiel laughed, replying, "I know. You are a white man."

Chris laughed, then became serious. "I don't know what happened. I started after an elk I shot and I went blind. It must be from the bear hitting me in the head."

"Can you not see the mountains or the trees around us or your own fingers?"

"I am like the bat flying toward the sun," Colt said.

Ezekiel slowly got up from his bed and walked to Colt's side.

He said, "The elk is ready. And the bread."

"Thanks."

Ezekiel said, "You do not thank your eyes. I am now your eyes."

Chris smiled and reached over feeling for the lad's shoulder, which he gave a pat, saying, "And I will be your strength."

Ezekiel said, "Then together we will be a mighty warrior."

"We must be," Colt replied, "we still have a long journey to make. There is good grass and water here for the herd, so we will wait a few days while you heal. We will first go to Fort Hall, so I can see a doctor and send a message over the singing wire to General Howard to let him know where I am. I have to get some new guns, too."

Ezekiel said, "The singing wire you said. Don't you mean telegraph?"

Thinking about the fact that Ezekiel was Nez Perce and spoke and thought in poetic terms, Colt realized the boy had still learned English from Christian missionaries. He spoke the language well and understood it even better.

It was less than a week later that the unlikely-looking pair rode by the parade ground at Fort Hall after putting the herd of horses in a large empty pole corral set up near the post stables. Colt still saw only blackness but sat his magnificent horse tall trying to conceal his blindness from any onlookers. With his reputation, he knew that all the human snakes around constantly viewed men like him for any sign of weakness or vulnerability.

His reputation had preceded him, so nobody said a word when Colt took Ezekiel to the mess hall and got him a giant meal of hot food. Chris left him there while he went off straightaway to the regimental surgeon. He was told by the boy that the dispensary was attached to the side of the mess hall, so he just felt his way with his right hand gliding along the chinked log walls.

"Mr. Colt, you have suffered a traumatic injury to the head and may have blood accumulating inside your cranium," the surgeon said. "I don't know, but you will be much safer staying here in a bed and giving this a chance to clear itself up."

Colt said, "Can't, Doc, got a lot of work to do. Am I going to be permanently blinded?"

The surgeon replied, "I don't know. You could get your eyesight back as quickly as it left. You probably have accumulated blood or a hematoma, a bruise of sorts, pushing on your optic nerve, but we do not know a lot about the brain. I had a trooper that got busted upside the head by a Shoshoni warrior, and he had the same thing happen. His eyesight came back in two days time. Another trooper had to be medically discharged with severe headaches, horrible ringing in his ears, and blindness that lasted the rest of his life. I do know that you could die suddenly if you have blood accumulating inside that thick skull of yours, and I order you to bedrest."

Colt said, "Sorry, Doc. I know you're a good 'saw-bones,' and I appreciate your concern, but I have to take a young Nez Perce lad and a herd of Appaloosas back to Chief Joseph, and I have to report to General Howard at Lapwai."

"How much scouting do you think you can do for the cavalry, Mr. Colt?"

Chris smiled through his darkness, saying, "Captain, I can only tell you that I know that any talents and experiences that the Good Lord has blessed me with have not been intended to be used in a blackened world."

"What do you mean?" the surgeon replied.

Colt said, "A grizzly is not given great strength and

long sharp claws and teeth to help him carry pollen from flower to flower."

Colt added, "Thanks, Doc," turned, and fell head-long over an examining stool.

Standing and dusting himself off, he walked straight out the door without touching the wall or even holding his hands out. Outside on the wooden boardwalk, Chris grinned to himself as he pictured the surgeon staring at his back in amazement. He was thankful that a slight breeze pouring into his face through the open door guided him into the fresh air. Colt made his way to the mess hall and walked in the door. Many eyes turned toward him as he stood in the doorway sum-moning Ezekiel with sign language.

As hard as he was trying to cover it, it was apparent to all who saw him that Christopher Colt, the famous scout and shootist, was blind. In fact, in the door of the mess hall, Colt, without realizing it, was speaking with sign talk to a group of dumbfounded soldiers standing three feet to his front. Ezekiel was actually off to his left, but the boy ran to Colt's side and led him out the door.

"All know," Ezekiel said. "You cannot hide your blindness, but I see no enemies here. These men all look at you the way our men look at Chief Joseph."

"I know," Chris replied, "but the word will spread around, and my enemies will come looking for me."

"Then you will be like the owl," Ezekiel said.

"I must be like the eagle more than the owl," Chris said.

"You shall be both, with my help."

"We have to get going, boy," Colt said. "I have to send a report to General Howard first, then we have to pick up some supplies and get you and the 'Palouses back to Joseph. Lead me to the commandant's office."

An hour later Ezekiel led Chris into the local mercantile. There were two of them, so they chose the larger one.

"Help ya, mister?" the storekeeper said as he adjusted a pair of worn suspenders that came slipping off his shoulders.

"I'm after a six-gun or two and some ammunition."

"Got this beautiful matched pair of Colt Peacemakers here with the eagle-butt grips," the man said. "Say, ain't you blind?"

Colt replied, "Yes, but only temporarily. Got something in my eyes. The doctor checked them out just today."

"How ya gonna manage shootin' without eyesight?" the man asked.

"I'll manage."

The storekeeper handed the guns, tooled double holsters, and gunbelt to Chris. Colt slipped them around his waist and pulled the pistols out of the holsters one at a time and felt the cylinders to insure neither gun was loaded.

He put the guns back in the holsters and faced toward the middle of the room.

"Anyone in front of me, Ezekiel?" Chris asked.

The boy replied, "No."

With blinding speed, Colt pulled both guns out of the holsters, the hammers cocking, as each gun slid forward at the waist. He dry-fired both, then deftly spun the guns backward into the holsters.

The storekeeper whistled in amazement. "Never seen anything like that in my life. By the looks a ya and that draw, you just gotta be Colt. Is ya?"

Chris smiled.

The man said, "How ya like 'em?"

Chris said, "They're called Colts, aren't they?"

The man laughed, then said, "They'll cost you about—"

Colt interrupted. "Sir, I don't have much with me right now. Do you buy directly from Colt Firearms?"

"Shore do."

"Sir, if you telegraph them, they will approve it," Colt replied. "Just tell them the guns, holster, and ammunition is for me, and they will replace all of it, plus add a ten percent commission to your account."

The merchant said, "Fair enough, Mr. Colt. I seen ya ride up on that horse a yourn and the look of ya already tole me ya was who ya say ya are, but thet quick-draw done it sure enough. I don't need to send no telygraph. I'll make a note of it with my next order. Now, how much ammunition ya want?"

"Do you have five hundred rounds of forty-fives you can spare?" Colt asked.

The man whistled again and said, "Shore, but do ya know what kinda bill that would run ya? Ya plannin' on startin' a war?"

"Maybe," Chris replied. "I might just have to."

Chapter 2

>>>>>>>>>>>>>>>>>>>>>

A Man Like Mecca

Colonel Rufus Birmingham Potter slammed his gray gauntlets down on the ornate hand-carved cherry table in his massive dining room. Three of his cut-throats stared in curiosity as the tall, wiry, gray-haired and gray-bearded land-grabber finished the note.

"Boys," he said enthusiastically, "Chris Colt, the one who killed my business partners, the Sawyers, killed those five new men who picked up that herd of Appaloosas they were taking to sell. Somehow he got blinded and only has one little red nigger kid with him and left Fort Hall yesterday headed toward Fort Lapwai with the herd of horses."

"Colonel," an ugly, curly-haired man said, "you telling me that he's blind?"

"Sure am, Curly, and virtually alone with hundreds of miles to travel," the rich crook replied.

Colonel Potter wasn't a real colonel. In fact, he had made it only as far as corporal, fighting for "the cause" in the Civil War. The only problem was that the only real cause he believed in was his own bank account, so he deserted and headed west, changing his name in the process, assuming the name of the phony Colonel Rufus Birmingham Potter. He still wore Confederate grays he had stolen when he deserted, and he played the role of the Southern gentleman to the hilt. Potter had his hands in many crooked deals in Oregon, Colorado, Utah, and other western regions. The Sawyer brothers had been tied in with Potter, General Custer, and several others to the infamous Washington Indian Ring. They stole Bureau supplies meant for reservation Indians and replaced them with inferior goods, pocketing the difference. Most of Potter's monies came from phony land fraud deals, especially salting old mines with gold, then selling them for exorbitant prices. His current projects, in fact, included salting mine properties throughout the Colorado Territory and selling off farming lands in Oregon.

He had let the five men, who were new to his operation, steal the herd of horses to sell to a contact of his in Colorado. There were several reasons for this. First, he was trying everything his devious mind could scheme up to start a war with the Nez Perce, so their rich ancestral lands could be stolen to sell to settlers. Second, he wanted to test the new men who had approached him about joining his gang. Because of Colt, they had failed the test.

Potter looked at his men and said, "That Colt cost me some money, and he killed some of our boys."

The latter remark stirred the three men in the room by nature of the fact that they all had grown up in the West and usually "rode for the brand." It didn't matter that most of them were totally crooked and would steal the pennies off their mother's eyes in the coffin. This Colt fellow had killed some men from their outfit. Not only that, he was now a blind target for the taking.

Potter went on. "I will pay a one-thousand-dollar bonus to the man who kills Christopher Colt and brings me his ears."

Curly spoke up. "Colonel, Will Sawyer and me rode the grub line one season. I owe that old Colt boy a debt myself. I'd like to go."

"Can't afford to spare you, Curly. You're my top hand. I've wired my associates in Salt Lake City and Colorado both. They've already sent a group of men to intercept him, and we'll send another group from here. Rip, you take six men and leave right away. He's going along the Snake."

Rip looked like a thirty-year-old man who could have raped his sister and killed the family hound just for fun. He was small but mean-looking and his twin cross-draw holsters were well worn. He stood and headed out the door with a grin on his face, not breathing a single word. If there was a killing to be done, and he could make one thousand bucks doing it, Rip Brangston didn't want to waste a single second waiting. He loved to shoot people, especially when he had a great advantage. It didn't matter to him that Chris Colt was blind; Rip just wanted to be the man who killed him. People would talk about him for years and everyone would fear him. That's what he wanted more than anything. It would make up for the whole childhood he suffered at the hands of his uncle who raised him and beat him continuously.

Rip had a gang together and was gone within an hour.

In the Old West, it was amazing how word would go around right away about the activities of just a few men who were considered living legends: Bill Hickok, the Earp brothers, Doc Holliday, William Bonney, Crazy Horse, Sitting Bull, Geronimo, Cochise, Clay Allison, the James brothers, and Chris Colt. As soon as folks learned that the scout had killed five more men in a battle, using guns and arrows, and using a knife, he killed a massive grizzly that blinded him, the word spread all over the West like wildfire. With each telling, as usual, the story grew in proportion.

Some people were so caught up in following the exploits of heroes and badmen that they actually spent money on telegrams just to pass the word on to friends more quickly. Because of that, the word about Colt reached the ears of his love, Shirley Ebert, in Bismarck less than twenty-four hours after he reported into Fort Hall.

Less than a day later found her driving a wagon with all her worldly supplies west out of Bismarck headed toward Oregon, where she would find and take care of her man who was blinded and obviously needed her. She did this despite all the warnings and scoldings from numerous people, including the wonderful banker and his wife who gladly paid her good money for her thriving restaurant business and attached house.

Shirley had grown up in Youngstown, Ohio, less than a day's ride from where Chris had lived, although they had never met there. In the mid and late nineteenth century the average person, over three fourths of all Americans, in fact, never traveled more than twenty-five miles from their birthplace during their life.

When she was a little girl, about eight years old, she was playing in front of her house. A little sparrow, not quite full grown, suddenly appeared on a limb a few feet from her head. A tiny drop of blood was showing on the side of its gray head. She smiled at it and held out her hand, and amazingly the little bird flew forward and lighted on her tiny hand. She cuddled the little bird and wiped the blood from its head.

Young Shirley, the sunlight playing on her then blond curls, fed some bread crumbs to the bird and petted it some more. She finally opened her hand and talked to the tiny creature and it cocked its head from side to side, as if trying to understand her words. It suddenly flew away and flew out of sight while she watched.

It had been an incredible experience and affected her entire life. Shirley Ebert had a soft heart but was also a tough woman. Like many people of her ilk, she was full of contradictions, gentle, yet tough; forgiving and kind, yet dangerous when cornered; and beautiful and dainty, but hard as nails when her mind was set. It was now set.

She would take a wagon and try to join up somewhere with a wagon train. Shirley had been kidnapped and repeatedly raped by Will Sawyer, the giant whom Colt had killed in the Yellowstone. She heard about that and smiled for days. She had also been held cap-

tive by the Oglala Sioux in the giant encampment during the Battle of the Little Big Horn. Shirley Ebert was
no idealist marching off to join her lover and thinking
everything would be fine if she just smiled and had
happy thoughts.

She knew what the risks were, but she had to reach
out to Colt like she had reached out to the little sparrow. It was something in her. Common sense be
damned, she thought. Shirley understood that she
could be kidnapped again or worse. There were bad
men and hostiles, grizzly bears, killing storms, rattlers,
and diseases, but her man was hurt, and he would
need her at his side. There was virtually nothing that
could have been said or done to keep her from setting
out for Oregon. Before leaving, she sent a telegram to
him at Fort Lapwai to let him know she was on her
way.

Shirley was also not stupid. She carried a Winchester
carbine with her, as well as a Colt revolving shotgun.
Under her skirts, she carried a Remington over-and-
under .41-caliber derringer. The little two-shot pistol
was small and easily hidden away but certainly packed
a wallop. By the time she had purchased hers, there
were already over one hundred fifty thousand satisfied
buyers of this dangerous little duster. If that were not
enough, she wore boots under her skirt, and tucked
into a holster in the right one was a Barns .50-caliber
boot pistol, which was loaded with a single ball. It
really kicked like a mule and would blow a hole
through a man big enough to drive a wagon and six-
mule team through, but Shirley had test-fired it and

knew she could handle it in an emergency. Most cap and ball percussion-type black powder pistols and rifles didn't have anywhere near the kick when fired as their more modern, breech-loaded cousins.

She hadn't reached the border of Montana Territory yet when she tied in with a four-wagon train of buffalo-hide hunters. She had the feeling that the men were probably really smuggling guns and alcohol to the Plains tribes. She didn't care.

Her mind was set on one thing, and although she didn't like the way several of the smelly bearded men looked at her, there was a code in the West. Women were a rare commodity. Even outlaws had lynched other outlaws for molesting women, so it was something that happened on very rare occasions. It had already happened with Shirley once with Will Sawyer, so she hoped that the odds would be in her favor that it would not happen again. On top of that, if any men wanted to bother her and knew she was Chris Colt's woman, they would think twice or thrice about such a dangerous undertaking.

The four teamsters were white men. All four were bearded and all four were very large men. They smelled and were gruff and dirty, but Shirley was single-minded in her mission. She had to get to her man and these men provided a little more measure of safety for the journey.

They were well into Montana and were making a nightly stop after several days of travel when the killing happened.

As the men sat around the campfire talking, drinking

coffee, and smoking, Shirley went to take a bath in the natural water tank that they camped near. Although the four men talked and joked with one another at the fire and could not see her out in the darkness, each of those men had images running through his mind of that beautiful auburn-haired woman in the nude, shivering in the cold night air.

It was the middle of the night when Shirley awakened with a start, someone's hand on her breast. She stifled a scream and sat bolt upright, as a rough hand, the size of a melon, clasped her mouth.

Ed Broderick had spent most of his adult life up in the mountains, ranging the Continental Divide, putting out traps in search of the elusive beaver. He had gotten into an argument when he was a shade over eighteen and killed a man, accidentally, when he picked him up and threw him headfirst into the steel rim of a stagecoach wheel. The posse that pursued him for killing the town mayor's son didn't give up the chase until Ed, who was named Walter Reeves at the time, made up into the "high lonesome." He fell in love with the mountains and was fed up with people then anyway. He stayed and fought Indians, grizzlies, and blizzards until the beaver really played out, and he was forced down to the flatland.

Right after lying down and wrapping up in his buffalo robe, he squinted his eyes and glanced at the rounded figure of the sleeping woman. He hadn't had a woman since his Crow wife, who went under three years past in a fight he had had with some Blackfeet. Ed felt his ears burning and got very angry with himself for his thoughts. She was a decent woman, albeit beautiful. She was also someone else's woman. In any event, she had no interest in Ed and he would not allow himself to think any romantic thoughts about her.

When Buster Boors went to check his team, he thought he got a quick glimpse of the naked woman off by the water tank. My, she was handsome, he thought. She was full of spunk, and he figured she was probably one handful under the blankets. He lay awake a long time just thinking about what she would be like in a bed.

Bubba Parrish noticed how pretty the woman they were escorting was, but he really had no truck with women. They scared him, and he didn't understand them. He felt a hell of a lot more comfortable with a team of mules or horses and loved driving them across the unforgiving prairie, always presenting some new challenge to be conquered each day. He had always been uncomfortable around other people and had been a loner ever since he ran away from home, back in Illinois, when he was fourteen. He had raised himself since then and had lost his virginity in a whorehouse outside Wichita, but the old woman he was with spent most of the time laughing at him. All in all, it was an unpleasant and humiliating experience.

Ezra Parker had been in and out of trouble with the law every time he drank. He had been wanted in numerous towns under different names and for a variety of reasons, but he was stone-cold sober when he made plans for Shirley Ebert. She was too beautiful and was full of fire. If he could conquer her, he would just simply threaten to hunt her down and kill her if she breathed a word of it to anyone. The threats had worked before with other women, it would work with this one, too. Besides that, it really excited him thinking about how much he could frighten her. He loved it when women cried and whimpered, and oddly, he thought, it reminded him in a way of how he used to cry and whimper when his overstrict pa used to give him severe beatings and whippings.

He had decided to wait until all were asleep, creep over to her bed, and put his hand over her mouth. When she awakened fully, he would show her his big knife and let her feel the blade against her skin. He then planned to lead her out away from earshot and rape her.

Shirley reached for her derringer and found it was missing. She heard a little chuckle coming from Ezra's barrel chest. He pulled the derringer out of his buffalo coat and pointed it at her, cocking it.

Ezra stood up and said, "Come with me, missy."

A quiet evil chuckle started to rumble from his chest, when Shirley suddenly screamed as two shots rang out and his body flew sideways to the left, then the right, then spun around with a large throwing ax stuck into the middle of his back. He fell flat on his face, dead.

Shirley twisted her head to see Ed walking toward her. Bubba sat up in his bedding spot and held a smoking Sharps buffalo rifle. On the other side, a rifle cocked, and she turned to see Buster holding a Henry repeater. Her mouth dropped open. Ed grabbed the handle of his tomahawk and pushed down on Ezra's back with his big right foot as he pulled and yanked on the hatchet. With a squishing sound and a crack, the blade popped out of the dead assailant's back.

Shirley felt a wave of nausea pass through her.

Ed looked down. "Ma'am, we apologize about that hapnin', but you ain't got to ever worry 'bout no man touchin' you what ain' yer man. I'm a hard man and so're these men here, but we don't harm womenfolk. Looks like ole Ezra thought different, but we changed his mind for him."

Shirley said, "Yes, you most certainly did. Thank you all very much. When I reach Fort Lapwai, I'll tell my fiancé about how you three saved me. I know that he'll appreciate you watching over me as much as I do."

"Wal, this is the West, ma'am, and we ain't asked, 'cause plenty of folks out here would ruther forget about yesterday and concentrate on tomorry," Ed said. "Why in the hell were you out here alone in Injun country, and why is yer man allowin' ya to do so? If'n ya don't mind my askin'."

She said, "Well, he got hurt and he needs me. He didn't know I was coming. I just left."

By this time Bubba had wrapped her blanket around her and he, Ed, and Buster escorted her to the fire. Buster threw some more sticks on and set the coffeepot on. They all sat down.

"You shore got sand, Miss Ebert," Bubba said. "What's yer fiancy do anyhow?"

"He's a chief of scouts for the U.S. Cavalry," she replied.

Curiosity peaked, Ed asked, "What's his name, ma'am?"

"Colt, Chris Colt."

"Good Lawd awmighty," Buster said. "Yer man is Chris Colt. Whooee! Miss Ebert, when you tell him 'bout ole Ezra there, please let him know I was on your side. I wanna keep my scalp."

"I should say so," Ed said. "Ezra got off lucky that we kilt him. If'n we let him live and Colt found out what he tried. Phwoo! I don't even want ta think about what woulda happened ta him."

Bubba chimed in, "Ma'am, if you are Chris Colt's woman, we are gonna take ya safely to Oregon."

Shirley gasped, "I can't have you men do that. It's days and hundreds of miles out of your way."

Ed looked off into the darkness, sipped his coffee, and said matter-of-factly, "There won't be any arguin' 'bout it, ma'am. Bubba's right. We're takin' ya safely to Mr. Colt. He's one hombre who I always wanna stay on the right side of. 'Sides that, it's the right thing to do. No argument, we're a doin' it."

She knew better than to argue, so she just said, "I can't thank you gentlemen enough. I just don't know what to say."

Buster said, "No need to say nuthin', ma'am."

She dropped her head down and wiped tears from her eyes. Ed cleared his throat, and Bubba poured her a cup of coffee, handing it to her. She sipped it and stared into the fire, her thoughts far away with the love of her life.

The next day they started into the foothills leaving the relatively easy travel of the prairie behind them. Shirley was excited, as she knew that her love was also in the rough mountainous country connected to this very land. Somehow, leaving the prairie and moving into land that was roughly similar in feature and connected by vast, winding chains of rocky peaks, she felt at least connected to Chris in a sense.

The way would be much rougher now, but that was inconsequential to Shirley. Her mind had been made to seek out, find, and care for her ailing man, and she was that much closer to her goal.

They had followed the Yellowstone and opted not to travel the Clark's Fork, like they first planned, but to continue due west toward the headwaters of the Yellowstone. Their goal was to make Fort Ellis and try for a military escort or even join a troop train in Fort Lapwai or Fort Walla Walla.

Screaming Horse had been in on the Battle of the Greasy Grass, or at least was joined with the giant encampment. The Battle of the Greasy Grass was where the famous Long Knife leader Yellow Hair, Long Hair Custer, Son of the Morning Star, as the Crows called him, walked the spirit trail along with all of the bluecoated soldiers with him. The *wasicuns* called it the Battle of the Little Big Horn. By any name, the battle was the beginning of the end for the people of the Lakotah and Chyela circles.

Screaming Horse's little band had journeyed from the Northern Cheyenne nation to the giant camp and only two of its warriors partook in the Sundance Ceremony in which Sitting Bull gave up so many pieces of flesh and had visions of "enemy soldiers falling into the camp."

The wrinkled old war chief had actually arrived at the big camp on June 24 and joined the Chyela circle, but he and his handful of braves had been out hunting to the west of the encampment when the battle actually began. Only two of his men got back in time to fire some shots at Reno's retreating command, after Custer and his battalion were already wiped out. Screaming Horse was embarrassed and angry that he and his braves could only watch the other braves, who had won so many battle honors, as they celebrated and carried on through the night, and for days after the death of Long Hair.

They had since been wandering from place to place in the Montana Territory almost hoping for a major skirmish with Long Knife troops, so they could win their own battle honors. The wily old man knew that the time was short for the life of the plains as his people had known it. Through traders and loyal *wasicuns,* they had learned that a great cry rang up among the whites over the death of Long Hair, and his journey would certain be avenged. The *wasicuns* were as many as blades of grass upon the prairie and anytime a red man pulled one up and tossed it into the wind, ten more would take root.

Screaming Horse's scouts were now headed north to

seek out and find Sitting Bull and Crazy Horse, who were rumored to be seeking refuge in Canada.

It was on their way toward the Bear Paws, far to the north, that the chief's scouts reported to him that they had found a five-wagon train with three buffalo scalpers and one woman. The second wagon had a long rope tied to the third wagon's team and was leading the team in effect.

"Hokahey!" Screaming Horse cried in Cheyenne. "We will take the wagons, kill the *wasicuns*, and the white woman will be my slave. Waken Tanka has surely smiled down upon us this day. My winter count has grown long and the *wasicuns* have taken a hold of Mother Earth and claimed that she is theirs. We will make battle with these *wasicuns* and have a victory dance tonight."

The five wagons had to make their way between a set of four piñon and cedar-covered hills. This was chosen as the ambush site. Screaming Horse only had eleven lodges in his circle, which included eight men of fighting age, twelve women, and a handful of old men and children.

The women, elders, and children hid among the cliffs overlooking the four hills and waited. The eight braves and Screaming Horse picked hiding places among the small trees dotting the hillsides. Two trees were felled at the narrow little pass between the two westernmost hillocks.

It was less than an hour later that Bubba, in the lead wagon, started to pass between the first two hills. He pulled out a plug of tobacco and bit off a chew.

As he placed the pouch back in his breast pocket, an arrow whooshed through the air and penetrated his hand, went into his chest, and through his heart. Bubba died instantly, his wagon still rumbling slowly along. From behind, the others could not have known he was dead, except for his head leaning to the side. He was propped upright in a sitting position, slightly leaning on the wagon's brake arm.

Ed, in the next wagon, muttered to himself, "Son of a bitch! Nippin' on a daggone bottle again."

He reached down and grabbed a rock out of the little wooden boxful by his right foot. He used the rocks to hit his mules on the rump when he wanted them to move. He threw the rock and it sailed over Bubba's head, hitting the left lead mule on the dead man's wagon. The mule, as well as the one next to it, bolted slightly from fright and the big wagon lurched forward. The jerk on the wagon jolted Bubba's body loose from the lever, and he fell sideways out of the box, his limp body hitting the ground headfirst. His left leg fell out to one side and the big heavy wheels rolled over it, breaking it in several spots.

When Ed saw this happen and the arrow sticking through the hand and in the chest of the dead man, his jaw dropped open. He had not quite reached the closed-in spot between the last two hills, but instead was a little bit in the open between the two pairs of earthen mounds. The only thing even close to him was a small rust-colored boulder next to the trail.

He stopped his team and grabbed his Sharps buffalo gun in one hand and Spencer carbine in the other.

Hoping he was out of bowshot, he stood tauntingly and looked at the little hills to his front and rear.

He yelled, "C'mon, ya red bastards! Come'n git me if ya can!"

Behind him, seeing this, Buster and Shirley grabbed their own weapons, Buster with his Sharps and Shirley jacking a round into the chamber of her Winchester carbine. She scanned the hillside and gave her Remington .41-caliber over-and-under derringer a pat under her skirt.

Ed looked back at the woman and his remaining partner and gave a reassuring wink. Just then, the rust-colored rock next to his wagon moved. It was a young warrior under a red blanket, and he sprang up into the wagon seat and drove his bone-handled knife deep into Ed's kidney, just as the buffalo hunter snapped his head around. The pain from the stab paralyzed the big man, his mouth contorting in a scream. The Sharps went off but the ball flew by the wiry warrior's torso. Shirley's Winchester boomed and the Indian flew sideways onto the back of the right drive mule. Ed spun around and stared in horror at Buster and fell backward between the mules.

Shirley immediately jacked another round into the Winchester and looked up into the rocks.

Buster's face looked frightened, but he turned and yelled to Shirley, "Don't you worry none, ma'am. I'll protect you!"

Suddenly he fell forward over the backseat of the wagon box and landed on the pile of supplies behind him. Three arrows were stuck up in the air, protruding from his broad back.

Shirley Ebert was scared, but more than that, she was angry, very angry. Her eyes roamed the hills back and forth, but found nothing.

She yelled, "Come on, you cowardly dogs. You brave warriors who make war on women! Come and get me!"

Knowing the pride of many warriors of the Plains tribes, she figured her taunts might keep them from killing her, too. She was tough-minded, like Colt, and she could not even think about the death of her new friends right now. She had to survive. No arrows came.

She hollered again, "I am the woman of Wamble Uncha! If I die, I will die fighting like he would! Come, fight me, you cowardly curs! I am only one woman! Are you scared to fight one woman?"

Her head switched around from side to side, scanning all the terrain in every direction.

Nothing happened.

She heard a moan and looked at Buster. Incredibly, he suddenly stood straight up and looked all around like he was in a daze. Two arrows came from nearby hills and buried themselves to the feathers in his side and chest. He collapsed and folded like an accordion, his bloody corpse flat in the bottom of his wagon box.

Shirley aimed her Winchester at a large bush on the side of the hill that would be a likely ambush spot. Using searching fire, without knowing that was a cavalry technique, she fired dead center into the bush, then quickly fired to the left and the right of her first shot. There was a moan and a warrior stood straight up on his toes, hands clutching at the hole where his windpipe had been. He fell on his side, legs and arms twitching, and his convulsing body rolled down the hill, his body coming to rest against the front wheel of Bubba's wagon.

She picked out more bushes and trees and started firing in the same manner. It was certainly understandable why Chris Colt would love this woman. She was cool while staring death in its jaws.

Screaming Horse and three of his warriors had seen Chris Colt from a distance during the Battle of the Little Big Horn, but had not seen his woman. They had heard of the pair of *wasicuns* who many said should have been born Lakotah or Chyela, but they did not know them.

None of his band could speak any English, but he heard the name of Wamble Uncha and figured that this woman was maybe claiming to be the great *wasicun*'s betrothed. She also, he concluded, might have been saying that because it was known that Wamble Uncha, the man called Colt, was great friends with Crazy Horse himself and was highly respected by even Sitting Bull. She may have been claiming to be his woman or his sister to win favor with her potential captors. In any event, he would not kill her. In case she was the woman or sister of Wamble Uncha, Screaming Horse did not want to suffer the wrath of Crazy Horse or any other of his allies who treasured that *wasicun*'s friendship. The woman would be taken without her shedding blood and would become his slave, and if she was the betrothed of Colt, he could pay a high price and buy her back if he wanted her. The only problem was that it looked like he would lose all of his warriors to her bullets if he tried to take her alive.

He slid back down the hill behind him from his hiding place behind a cedar on the first hill's crest. The wrinkled old man easily vaulted onto the back of his yellow and white pinto pony. He held a coup staff in his left hand and had a thick bull-hide shield on his right arm. He cantered the pony around the base of the hill and came into view to her front. She aimed the Winchester at the old man. He raised one arm and gave some signals in sign language. In less than a minute a group of warriors came out from behind the hills on horseback and surrounded her. They slowly walked their horses closer. Shirley fired and the top foot of Screaming Horse's coup staff disappeared. He ducked and his horse reared, but dropping the staff, he held his hand up to his warriors and signaled them not to shoot.

He walked his horse slowly forward, and she held her rifle leveled and aimed at his midsection. Screaming Horse kept coming and Shirley looked around at the other warriors, calculating the odds against her. Finally, she lowered the weapon and set it next to her by the wagon seat. Screaming Horse rode up to her and extended his hand and she resignedly handed him her rifle.

As soon as he had it safely in his hand, a scarred brave named Quills in the Face gave out a loud whoop and swept down on her to count coup and capture this woman for himself. Nobody got a chance to figure out why, because her hand swept down and yanked the Barns .50-caliber boot gun from her right leg. She cocked it and grabbed the stock with her left hand and blasted him in midchest. His body flew backward off his horse as if yanked with a lasso. Screaming Horse shook his head because the blast from the gun went right by his ear, which was now ringing loudly. He looked back and saw a hole through Quills in the Face that actually showed the ground under him. The chief looked at the *wasicun* woman with awe and new respect.

Screaming Horse grinned and stuck out his hand again. She laughed and handed him the Barns boot pistol. He stuck his hand out once more as if asking if she had any more firearms, and she pointed at all the remaining warriors surrounding her. He dismounted and climbed up on the wagon box, grabbing her by the wrist and dragging her down to the ground. She reached up under her skirt and yanked out the derringer, but he grabbed her hand before she could bring it to bear.

Several other warriors ran up and grabbed her, pinning her to the ground while she was searched for more weapons and binding her hands behind her back by a leather thong.

She was stood up and she defiantly stared into the grinning eyes of the old war leader.

She said, "Are you Sioux?"

Then remembering their word for themselves, she said, "Are you Lakotah?"

He pointed to himself and his followers and said, "Chyela."

She smiled, remembering their name for their tribe and she said, "Cheyenne."

The man pointed to himself and his followers again and said, "Cheyenne," then repeated the gesture and said, "Chyela."

She nodded in understanding.

She looked at him and said, "Do you speak English?"

He gave her a quizzical look.

She said loudly, "Do any of you speak English?"

Nobody understood.

She said, "Man, me, Wamble Uncha."

Screaming Horse grinned in recognition again and said, "Wamble Uncha," and made a gesture with his groin while he pointed at her.

Her face flushed in embarrassment, but she nodded her head affirmatively. She thought he understood now, so she felt she would be safe. The old man said something to his men and they all laughed. He then slipped a lasso over her neck and held the other end while he mounted again.

She was led off by a noose around the neck, for the second time in her life. The first time had been with Crazy Horse. While the chief proudly led her off toward the lodges, she passed women and girls carrying baskets and three leading horses with travois attached, on their way to the battlefiled to strip the bodies of the dead enemies and collect war trophies.

Several women smacked her with sticks, and Shirley, despite the thong around her throat, kicked at them and spit on them as well. They taunted her as they walked on, but did seem to decide to keep a respectable distance from her.

Ten minutes later they arrived at the lodges of

Screaming Horse's band. The expedient village had been set up along the banks of a small mountain stream in a grove of quaking aspens. Several dogs nipped at Shirley's heels as she passed between the tepees, still in tow behind the chief's pony. She kicked them, too.

The chief stopped by the farthest lodge and slid off the paint. He took her to a post outside the tepee and tied her thong to it, then tightened the noose part of it around her neck. His wife came after about ten minutes and went inside the tepee. Shirley could hear the two arguing, it seemed, through the thick bison hides. Several dogs came up and sniffed around her but seemed friendly enough. The woman came out of the lodge and threw several meat scraps to the dogs and Shirley. Shirley picked up one and threw it back at the woman, who just laughed and went back inside the tepee.

Shirley waited and watched. It got dark and the temperature dropped sharply. She felt thirsty and cold. Within two hours, all the braves and women and girls had returned to the village with much booty. They brought the wagon mules with them and most of the goods. She spotted a number of men carrying new Henry carbines, so her hunch about the hide hunters smuggling weapons was correct.

A large fire was lit and there was laughter, dancing, and celebration. After that various painted warriors stood up and she could tell that they were telling about their exploits and acts of bravery during the so-called battle. It was all these people had, she guessed. They had to know that the end of their ways was coming. During the evening women, children, and warriors drunken with enthusiasm would walk over to her and taunt her. If they got within kicking or spitting distance, however, they learned to show Shirley Ebert a little more respect.

Finally, the fires were just glowing embers and all in the camp had returned to their lodges. Dogs had curled up in tight balls, their tails wrapped around their noses. In many cases, the dogs slept around the big fire circle where heat was still being radiated. Others slept outside the tepees of their masters. The night turned cold.

Shirley lay curled up in a ball, her bound arms cramping. Her teeth were chattering and she felt frozen all the way to the inside of her soul. The woman knew that she would not make it through the night, at least not alive, she wouldn't. She would have to do something or die.

The old woman came out of the lodge carrying an earthen bowl of steaming liquid. She looked around and shivered, then set the bowl down in front of the white woman so Shirley could bend forward and drink it. Shirley looked up at her and smiled. The old woman ignored the friendly gesture and turned back inside the tepee.

Shirley, hands still tied behind her back, bent forward at the waist and stuck her mouth down into the bowl of steaming stew. She slurped it up like a dog but stopped after hearing several dogs growling. Two dogs, teeth bared, wanting the stew, growled at her. The larger of the two inched forward toward the bowl, his nostrils flaring smelling the pungent aroma. He was almost there when Shirley butted him with the side of her forehead hard enough to make him yelp and jump back.

The smaller of the two inched forward but suddenly lunged for her, teeth bared. She butted him straight on with the top of her head and he jumped back, blood running out of his mouth. His tongue started lapping it up over and over. One tooth was bent painfully to the side.

Still, the two dogs, ribs showing slightly, tried to creep closer to the bowl, though more cautiously. Suddenly Shirley smiled and turned around, soaking her hands and leather bond in the bowl of steaming broth. She soaked them for several minutes, keeping the dogs away with her feet. Shirley then turned around again and kicked the bowl over, the broth soaking into the cold ground. The two dogs rushed forward and started licking the spot where the bowl was spilled, and Shirley spun around once more and inched backward toward the curs with her hands outstretched behind her.

She felt a tug, then another, and looked back to see that the two hungry animals were now starting to chew on the smelly rawhide. She pulled while the two dogs bit into the leather thong, and she tried her best to keep her shivering down as much as possible.

Finally, after several minutes of the two chewing and trying to get as much of the stew-soaked leather into their gullets as possible, the rawhide rope snapped and freed Shirley's hands. She rubbed her wrists and beat her arms across herself as quickly as she could.

After a minute she removed the thong from around her neck and almost dived through the door of the lodge. The old chief and his wife were lying under a thick buffalo robe, and they both sat bolt upright. Shirley's eyes met theirs, but she went directly to the fire and rubbed her body all over trying to warm up. She picked up a bowl and poured herself some more stew from a pot still by the fire. She drank the broth while the two just stared at her. Not a word was spoken.

The white captive spotted another thick buffalo robe across the fire from them and she, still staring at the two, wrapped up in it and curled up close to the fire. They looked at each other, then back at her, finally laying their heads down and going to sleep.

They must have reasoned that she had nowhere to go anyway. The wife realized that the *wasicun* woman was probably thankful that the old man owned her instead of some young buck full of lust. The chief's wife had heard that the captive was the woman of Wamble Uncha, so she knew where her heart must be.

Shirley pulled the buffalo robe up over her head, then with her eyes finally hidden from all others she silently wept, long and hard. She finally stopped and thought, she had survived so far and must continue to do so. She knew that Chris would find her somehow, some way. If anybody could, it was Christopher Columbus Colt.

Randolph Webb and his gang had been in Colorado Territory working on pushing miners off promising claims for the colonel when he got the message. Webb left immediately with ten henchmen and thugs. Their intention was to run in with Colt somewhere near Boise Barracks. The message was simple: kill Colt and all the horses he had with him and make it look like it had been done by Indians. As with most criminals, Colonel Potter was too ignorant to realize that no Indians would believe that any other group of Indians would kill a herd of horses. That would be like a banker taking over another bank and burning all its money.

Randolph Webb wasn't anxious to tangle with Chris Colt but Moose Connors would love it. He was that type. He had heard that Colt had killed the giant Will Sawyer in a gun battle, so he wanted to take him on with knuckle and fist. Moose was one of those behemoth men who could lift a boulder when other men couldn't budge it. He loved to fight more than eat, probably because everybody else was always much smaller and less muscular than he. Moose had always been big and was always a bully. He found out as a child that he could intimidate everyone, and in his early teens, even started beating his own father.

Webb took nine other men with Moose. The men all had thoughts of the thousand-dollar bounty, except for Moose. From the beginning of the trip, he talked incessantly about how he was going to kill Colt with his bare hands. So disproportionate were the boundaries of the scout's abilities in legend already, these men didn't take into account the fact that he was not only outnumbered and virtually alone, but was totally blind as well.

*   *   *

Clay Sampson was a ladies' man and a businessman. He had come to Salt Lake City to set up operations for Potter there. Most of his time had been spent in the local brothels, however, and he hadn't really recruited any thugs yet for Potter. It was just as well with him when he got the message, because he wanted the thousand-dollar bounty himself and more importantly the reputation of being the man who killed Chris Colt. Clay set off from Salt Lake City by himself and pointed his horse's nose in the direction of the Camas Prairie region of Idaho Territory. He was indeed a businessman and his business was killing people. Clay wasn't so much a shootist in the conventional sense in that he accomplished most of his killings at a distance and in the back. He didn't care as long as he could make money from his handling of firearms. Duels in the street and such were ridiculous to him, and he could not understand why two men would risk their lives over such a silly notion. To him, if you wanted to kill a man, it was so much easier to select a good ambush site, hide, and put the sights of a good long gun on the middle of the person's back, then squeeze off the shot. You still got paid, but you didn't take a chance on getting shot like the gunslingers with the pistols. Clay carried a Sharps .50-caliber buffalo gun with a scoped sight for most of his shooting. He also carried a Winchester .44 lever-action rifle with a seventeen-round magazine for his closer work. The Winchester .44 carbine looked similar to the same caliber rifle, but only held thirteen rounds and had only a twenty-inch barrel. The .44 rifle had a twenty-four-inch barrel.

If he was forced to use a short gun, Clay wore a black broadcloth suit with a pair of Smith & Wesson Pocket .38s in shoulder holsters tucked out of sight under his arms. The two little guns were lightweight and easy to hide or carry in a coat pocket, if need be. His goal was to take care of his quarry with the longer-barreled weapons anyway.

Chris Colt, chief of scouts, rode his trusted friend War Bonnet, trailing a very brave young Nez Perce warrior, barely twelve years old but with the heart of a thirty-year-old dog soldier. Colt could not see, but his other senses were heightened, and he continuously practiced his quick-draw while they rode, dry-firing his Colt .45 eagle-butt Peacemakers. Chris trusted Ezekiel to let him know if they approached a low overhanging branch, and he trusted his horse to follow Ezekiel's and keep him out of trouble.

The mother-of-pearl grips on his revolvers each had a hand-carved eagle with a rattlesnake clutched in its beak and in its talons, the symbol of the country of Mexico. Apparently some designer at Colt Firearms liked this engraving.

Colt had miles to go on his mission to return a herd of horses and a small boy to an enemy chief he was supposed to be scouting against for the U.S. Cavalry. The woman of his dreams, the love of his life, was dragging a travois behind her, the slave of an old Cheyenne chief, who was leading his band toward Canada.

Rip Brangston, a small, mean-eyed gunfighter, was leading six men from Oregon to intercept and kill Colt and his little charge. Clay Sampson, a sharpshooting dry-gulcher, was on his way from Salt Lake City to intercept Colt and kill him from ambush. Randolph Webb and ten more killers were on their way from Colorado Territory to find and kill Chris Colt first. One of those ten men was a giant of a man named Moose Connors who dreamed of killing Colt with his bare hands.

Was the chief of scouts at a disadvantage? He was pushing a herd of prime Appaloosa horses and was accompanied by a twelve-year-old Nez Perce boy who was acting as his eyes, because Colt was totally blind. Was he at a disadvantage though?

If Colt had known all who were coming after him at one time, he would have told them one and all, "Boys, you want me, you better go get some reinforcements."

While Chris and Ezekiel followed the lazy winding Snake, letting the horse herd graze occasionally along the way, Shirley Ebert walked blisters on her feet and worked her fingers to the bone getting closer and closer to the Canadian border. She would stop and look off toward the west wondering about the fate of the man she loved so much, until a stick across the back from her captor or his wife would snap her back to reality and the backbreaking chores of a slave. Shirley would have given anything to know that Chris was safe, but she held a deep belief that Colt was a special man. She knew that he would endure and survive any trial and end up as a winner. If only she knew where he was.

Chapter 3

>>>>>>>>>>>>>>>>>>>

Dancing on
Quicksand

"We are leaving a big valley," Ezekiel said. "We now go into a narrow canyon."

Colt said, "Where does the sun now stand?"

"It's about noon," Ezekiel said with a chuckle.

"Educated coyote pup," Chris said.

Ezekiel laughed.

The scout said, "Son, you make sure your eyes are like the eagle's. Watch for sunshine reflecting off a rifle barrel. Anything out of the ordinary."

Ezekiel said, "If I do see someone in ambush, I will yell 'jump left' or 'jump right' to let you know which side of your horse you can jump off."

The two rode forward, and the herd of Appaloosas filed into the narrower terrain naturally as the rugged land closed in around them.

Colt said, "Tell me how the land looks."

Ezekiel replied, "To our front and to our right the land goes up high and is all rock. The river is a little below us on that side. On our left, the land walks softly toward the sky but big pieces of rock stick up all along its side like knives sticking up through a tanned hide. There are trees all over its back like a blanket to keep it warm in the winter. Where we ride is long grass and there are bushes along the trail and sometimes small trees and rocks."

"Watch the knives sticking through the hide, and watch the ears of your horse."

"He will smell or hear someone before my eyes can find them," Ezekiel said, understanding.

Colt replied, "If you watch his ears, they will aim at him like a rifle and tell you where he is. You must also watch for many men, not just one with a rifle. Someone will probably want to kill me if they heard I'm blind."

Ezekiel said, "Colt with no eyes is like the grizzly with one ear cut off. It might be hard for him to hear us, but I would not whisper near him."

Minutes later Colt spoke. "I feel the sun. Is it out?"

"There are no clouds."

Chris replied, "I feel bad feelings. Be like the eagle."

Ten minutes later Chris heard Ezekiel shout, "Jump! Jump!"

Chris dived to his right and his face tore into a thick bush as his hands came up protectively. He hit the ground and immediately curled into a shoulder roll. He felt himself on a steep hill, heard a loud crack of the bullet going overhead. Still rolling downhill through thorn bushes, he heard the muffled report of the gun a few seconds later. It was a Sharps buffalo gun, fired from what had been his left front. Colt slammed into a tree with his back and grunted in pain, the wind leaving him in a rush.

He lay there fighting panic, his breath coming in short order. Colt strove to control his panic. Someone had just tried to shoot him and narrowly missed. He did not know if he was in the man's sights right now. His hand went out to his front, sides, and rear. He could tell that he was in thick bushes on the side of a steep hill.

Chris waited, sweating, fighting to remain calm as he listened and wondered if he was hidden from view. He waited five minutes, ten minutes, more. A horse approached, slowly. Was it Ezekiel? Colt thought and reasoned. Ezekiel would have rushed to his side. The horse pranced. He could picture it by the sound of its feet. Indian ponies didn't prance. Was the boy dead?

The horse got closer and Colt hugged the ground, hoping beyond hope that he could not be seen. It wore shoes, he heard them click on stone. It was definitely a white man. Directly above him the horse stopped. Colt's heart pounded in his ears. His ears strained for the slightest sound.

Suddenly he heard a Winchester being cocked, followed by a voice saying, "Gee, pardner, I wonder why there's a big mark here going into these bushes on this hillside. Heard you were blind, Colt. How about if I set fire to this brush and shoot you when you run screaming out, on fire?"

Colt's heart leapt in his throat. Fire! He heard a match being struck, and he sprang into action.

In his mind's eye, Colt had pictured the horse, and

when the man spoke, he did the same thing. He pictured where the man sat his horse, so Colt jumped up, firing both Colt .45 Peacemakers. He dodged to his left and kept firing right and left of where he had heard the voice, then jumped right, still firing. He heard bullets making solid impacts and a bullet screamed past his left ear at the same time he felt the muzzle flash heat on his face. Something crashed in the brush and came at him rapidly. Colt quickly holstered his guns, put his hands up, and felt something slam into his body throwing him backward. He felt his head hit the ground.

Colt heard the brush burning in front of him, jumped up, and grabbed both guns from the holsters. His head swam, and he felt nauseated.

Small hands pulled him farther down the hillside.

"Be still, Great One." Ezekiel's voice came out of the blackness. "They are all around us."

As Colt's senses cleared, he realized the crackling sounds were a small fire, and he felt coolness on his skin away from the fire, a damp coolness. The crackling sounds made slight echoes. Colt had the distinct feeling that he had awakened from a dream.

Colt whispered, "We are in a cave."

Ezekiel said, "Yes. Do you know what happened?"

Colt said, "No."

The boy said, "You are the warrior all say you are and more. We rode where the trail came along a cliff. Father Sun gave me a warning by shining off the barrel from the closest rocks to our front. By your right side was a hill with many thick bushes with tiny knives on their arms and legs. The hill was steep. Where I was was a cliff with rocks below and the mighty River of the Snake. When I started to yell, my pony jumped and lost where his foot wanted to be on Mother Earth. I could not yell to jump left, because I was in the air, then falling many feet below to my death. My pony did die on the rocks, but I fell into the angry water. I saw you jump off the hill when I yelled. I swam against the angry water and my muscles kept saying to quit and make the spirit journey but my heart kept telling me to swim like a mighty warrior would.

"I made it to the rocks on the other side and pulled myself up into the rocks. I lost my weapons. I climbed up higher and higher until I was looking across the river at where you were in the bushes on the hill.

"I saw a white man in a black suit and black hat and black boots ride up the trail on a big red horse. He looked all around and held a rifle across his saddle. He kept looking down at the bushes along the trail, and I wanted to know if he saw you. Then he cocked the rifle and spoke to the bushes. He then put a cigar in his mouth and lit a match, and the mighty Wamble Uncha stood up right below him in the bushes and fire came from both of your hands. Each time your guns spoke, a bullet found a place to go into the man and into his horse. His gun fired by you, but he was hit already many times and so was his horse. They were both dead, then the horse and man fell and the horse hit you and you fell backward and hit the hill where the bushes didn't grow. You have been asleep for many hours."

Ezekiel poured a cup of coffee for Chris and handed it to him and went on, "I counted bullets and the holes in the man and horse. You shot ten bullets, and there were three holes in the horse and four holes in the man."

"I feel very bad that I killed his horse."

Ezekiel said, "It was a good horse and was very proud, like yours."

Colt sipped the coffee.

Ezekiel went on, "We are across the river in the cliffs and rocks, where I found this cave. It goes through a big rock and behind it is a small canyon with grass and water. I dragged you with War Bonnet and found a place to cross the river with the herd. The horses went through here and are in the canyon. They can only leave this way. Before Father Sun climbed under his robe, seven white men with guns came. Their leader is small like the antelope."

"They see us?" Colt asked.

"No," the boy answered. "All were hidden and I watched. They found the dead man and his horse, but not his guns, for they are now mine. He made the river steal my knife and bow. Many come now to kill the mighty Wamble Uncha, but they will find that even with no eyes he can still see with his spirit. I am setting down a plate of food. Do you smell it, Colt? It is good. I have watched you cook."

Chris ate a hearty meal of bacon, biscuits, beans, and he and the boy each had a can of peaches. The lad had found these last items in the dead man's saddlebags. The food was horrible. The biscuits were dry and the bacon and beans overcooked, even burned, but the peaches and coffee made up for it.

"Thanks. It's good," Chris lied. "How about some more coffee?"

Ezekiel poured him some more and said, "It has snowed outside the cave. The hidden canyon has no wood. I must go across the river and fetch us more firewood."

Colt said, "You are right that we must hole up here, but it is too dangerous for you to hunt for firewood alone. You must stay."

Ezekile said, "I must go, Colt. We will freeze. If we do not obey the tribal laws of the mountains, they are offended and become our enemy and will kill us. If we treat them with respect, they will be our friends."

Colt could not argue with the simple logic of the boy whose people lived one with nature. Ezekiel prepared to leave when Colt's words brought a big warm smile to his face.

"You will freeze going across the river through the water. Ride War Bonnet. He can outrun anything they have anyway. I guarantee it."

"War Bonnet could take me safely through the middle of any battle," Ezekiel said enthusiastically. "He is indeed a spirit horse."

"Careful," Chris said.

Fifteen minutes later, riding bareback, Ezekiel left the confines of the warm cave and ventured out into the freezing night wind and blowing snow. Before leaving, he had walked Chris around the cave and let him feel and touch where the small balance of their firewood was kept, the food, his weapons, and bedroll. As Colt walked around and touched things he tried to picture every detail as if he could see it. Without his vision his other senses and his concentration seemed to be even keener than they normally were. Colt even tried to picture colors on every little log he felt for the fire. He pictured knots in the wood and spots where the bark had been rubbed off. As he smelled the aroma of the coffee he drank, he tried to picture the steam curling off the top of the cup and the smoke from the fire swirling up toward the top of the cave where it would drift to find an escape.

Chris waited about an hour and finally decided to turn in, secure in the knowledge that he always slept lightly. When Ezekiel got back with the firewood he would awaken before the boy could even reach the cave.

The gunshot smoked from Crazy Horse's barrel and one of Custer's men toppled backward from the cavalry charger. Hundreds more were charging the Lakotah war hero from the front and two sides but he was unable to reload quickly enough to be very effective. Colt sat his magnificent paint, a gift from this very man, not knowing what to do. He had to save his friend and brother, but he could not fire at Americans. Finally, he threw down his weapons and charged down the hill toward Crazy Horse. Looking at his friend's handsome features he wondered at how Crazy Horse had never allowed himself to be photographed or have his picture painted. Of all the warriors Colt had seen, Crazy Horse was one of the handsomest, most muscular, and most striking in appearance. A single eagle feather was worn down and cocked to the side in the back of his braided hair. He had a hawklike nose, high cheekbones, and intelligent eyes. He stood right at six feet in height, his frame heavy, but his build whipstock lean, with muscles and sinew like steel cables all over his arms, chest, back, and legs. He always wore a red lightning bolt zigzag from forehead down to chin when in battle, and he was covered with a fine, gray clay dust.

Colt heard many shots now from the cavalry, and he suddenly realized it was from across the river as he sat bolt upright. *Ezekiel.*

Chris's ears strained to listen for any sound, and he crawled on hands and knees toward the door of the cave. Above the sound of the churning river below, he heard a couple of muffled shouts far away. Finally, another far-off gunshot, followed by two more.

Chris spun and stood, holding his hand above his head to keep from hitting it on the cave roof. A giant boulder protected the door of the cave from detection across the river and Chris remembered that the cave and mouth were high—twenty feet in some places. He walked as quickly as he could manage and located his weapons and supplies. He dressed for cold weather, including his buffalo coat that kept him warm on the coldest of days or nights. He felt with his hands and checked the loads in his guns and pistol belt, grabbed up his rifle, and moved for the door.

Colt felt his way with his right foot and stepped out into the cold night. He felt along the giant boulder and worked his way along it until he was around it and facing across the white-water course. He heard another shot, followed by many mixed rifle and pistol shots. This was followed by the sound of many distant shouts and muffled curses.

Chris's mind started to race, but he quickly calmed himself. He felt trapped, but worse than that, he felt totally helpless to assist his young charge who apparently was in deep trouble right now. Chris now heard the young brave riding full out on War Bonnet directly across from him, followed, seconds later, by what sounded like four men on shod horses.

As Ezekiel rode directly across from him the boy started shouting, "The grouse! The grouse!"

The words suddenly struck Colt full in the face, and he froze in place. There must have been a moon out and the boy spotted him. When in doubt in a situation like that, the best thing to do would be to freeze. Moving would make it much more likely for him to be spotted.

When all the horses passed by and went out of hearing down the river, Colt made his way back into the cave and removed his coat and Hudson's Bay blanket leggings. The white leggings had green and pink stripes on the bottom and were flared out Sioux style. He wore them as chaps in the winter, as they helped keep his legs warm.

Using his hands for eyes, Colt tossed out the old pot of coffee and made a new one, figuring the young boy would probably be very cold when he returned. If he returned.

While making the coffee, Colt grinned to himself. He knew what the boy was thinking and he thought about the lad's courage. Running by and yelling, "The grouse," Ezekiel knew that the men behind him could not hear his words and would figure it was a war whoop anyway. Colt knew that a mother grouse would pretend like she had a broken wing and was crippled and would crawl away from her nest with her children in it with a coyote, fox, or some other predator after her. This was done until she had lured the animal far enough away from her nest that it would not realize that there had been a nest nearby with young ones. Once the bird got the predator far enough away from her family that she knew they were safe, she would suddenly seem miraculously healed and would take flight.

Colt figured that Ezekiel must have seen him, because he wouldn't yell if Colt were still inside the relatively soundproof cave. Colt must have been standing there silhouetted against the boulder, which was probably pure white almost. In any event, Ezekiel was letting Chris know that he was leading them away from their hideout. The boy would return later when it was safe.

Chris made himself some elk steak and heated up biscuits they hadn't finished earlier. He downed these with coffee and waited, rolling and lighting up one of his rare cigarettes. Colt guessed it was precisely dawn when he heard the hoof steps of his horse approaching.

His heart lightened a little as he listened to War Bonnet climbing up the rocks from the river and entering the cave. One of the first things Chris learned after becoming blind was to learn to identify the sound of his horse.

War Bonnet entered the cave and Colt said, "Sounded like you had a war last night, boy. Are you okay?"

War Bonnet whinnied and a horse outside whinnied. Colt made his way to War Bonnet and felt for his nose and petted the big paint, ready to pinch his nostrils if he started to whinny again.

A voice from the door said, "Now, ain't thet purty. Ole Chris Colt feeling around with his hands to pet his big red nigger horse. Too bad thet red nigger kid's still bein' hunted down by my partners. Guess I'll have to collect the bounty on ya all by my lonesome. I tole them idjits all we had ta do was foller yer horse and he'd take us right to ya."

Colt said, "What happened to the boy?"

"Ran into one of our boys out takin' hisself a water," said the voice. "The kid was leadin' yer damned horse all loaded down with firewood, when Paul's jest standin' there lettin' his water out and sees 'im. What's thet little red nigger do? Jest a little kid. He pulls up a Winchester and puts one right betwixt ole Paul's peepers. Then the little red devil unloads thet firewood right quick and hops aboard that white devil horse a yourn and tries to stampede our horses. Then he swings the horse aroun' and instead of runnin', he swings down around thet horse's neck and runs right through our camp and puts a .44 through Chester's right thigh and takes off whoopin' and hollerin' like a damn banshee ghost or sumthin'."

Colt said, "Seems to me, you should have gotten the message."

"What's thet, Colt?" the man said, earing back the hammer on his Russian .44.

Colt didn't miss the clicking sound. He would have to make a move shortly.

Chris Colt's hands swept down with blinding speed and his guns came up in one fluid motion while he stepped to his left bumping onto War Bonnet's flank. He quickly stepped to the right while firing over and over blanketing the area where he thought the shooter to be. Colt's ears rang as he heard his own guns and the other man's going off in the confines of the solid rock room. He was sure that he heard bullets hitting flesh. He heard a body slam into the boulder and slide to the ground. Was the man dead though? he wondered. Colt's life depended on it. He heard the man's gun being cocked and Chris fell to the ground firing his right handgun straight ahead and parallel to the ground. He fired the left, then the right again. He rolled to his right and his head hit a hard log on the woodpile.

Not again, Chris thought, as he lay there in blackness listening to his labored breathing. His head ached from the blow to the temple on the woodpile and a wave of nausea passed through him again. He heard a wheezing sound and bubbling. Then there was no sound at all, except his heart beating in his ears. Feeling a sharp headache, Chris crawled forward on his belly until he reached the shooter in the cave door. Colt reached out and felt the man's body. Locating the

neck, he felt no pulse. His hands checked the body and
found bullet holes through the left cheek, left forearm,
stomach, groin, right thigh, right shoulder, and right
side of the chest, and three fingers had been shot off
the left hand.

Colt could not believe his accurate shooting.

There was a sudden flash and Chris drew his guns,
then holstered them. He made his way to War Bonnet
and felt his horse for bullet holes but found none. In
the meantime, he kept blinking his eyes against the
pain. The light flooding into his eyes was blinding and
Chris laughed over it. He walked to the canteen and
poured water in his eyes, shaking his head from side to
side. The headache was gone and so was his blindness.

It took a while but Colt was seeing as good as new
within a half an hour. Chris figured the blow on the
woodpile must have caused it, and he didn't know if it
was permanent. For the moment, he had his vision
back.

He looked around the cave and at the dead man on
the floor.

Suddenly he thought of the man's horse and he went
outside into the morning sun, after first drawing two
thick coal marks under his eyes to prevent snow blindness or any injury to his sensitive "new" eyes. Colt
silently said a little prayer of gratitude while he walked
down and picked up the reins of the dead man's stocky
blood bay horse. He led the gelding up the rocks to
the cave, while Chris admired the world all around
him.

Below him the Snake River churned from his right

to his left in big angry foamy swirls. Ice had formed along the edges of the river wherever the water had been reasonably still. The rest of the beautiful country-side was covered with a thick blanket of snow. On his side of the river, the country was nothing but steep rock walls and little clefts running down from high granite cliffs. On the opposite side, there were mountain ridges but the land sloped up a little more gently and was covered with snowcapped evergreen trees and quaking aspens. Every couple of acres had at least one rock outcropping jutting up in the midst of the greenery. The drop to the river was abrupt—maybe fifty feet down vertically. Looking far to his left, Colt saw where the river turned back away from him and the rapids seemed to disappear.

He led the horse into the cave, fighting the panic-stricken animal once it smelled the blood of its owner, which it had to step over. Colt picked the body up and draped it across the saddle, while covering the horse's eyes with the man's slicker. He unsaddled War Bonnet, rubbed him down with a blanket, and led him back to the meadow to graze. Colt checked on the other horses while he was there and returned to the cave where he cleaned his Colt .45 Peacemakers. He was now able to truly admire the hand-carved ivory grips showing the bald eagle on each holding a rattlesnake in its beak while perching on the serpent's long body. The silver barrels also had hand-engraved floral designs on them. The holsters and belt were black and also bore hand-tooled floral designs.

Colt cleaned all his weapons and loaded them. Then he dressed, garbing himself for combat.

Chris poured another cup of coffee and whistled for War Bonnet. The big stallion trotted into the cave and up to his master. Colt saddled him and led him toward the door of the cave. As they neared the entrance, War Bonnet laid his ears back and feinted a bite at the blood bay gelding, which turned and walked out the door intimidated by the big paint.

Colt checked the bonds on the dead man's body to make sure he was securely tied to the saddle. Grabbing the lead line on the dead man's horse, he swung up onto the back of his beloved paint and gave War Bonnet the reins, as the big stud picked his way carefully down the rocks toward the roaring river. He turned left at the river's edge and headed toward the bend farther upstream and the ford Ezekiel had been using.

The world was white and black and blue and green and Colt reveled in it. Even though Ezekiel was in trouble and Colt had to tangle with a bunch of gunmen, he couldn't help but enjoy and appreciate having his sight back. He didn't know if he would suddenly go blind again or not, but Chris wasn't the type to worry about things like that. If it happened he'd deal with it at that time, but he had a feeling that it wouldn't happen.

He saw a golden eagle soaring high overhead swirling around in lazy circles looking at a frozen world down below. If he could fly like that, Colt thought, he would be looking down at Ezekiel right now.

Chris thought back to a dreamer he knew in his

National Guard unit in the Union Army. The man told Chris that someday man would be able to fly like a bird. If that were not enough, he also said that someday buggies would drive around without horses pulling them. The man couldn't explain how such things would be powered, but he asked Colt to consider how far man had come already and the many inventions that men had come up with. Chris thought about it, back then, and wondered if such miracles would actually come about sometime in the future.

Colt crossed the river and looked back to see the dead gunfighter's head and shoulders were completely underwater. When they came out on the far bank, Chris picked up the trail of the killers and his young partner.

Rip was a weasel and had been one his whole life. His mother had been a common prostitute who worked the tent cities that popped up all over the mountains of the West in mining communities. Anytime some prospector made a strike that turned out to be more than a glory hole, within weeks, other miners, tradespeople, and hangers-on of all types were attracted to the area like it was a giant magnet. Rip's mother was handled by a very rough man named Mike Caudill. He took a group of women around from mining camp to mining camp, depending on recent strikes and availability of money. Caudill set up a large tent and partitioned it off simply with ropes and blankets hung over them. Each bay had a hastily constructed wooden bed frame and small mattress, pitcher and bowl, and prostitute, many of whom were disease-ridden.

Caudill made Rip do chores from the time he could remember and he beat the boy unmercifully, usually just out of meanness. He also took Rip's mother anytime he wanted to sate his own sick desires. On several occasions Mike tried to sell Rip to miners as a sort of slave or indentured servant and once it was to a man who had very strange secrets. In every case, however, Rip's mother intervened and begged Caudill to let her keep her son. She would usually convince the man with sexual favors, but that was only a temporary stopgap measure. Within short order, he would beat the boy again and try to sell him off to someone else.

When Rip was thirteen years old, he took a gun and holster from the edge of a bed while the very drunken man was in the bed occupied with one of the other tarts. The man was small and the holster almost fit Rip around the hips. He punched a hole in the leather with a knife and was able to make it fit. He hid the gun and gunbelt and sneaked out after dark every night to practice dry-firing it. He then would replace the bullets and hide the gun again.

One night Mike Caudill had been drinking heavily. He beat Rip first, then his mother. Rip ran to the hiding place behind the outbuilding and got his weapon. When he returned, he waited until Mike was busy in the cubicle with his mother. Rip ran in and shot the man, unloading the pistol into his tormentor. Unfortunately, one of the bullets passed through Caudill's left arm and pierced the heart of Rip's mother, killing her instantly. Mike wasn't dead yet, so Rip, staring in horror at his dead mother, grabbed a knife and slit the wounded man's throat, running out into the night and starting a future of running from the same brutal scene over and over again. No matter where he went Rip was haunted by having killed his own mother and he tried to rid himself of the memory by killing as many people as possible, especially in stand-up gunfights.

Unlike Clay, Rip liked to face down men with reputations and shoot it out with them. There were several reasons for this. First, he enjoyed killing. Second, he wanted to make himself feel that he was somehow worthy. Maybe with a gun he could intimidate all men so no other would abuse him the way Caudill had or take sexual favors from someone close to him. Third, although he had never put a gun up to his own temple, a big part of him wanted to die and get rid of the pain.

He looked at all the tracks in the snow around the thicket. He and what was left of his gang had been searching all through the thicket where the tracks led and still could not find the Indian boy. The boy had made many tracks but all of them went into the five-acre thicket but there were no tracks coming out. The boy had simply dived off the big paint horse when he saw he was in a box canyon and run into the thicket. He couldn't have gotten out.

Chester lay not far off moaning in delirium because of loss of blood and the severity of his thigh wound. Paul was dead back at the campsite and now Rip wondered what had become of Woody. He had gone off after War Bonnet when the scout's horse shot through the group, saying the big paint would lead him right to Colt. As Rip considered the possibility, he figured Woody probably was right, but he just didn't like being told what to do.

He was getting fighting mad now, because Woody had been gone too long, Paul was dead, and Chester would be dead within hours. He only had three other men with him, and they hadn't even tangled with Colt yet. All the damage had been done by a little Indian kid. What would happen, he wondered, if and when they located Colt himself. Maybe this time Rip was going to die, he thought. He laughed to himself nervously and a shiver ran up his spine. He shook for a second and a sob escaped his lips.

Rip self-consciously looked around to make sure none of his gang members heard him. His eyes stopped at the sight of Woody's blood bay gelding walking slowly toward him carrying the carcass of its owner. Rip gave out a whistle and the other three bounty hunters trotted up and stared in amazement. Rip gulped as he looked at the body draped over the high cantled Mexican saddle. Woody, his head and shoulders covered with a thick sheet of ice, was staring in death at the snow in front of the horse's path. The shroud of ice over his face made the whole scene even more dramatic.

One of the men said, "I'll be damned."

All eyes looked up a little beyond Woody's horse and to the right at the far edge of the clearing, and they stared at Christopher Columbus Colt sitting proudly on the back of his sixteen-hands-tall gift from Crazy

Horse. Colt wore his floppy-brimmed leather hat, a buffalo coat, elk-skin-fringed gloves, and yellow-striped blue cavalry trousers with his Hudson's Bay blanket winter chaps overtop. Over the buffalo coat, Chris wore his black gunbelt and holsters sporting the twin ivory-handled Colt .45 Peacemakers. In his right hand was a Winchester .44 carbine.

Colt sat calmly but the big paint pranced nervously in place ready for the adrenaline rush of battle. He could sense it. This well-muscled steed dancing in place simply added to the awe and fear in the gun-fighters' minds as they looked at this dangerous enemy whose reputation was legendary in proportion. War Bonnet, with three bright red coup stripes around each upper foreleg, eagle feathers in his mane and tail, and red handprints on both rumps, made the ruggedly handsome chief of scouts/gunfighter look even more formidable.

One of the men looked down at the face of Woody as the horse passed between the men.

Gulping, he raised his hands, his left one still holding his reins, and yelled, "Colt, I want no part of this anymore. Your medicine's just too powerful for me, partner. I heard the weather is really good down in Texas."

Colt nodded, letting the man know with a look that he made a wise decision.

Rip, angered by this treason, hollered at the big man as he started to ride away, "You yellow-bellied coward! No one cuts out on me!"

The big man turned, and Rip yelled, "Draw!" as his right hand swept across his body, cross-pulling his gun.

It suddenly bucked twice in his hand as the rider flew backward off his horse, a crimson stain spreading across his belly. He lay on the ground writhing and screaming in obvious pain.

"Scream and die, you yellow cur!" Rip hissed.

Colt said, "I have a question. Why are all you men after me?"

Rip hollered back, "Sure, you're entitled to know before you die. Colonel Rufus Porter, out of the Wallowa Valley in Oregon, is our boss. He offered a thousand coin for your right ear. Since I'm going to collect it, I don't mind telling you. Now, I got a question for you. How come you ain't blind?"

Colt smiled and said, "God Almighty wants me to see good, so I can kill plenty of rattlers and other vermin! Now you boys came to the ball, who wants the first dance?"

Rip gave the other two warning glances and quietly said, "He's mine."

He dismounted and removed his coat, after adding two bullets and ejecting the spent shells from killing his ex-partner. He spun the right handgun several times and shoved it into the holster on the left side of his abdomen. He wiggled his fingers and licked his lips.

Rip shouted, "It's my dance. I heard you were plenty fast with a gun. I'm ready to waltz. Why don't you try giving me a spin around the floor?"

Colt said, "Okay."

He raised the already-cocked Winchester and fired

right into the middle of Rip's chest sending the puny little gunfighter spinning through the air. Rip landed on a snow-covered brush and hit hard on his backside, eyes staring at Colt.

Weakly he yelled, "You cheated! I wanted to know . . . who's faster!"

"Who cares," Colt said, and rode slowly forward.

He now felt the exhilaration of combat and purposely did not recock the Winchester. Taking note of this, both frigthened but tough remaining gunfighters decided simultaneously to try their luck.

Colt dropped the rifle across his saddlebows and drew the twin Colts. His hands, as usual, were a blur and came up from the holsters, the webs of his thumbs as the guns slid comfortably into his hands. His index fingers quickly squeezed off both triggers and the two would-be killers spilled backward from their saddles. One had been shot right between the eyes, although Colt had aimed at the center of the man's chest. The other man took a .45 slug through the heart, dying instantly.

War Bonnet wanted to gallop toward the enemy, maybe from his conditioning with Crazy Horse. The echoes of the gunfire and the frightened whinnies of the horses died down and only the moans of the first gunman who tried to leave broke the stillness of the after-battle calm. Chris automatically ejected spent shells in all three weapons and reloaded. Only then did he move forward holding War Bonnet to a slow controlled walk.

When he made sure that Rip and the other two were

dead, Colt dismounted with his canteen and tended to the wounded man. He quickly bandaged and assessed the gut wounds. Colt poured some whiskey on the wounds, which he always carried for just such a purpose.

The scout said, "Mister, you got a chance. Looks like the first bullet mushroomed when it hit your belt buckle. The hole's big, but it didn't go in too deep. That shot apparently spun you and the second bullet tore across the muscle and made a slash-type wound. You know how to get to the nearest town?"

"You're helping me, and I was coming to try to kill you."

"A man can always change. You know how to get to the nearest town?"

The man said, "Sure, less than a day's ride. Mr. Colt, I'm a hard man, but this was my first and last ride on the owl hoot trail. If I live through this, I give you my word, I'm going to become a useful citizen in Texas, punching cows the rest of my sorry life."

Colt smiled and heard footsteps coming from the thicket.

He didn't even turn but said, "Found a good hiding place, huh, kid?"

Ezekiel, grinning from ear to ear, said, "The Great Spirit has smiled upon you and told your eyes to see once more."

"Yes," Colt said, "but being blind can be good too. Sometimes you can see many things when your eyes don't work."

Chris thought about Shirley Ebert and made up his

mind right then. He was not a coward, and he would not live his life afraid to fall in love again. He loved the crimson-haired woman even more than he had loved Chantapeta, and as soon as he finished the Nez Perce campaign, he would return to Bismarck and ask her to marry him.

At that time, Shirley fell and pulled a thorn out of the side of her calf. It had been buried beneath the deep snow. She stood again and tugged on the heavy travois, walking toward the winter village site Screaming Horse had decided on in the Valley of Many Smokes, the Yellowstone Valley. In the spring, when the killer mountain snows and blizzards were gone, he would lead his band to Canada and join up with Sitting Bull.

Screaming Horse's sister lashed Shirley across the back with a switch, and Shirley turned, teeth-clenched, and dived headfirst into the woman's midsection, knocking her backward over a log. The woman, struggling for air, tried to stand and Shirley's kick caught her full in the face, bloodying both lips. The Cheyenne braves laughed and chuckled, as Shirley brushed herself off and picked up the end of the travois and continued on.

She would do what she had to do to survive, she thought, but she would be respected while she survived, no matter what. Shirley wondered where Colt was and when he would come to save her. She could not give up hope.

*　　*　　*

Ezekiel and Chris rounded up the horses of the killers, after sending the wounded man on his way, unsaddled the horses, and salvaged what they could use from the saddlebags. They pushed the horses ahead of them and set out to rejoin the rest of the herd at the cave.

An hour later the unlikely friends were on their way west along the Snake. Chris Colt scanned the mountains and valleys, arroyos and gorges, admiring the sight of every tree, every rock, every flake of snow. His experience made him realize just how vulnerable he, and any man, really was.

On the other hand, he was pleased with himself. He had been confronted with a problem that would have made many men give up, but he took it in stride. He had excelled, even in blackness. A blackness that could have created panic and death. Instead, it had become a blackness of knowledge, a screen of darkness that blotted out any distractions to the thinking process.

In that darkness, Chris Colt had come to realize how much he really loved Shirley Ebert. He was, in his blindness, finally able to see that the only thing keeping him from experiencing true love again was a fear of losing the woman he would give his heart to. He had loved Chantapeta and Winona, loved them with all his heart and soul. They were suddenly and viciously snatched away from him. Chris tried to deal with their deaths and their absence, and he thought he had handled it better than most would have. During his blindness, however, he finally realized that he had been wearing a thick bull-hide shield to keep him from getting hurt again over the loss of loved ones. Now he realized his bull-hide shield was also keeping him from loving totally and fully with complete commitment of heart, mind, and soul. Now he would cast the invisible war shield down into the swirling angry waters of the River of the Snake. He would love without fear of losing. He would love the way men and women should love.

Several days later Colt and Ezekiel were pushing the herd through a wide valley, when the riders came.

The eleven men came from the south, riding side by side, as if to overtake the man and boy and sweep over them like ashes over a cabin floor. Colt stopped his horse and nodded toward a draw near the river.

"Boy, get down there and find a hiding place," Colt said.

"Hell no," Ezekiel responded firmly, shocking Colt with his harsh, grown-up words. "I'm young, but I am a warrior. If you and I are to die and make the spirit journey, I will die fighting here with you, not running and hiding like a rabbit."

Colt grinned. He reached into his saddlebags and pulled out makings, rolling two cigarettes. He handed one to Ezekiel and lit them both. The boy cocked the Henry .44 repeater Colt had gotten off one of the dead killers, after losing the one given him by Chris Colt. The scout had gotten a Winchester .44 carbine and a few other guns when he bought the twin Colt Peacemakers.

Colt also removed the Colt revolving shotgun from his left saddle scabbard. In the right scabbard was his Winchester. His Cheyenne bow and quiver of arrows were tied with his blanket roll behind his saddle. Extra guns were in his saddlebags and assorted weapons were hidden in different places. It looked like Colt might need them all.

The group of would-be assassins rode closer while Colt and Ezekiel, looking calm, smoked their cigarettes. The young boy also reached into his parfleche and pulled out a small metal jar. He reached in and daubed red greasy-looking material on his fingers. Within seconds, he had drawn two red stripes across his face from ear to ear.

Chris, accepting Ezekiel's declaration, told the boy his plans. The Nez Perce lad liked the idea and was anxious to carry it out. He shook hands with Colt, tossed his cigarette down, and took off after the horse herd at a gallop. Two of the distant riders took off after him but were apparently called back by a yell from their leader.

War Bonnet sensed battle and began prancing in place again. Chris just sat there sizing the men up as they neared, but to them he looked like a rancher calmly looking over his herd while enjoying a relaxing smoke. Colt knew that he would have to take swift action, and he catalogued each man in his mind by the man's appearance and demeanor. He was actually setting priorities and deciding who would get shot first, second, third, and so on.

The man who looked like he hollered at the others who were going to chase Ezekiel apparently was the leader, so he would go first. The big man would be last, as he would probably be the slowest.

The men kept approaching and Chris gave his twin Colts a reassuring pat. He clutched the Colt revolving shotgun like it was a wife and knew that it would make all these men have pause for thought. In fact, he thought, he would be smart to hold it down low behind the swells and saddle horn just to offer him more of an opportunity for surprise against the many gunmen.

They reached Colt and drew up, still in a broad line, about thirty feet to his front.

Webb said, "Howdy, mister, sure got a lot of Appaloosas there."

Colt said, "Let's cut the small talk, boys. We all know why you're here and you know who I am. Now, who is your leader?"

Webb said, "I am."

With that, Chris whipped up the revolving shotgun and blasted Webb backward out of the saddle with a double-aught blast in the middle of his chest. Not bothering to turn his head at the sound of Ezekiel whooping and hollering, he fired into the man next to Webb's horse, just as the gunfighter started to clear leather. Chris then swung the scattergun to the left end of the line, where another had his gun out already, and Colt spilled him from the saddle, with the man's head opening like a dynamited watermelon.

Colt felt a bullet whip by his ear, and he blasted the shooter while drawing his left handgun at the same time. He put a bullet in the right lung area of another man and turned his head quickly as he noticed all the gang members' horses starting to rear and panic.

The herd of Appaloosas were bearing down on the

flank of the line of gunmen at full gallop, Ezekiel whooping and hollering behind them. The herd ran into the line and caused the shooters' horses to wheel and want to stampede with them.

Holding his carbine in his left hand, Ezekiel wrapped his right arm around his horse's neck and his right leg over its back, while he swung the rifle up under the horse's neck, aimed, and fired with his left hand. In the meantime, not wanting to hit a horse accidentally, Colt dropped the shotgun and grabbed his right-hand Peacemaker, continuing to spill gunmen from their saddles.

It was all over in less than a minute. The herd swept by and Ezekiel swung back around and returned to Colt, who gave him an approving wink and a nod. They faced all the supposed killers and saw men lying all over the ground before them. Several moved slowly but were quite wounded. Finally, Moose stood up and just grinned, shaking his head and shaggy beard from side to side. A small trickle of blood ran down the right side of his head, where he had either been creased by a bullet above the hairline or had struck his head falling off his horse.

He yanked his gunbelt off and signaled for Colt to dismount. Moose was properly named. Big and strong, his scarred looks showed a life of hard living and toughness. The same could be said for Colt, except the scout had a twinkle in his eyes and a look of intelligence, both of which endeared him to good people. Moose Connors, on the other hand, had a look in his eyes that would strike only fear and revulsion in people.

"Well, you're the mighty Colt, huh?" Moose hollered. "You're the one what shot Will Sawyer! I can see you're not blind like they said, nor are you shy of the legend of your shooting, but I come to take you apart knuckle and skull! Or are you a sceered a me?"

The challenge to his ego didn't phase Colt, but the big man wanting to fight him without weapons did. Colt was amazed. He thought to himself, I know I'm not *great*, but I wouldn't pick a fight with me. Why do so many of these idiots try to pick a fight?

Chris Colt felt the rage building in him and just grinned. Moose had a lot of fat on his body, but it was quite obvious he had plenty of muscle too. The scout was nowhere near the size of Will Sawyer, who had stood over seven feet tall. Colt found some relief in the fact that Moose was more like a normal-sized behemoth, maybe six feet three and 280 pounds or so. He definitely would be a handful, to say the least.

Ezekiel watched with interest, wondering why Colt didn't shoot this big man and be done with him. He didn't care, though. Colt had become his hero and would handle the situation, coming out on top no matter what. Ezekiel wanted to become that kind of man himself. What the young Nez Perce didn't know was that, in Colt's eyes, he was becoming that kind of young man.

Colt stripped off his guns and handed them to Ezekiel.

"What are you doing?"

Colt didn't even look his way.

He just smiled and said to himself, "The hell with it. Heeyah!"

War Bonnet lunged forward, bearing down on the giant Moose Connors, who stood growling like a mad dog. The big paint swept by while Colt, with a mighty war whoop, dived headfirst and crashed into the big man, his body propelled at great speed.

Chris's dive sent the big man crashing backward with a thud, while Colt rolled over him and came up on his feet. His left shoulder was hurting and a knot on his forehead was forming from the dive.

Moose came forward with a roar and Colt stood his ground. The big man had his arms outstretched and wanted to sweep Colt up in a bone-crushing bear hug, but the scout dropped to the ground at the last second, his left foot catching the front of Moose's left instep, and Colt's right foot kicking the back of Moose's left knee, sending the behemoth forward onto his face.

Colt rolled to his feet as Connors, furious, came off the ground with a lunge and a scream of fury. His right shoulder crashed into Colt's washboard stomach. The scout's feet lifted off the ground and he slammed to his back with all of Moose's force. Colt felt the air leave his lungs and he couldn't get his breath. He fought the panicky feelings knowing he would breathe in a short time.

Moose clawed at Chris's eyes and howled like a banshee.

Chris clapped the palms of both hands on Moose's ears, twice in quick succession. Moose grabbed his ears in pain but recovered too quickly and a fist the size of a small turkey slammed into the chief of scouts's face, knocking loose several teeth and splitting Colt's lips.

Colt knew he couldn't take many punches with that much power. He shook his head and saw Moose raise his meaty fist for another punishing blow. Colt's right hand went down and grabbed the giant's crotch, squeezing hard and twisting. Moose grabbed at Colt's hand and screamed in pain, falling back from the scout and landing on his side. Colt rolled out to the side and jumped to his feet while the big man rolled on the ground holding himself and moaning.

He suddenly jumped to his feet in complete rage. Spittle started foaming out of his mouth and he was chugging like a locomotive going uphill. Head down he ran at Colt who deftly sidestepped and whipped out a right cross that smashed the big man's nose.

Chris's belly ached and his lips were swelling rapidly, when he sensed a presence.

Seventy or eighty war-painted Indian warriors appeared from two different draws, one to the left and one to the right. They were spread into equal groups, riding forward in two lines. Colt didn't care. He kept fighting, but he noted that the braves were not Nez Perce and they had rounded up all the Appaloosas. They looked to him to be Paiutes or Bannocks.

"Looks like we're both gonna lose our scalps anyhow, Colt," Moose sputtered.

"Speak for yourself, big man," Chris said and swung a hard right that caught Connors on the left ear.

The big man reeled and came forward head down again. Colt stood his ground, shooting his arm through

the giant's outstretched left arm and running it behind
the man's back, while twisting his body to the side. He
stepped across with his right foot and twisted suddenly,
sending the big man flying over his right hip and crashing on his back with a thud. Moose got up slowly and
Colt kicked him full power in the already injured groin.
Connors's air escaped with a rush, and Colt battered
his face with a punch that sent shock waves through
his arm and to the shoulder.

The big man was now teetering with blood streaming
from his mouth, nose, and left ear. Chris stepped in
swinging with both hands while the big man did the
same, but most of his arm-weary blows struck Chris on
the shoulders and the forearms. Moose grabbed both of
Chris's arms, so the scout lunged forward and butted
the man with the top of his head. This broke Moose's
grip and tore the left side of his face open with a long
wide gash, exposing the left cheekbone. Blood streaked
down his face and Colt hit him with a right cross that
he stepped into with all his power and weight.

Moose Connors didn't fall back or sideways. His eyes
just simply rolled back in his head and he slowly folded
up like a carpetbag suitcase and lay on the ground, out
cold.

Chris turned to face the Indians, two of whom had
grabbed Ezekiel and were holding his weapons and the
reins to the boy's horse.

Chris spotted the chief of the warriors and recognized him.

Colt said, "Buffalo Horn, you scouted against the

Lakotah and Chyela for the white eyes. Why are the Bannock painted for war?"

Buffalo Horn said, "We kill *wasicun* and drive from lands Everywhere Spirit lets Bannock live and hunt on."

Colt smiled and said, "Thought you saw firsthand how many *wasicuns* there are and how much power they have. You sure you want to disobey the white grandfather in Washington?"

"Tha Bannock are not children. No tell obey white eyes," Buffalo Horn said. "We fight. We kill white eyes. We take horses Nez Perce, too."

Buffalo Horn nodded and about fifty guns were cocked and pointed at Colt. He froze and took one step, hearing something behind him. He turned and saw Moose Connors, half awake, half out, but standing. The man had drawn a Reid's "My Friend" Knuckleduster .32-caliber derringer and was aiming it at Colt, ignoring the numerous red men all around.

The chief of scouts rolled forward in a somersault, his right hand shooting behind his neck and down the back of his shirt. As he came to his feet, Moose's .32 went off and flipped Colt's hair as Colt's bone-handled Bowie knife spun over twice in the air and buried itself to the hilt in the center-left of the big man's chest.

Colt walked over to the big man and stepped on his chest, roughly jerking the big knife free, which he wiped on Connors's jeans.

He turned and faced Buffalo Horn, who was pointing a brass tack- and eagle feather-decorated Winchester carbine, looking much like Colt's.

The chief said, "Throw knife, weapons down."

Chris didn't move, gauging his actions.

The chief nodded and Ezekiel was butt-stroked off his horse and landed, moaning, on the ground. The warrior who did it fired into the ground next to the boy's head. Ezekiel jumped up and spit toward him. Colt grinned, but he surrendered his weapons. He and the Nez Perce were grabbed and bound by rawhide thongs.

As he was bound, Colt noted that two of the wounded gang members had crawled off during the fight with Moose and would make it back to the white man's world with their scalps. The rest were not so lucky. Three still lived and were quickly dispatched and scalped like the others and stripped of weapons and valuables.

Chris and Ezekiel were placed on their horses and led off by the group of warriors. They traveled into some broken hills for about an hour and came to a circle of lodges, with women and children rushing out to greet the Bannock warriors and the herd of well-bred Appaloosa horses.

The white man and his young red charge were taken off their horses and tied, arms in the air, to the thick limbs of two trees side by side. The warriors went off to talk to their families and admire the spotted ponies they had stolen. Some paraded around the village showing off the scalps they collected thanks to the fighting ability of the famous chief of scouts.

Chris couldn't feel his arms by the time Buffalo

Horn walked over to him and Ezekiel. The chief strutted up to the white man, a haughty look on his face.

Colt said, "I heard you were highly respected by General Miles and No-Hip-Bone (General Terry). I am on my way to be chief of scouts for General One-Arm (O. O. Howard). I was told he wanted you and your warriors to be his principal scouts. Why do you do this?"

Buffalo Horn grinned. "I will scout for One-Arm. You will not. You will smoke the pipe with your grandfathers."

Colt smiled and said, "Oh, want to get rid of your boss before I even get there. I suppose it would be easy for a yellow bitch dog like you to kill me while my arms are tied to a tree. It is not the Lakotah way, but I suppose the Bannock—who are suckled by coyote bitches—do fight like this."

Buffalo Horn snarled and his fist lashed out striking Colt full in the groin. Chris felt tremendous pain shoot through his groin and intestines, but he refused to show any discomfort whatsoever. His only chance was to shame this chief into untying him.

"Yeah, I was right," Colt managed. "Can't fight me like men. The Bannocks tie me up and kick me. Why don't you stand back by those trees yonder where you can hide and shoot me over and over again with your rifles? Maybe I won't kill too many of your warriors."

This last challenge was enough for Buffalo Horn. His lips curling back over his teeth, he stepped forward, pulling out his antler-handled razor-sharp knife.

He pushed the blade up against Colt's throat and a small line of blood appeared.

Chris allowed a smile. "You cowards cut tied-up enemies, too, huh?"

The chief swung the blade in a wide arc and cut through the rawhide holding Colt's right arm, then the left. Next, he cut through Ezekiel's. He nodded and several braves dashed forward grabbing the two and leading them toward the lodge circle. Colt and Ezekiel rubbed the circulation back into their wrists and arms as rapidly as they could. They knew that they would need their arms.

They were pushed into the center of the circle of lodges and were surrounded by braves.

Buffalo Horn stepped up and said, "The Bannock give enemy chance live."

Buffalo Horn nodded and a warrior ran his horse out one hundred yards away from the camp and tied a feather to a tree branch. He returned to the group.

Buffalo Horn said, "You run. Go by feather. Bannock come. Burn you in fire."

A number of warriors started whooping in excitement and anticipation and Colt suddenly started whistling just like a red-tailed hawk. The assembled braves stared at Colt in wonder, then started laughing at him making bird sounds at a time like this. Colt nodded at Ezekiel, and the two took off running as fast as they could. One hundred yards was not very far.

They passed the feather in less than a quarter of a minute and ran as quickly as they could across the snow-covered meadow. As soon as they went by the feather, they heard a great many shouts going up behind them and turned their heads to see many braves, weapons in hand, chasing them across the flat area. Colt reached over and grabbed the back part of Ezekiel's breechcloth and held on to it, helping the younster run faster.

"Let us turn and fight," Ezekiel cried. "I do not wish to be struck down while running like the rabbit."

Colt yelled, "Just run, boy. We will run like the antelope."

Colt smiled as he saw the fast-approaching Bannock warriors and the magnificent black and white paint horse charging through their midst. It had a long braided tether rope trailing behind it, with a thick tree branch attached to it.

Ezekiel looked back and laughed.

"War Bonnet!

"My friend won't let us die that easy," Colt said.

War Bonnet was upon them in seconds. Shots and arrows began to trail him. Colt swung up onto his back, spun, and grabbed Ezekiel by the forearm and yanked him up behind. The two leaned over and felt the stinging winter wind in their faces as the big paint swept across the snow-covered ground. Colt looked back several times and saw some warriors already mounted and in pursuit.

Ezekiel yelled in Colt's ear, "Mighty One, they come now. War Bonnet cannot carry us both to safety. I will jump down and fight off as many as I can."

"Bull feathers!" Colt hollered. "We've come this far together, son. We'll make it all the way or die."

Chris pushed War Bonnet off to his left front, quartering toward a rocky tree-covered ridge line with steep cliffs overlooking the winding Snake River. The chase continued for an hour with many warriors closing in as the big-muscled horse started feeling the weight of two riders. The terrain was getting rougher now as they neared the cliffs, so Colt took a good hold of the horse's mane with his left hand. They started dodging in and out of boulders and trees, but the Bannock ponies were mountain horses and accustomed to such maneuvers. They still gained ground slowly, almost imperceptibly.

A mile along the cliffside area, Colt slid to a stop suddenly. The rocks had given way to a steep drop-off confronting the two for a long ways down. Colt looked down at the water that churned but swirled lazily down below.

"Can you swim?" Colt asked.

"I am Nez Perce."

Which meant to Chris that either the boy could or it didn't matter to him, as he had a great deal of pride and would teach himself quickly.

Colt said, "Hang on!"

He turned the big paint and charged back at the oncoming braves, overwhelming the warriors and almost stopping their charge. Chris suddenly slid War Bonnet to a stop and pulled on his reins to the right while pushing on the left shoulder with his left knee and squeezing his right calf into the rib cage. The horse reared and did a rollback, turning his body in midair up over his hips and took off toward the cliff edge.

The warriors, now with renewed hope of the two valuable scalps, pushed their war ponies even harder. Reaching the edge of the cliff, Colt kicked War Bonnet hard in the ribs and the mighty horse jumped out into midair, and the three fell toward the cold water below. It seemed like they fell for minutes. Colt and Ezekiel pushed off the big horse before all three splashed into the water and went down deep.

They came up several yards downstream and swam across the river, the current carrying them out of effective aiming range of the arrows and bullets that tore angrily into the water all around them. Across the river was a large flat forested area and Colt quickly mounted up and pulled the boy up behind him and took off for the wooded haven. Up on the cliff, the warriors watched in disgust and anger, blaming one another for letting the two escape. They could not get down to the river and there was no fording spot for miles.

Colt was into the woods in minutes and quickly wheeled the horse and ran back upriver paralleling the watercourse.

Teeth chattering, he turned his head and said, "There is no place to cross, so we will go back upriver and swim back across and head into the woods. We will make a fire and get warm. Tonight we will get our guns and horses back. Can you keep yourself warm with your mind?"

"No, I am very cold," Ezekiel said. "But I am Nez Perce. I will be okay."

Chris galloped the horse full out and laughed, saying, "I figured you'd say that."

The two ran upriver for a mile and then went back into the water swimming across to the enemy's side again. Colt pushed War Bonnet toward a nearby hilly, tree-covered area. As soon as they got in where Colt thought they were safe he slid to a stop between four hills.

Ezekiel didn't have to be told what to do. He immediately started grabbing dry evergreen needles and pinecones, along with what the mountain men called "squaw wood," dead branches and tinder at the base of trees. One thing the Bannocks had not removed from Colt's boots were some matches he kept in a tiny leather pocket. They had all been dipped in hot candle wax to waterproof them, and Chris prayed now that the wax worked. Colt and the boy both were turning blue already, but the first match lit immediately and caught the tinder.

The two blew on the small fire and the flames caught quickly, building to a roaring, snapping fire in seconds. They stood next to the fire and started removing their clothing, steam already pouring off the wet garments and their hair. Colt, every few seconds, stepped away from the fire and grabbed sticks to hang their clothing on. If the smoke was spotted, they would soon be dead, but Colt had no choice. They had to survive. Fortunately, the Bannock chief had let them keep their winter clothing on while tied.

They spent over an hour drying out and getting warm again, as well as getting War Bonnet dry and warm, too. Colt and Ezekiel kicked snow over the fire and mounted up, moving deeper into the woods. They rode another mile and a half into the woods away from the river and built another fire.

This fire was smaller and they started looking for sharp-edged rocks, finally finding two. Using these rocks as knives, they made two pointed spears from hardwood saplings. After that, the two sat down and ate some wild onions they dug from the cold earth. The onions made them thirsty, so Ezekiel ventured into the trees and came back with sassafras roots, while Colt stripped some birch bark off some birch trees. Colt fashioned the birch bark into two bowls, which he filled with water and put in the fire with the sassafras roots shaved into it. He knew that the fire would not burn the birch above the waterline and would simply bring the tea to a boil.

The sassafras tea tasted good and Colt hated to finish it. The two put out the fire and mounted up on War Bonnet's back and headed toward the Bannock camp. It was less than an hour until dark.

They arrived at a knoll just south of the village right at dusk and left War Bonnet at its base, crawling up on hands and knees, careful not to skyline themselves. Chris was glad to see that the sky was painted with crimson and scarlet streaks mixed with blue and purple. There should be no snowstorm the next day.

The horse remuda was in a grove of trees on the far side of the village. Smoke came from the openings at the top of each lodge and most people were inside, ready to eat their evening meals and not wanting to feel the chill of the winter night. There were three guards on the horse herd and all three were vigilant.

Colt and Ezekiel whispered plans together as they looked at the terrain still visible around the herd and the village. As soon as full darkness arrived, they crawled down the back of the knoll and started in a large circle around the wooded area that held the remuda.

Colt led War Bonnet and the two moved through the darkness of the trees, always vigilant, and moving in a wide semicircle, always keeping the Bannock camp to their right.

At one point, they were directly downwind from the remuda and Colt quickly put his hands over War Bonnet's nostrils to prevent him from whinnying to the other horses. They found a place to leave the big paint, well away from the herd, and the pair moved forward through the trees.

As they reached the herd and spotted the first two guards, they saw that one was not much older than Ezekiel.

Colt sat down on a fallen log and removed his boots and left sock, praying that he would not step on any unexpected cactus plants under the snow. He found a small rocky area and filled the sock with stones, tied the neck of it, and handed it to Ezekiel. Colt pointed at the younger sentry and the Nez Perce slithered off into the darkness.

Colt, instead of going around the herd, dropped to all fours and crawled under and between the Nez Perce and Bannock ponies, headed toward the other sentry.

The one Ezekiel stalked sat on a large rock and over-looked the herd, occasionally turning his head to look into the woods and watch for potential enemies. Ezekiel crept to within fifteen feet and waited behind a tree. Knowing that an enemy can feel someone staring at his back with the underdeveloped sixth sense all people have, Ezekiel did not stare at his quarry. Instead he looked slightly to the man's side so his gaze was not directly upon the guard. He had been told this before by no less than Joseph, but when Colt issued the same warning, the words stuck with him.

After the sentry looked around at the surrounding woods and turned his attention toward the herd Ezekiel went forward and swung the stone-filled sap. It crashed against the temple of the young Bannock brave and Ezekiel heard bone break as the Indian landed heavily on the snow.

Colt moved under the horse's belly closest to the sentry and came off the ground with a low growl, as if he were a rabid coyote. That was all he needed to keep the startled brave from giving out a signal cry. When he realized it was a man, the sentry tried to scream out but it was too late. His windpipe was already crushed by the forearm crashing into it. His feet went out from under him and he landed hard on his back choking from the vicious blow across his Adam's apple. He saw the figure of the tall white man looming above and he reached for his knife but suddenly the man's foot came down on his face with full force. He heard the bones break in his face and felt and saw a bright explosion of color in the blacknesss inside his head. He was no more.

Colt grabbed the dead sentry's rifle, while Ezekiel

slowly went through the herd looking for his own horse and Colt's saddle.

Chris crawled among the horses once again and headed toward the other sentry. He made it in a few minutes but had to wait, as this man looked all around carefully. Colt figured he was in trouble, as this brave was too careful about his work. The scout was relieved though to see that the careful preparations were made so the man could relieve his colon. The sentry removed his breechcloth and squatted down next to a tree about ten feet from the herd. Colt came up silently behind him and clubbed him full power with the butt of the other sentry's rifle, a beat-up old Henry.

Chris stood and looked across the backs of the horses and spotted Ezekiel. He gave him a wave and the boy went through the herd more quickly finally finding his own horse, for which he quickly fashioned an Indian war bridle out of rawhide-braided tether line. He simply made a loop over the horse's nose, and twisted it into the horse's mouth with an overhand knot under the chin. Both ends were brought back as reins, and he was able to ride. Grabbing a handful of mane, he swung up on the horse's back and slowly moved around the herd. At the edge toward the village he found Colt's saddle and blanket and waited there until the scout arrived.

Colt patted him on the back as congratulations for doing a good job and the lad handed the big scout his sock back. Because of his adrenaline, Colt had not noticed how cold his feet were, but he now did as he rubbed the foot and replaced the sock. Ezekiel rode into the darkness and returned, minutes later, leading War Bonnet.

Luckily, Colt's saddlebags were still there, so he reached inside and pulled out a fresh dry pair of socks and put them on, then his boots. He then changed his mind and removed them and put on a pair of porcupine quill-decorated moccasins.

He smiled at Ezekiel and said, "You stay back here, boy. I'll be damned if they're going to keep my weapons."

The night was getting very chilly, so Colt also pulled his Hudson's Bay blanket leggings out of the saddlebags and put them on over his gold-striped blue cavalry trousers. He pulled out his Cheyenne bow and quiver of steel-tipped arrows from his blanket roll and strung the bow. Ezekiel retreated to the safety of the trees, leading War Bonnet while Chris Colt moved into the shadows of the Bannock lodges.

He slowly crept through the darkness of the village from tepee to tepee listening for the familiar voice of Buffalo Horn. When he located the tent, he heard an argument going on between Buffalo Horn and, apparently, his wife. Colt saw a shadow, two lodges down. He froze. Suddenly the tepee's buffalo-hide door flew open and Buffalo Horn stepped into the night.

Colt could not move, he was too close. The chief looked around, not seeing Colt right to his left rear next to his own lodge. He moved toward the lodge where the other person had just exited. Colt strained his eyes in the darkness and saw Buffalo Horn talking to a woman, a young one. The chief put his arm around

her and the two sneaked off into the trees. Colt could
barely see them outside the circle of lodges. Soon they
were making love.

The chief of scouts grabbed the door of Buffalo
Horn's tepee and went inside quickly. His wife was big
and ugly. She looked into Colt's eyes with utter shock.
He leveled the arrow at her ample midsection, and she
knew not to make a sound. He spoke to her in hurried
sign language, telling her if she spoke he would kill
her.

Colt laid her on a buffalo robe and gagged her, then
tied her hands behind her back, and tied her feet together. He covered her with another buffalo robe, including her head. Chris looked around the lodge and
found his weapons in one corner. He smelled the stew
on the cooking fire and figured it was dog, so he decided against it. That was a taste he had never quite
acquired.

Colt put on his double holster gunbelt and grabbed
up his arsenal of weapons, putting them into their various hiding places. He also found Moose Connors's .32
Reid's "My Friend" Knuckleduster derringer and
shoved it in his pocket. The derringer was unique in
that it could also serve as brass knuckles with the
round metal ring that was part of the grip. There was
no barrel. The bullets fired right out of the cylinder.

Colt went out the door of the tepee and heard the
woman trying to scream from under her blankets but
her yells were barely audible. Colt grinned as he
strained his eyes in the darkness and saw that Buffalo
Horn was still quite preoccupied with his lover. He

quickly moved back toward and through the remuda, rejoining Ezekiel under the trees. There, Colt removed his moccasins and replaced his socks and boots. War Bonnet was already saddled and Colt was impressed at the things Ezekiel had learned just from observation. Just out of habit though, Colt double-checked the girth and breast straps, saddle blanket, and saddle fenders to insure nothing was twisted or binding against his friend's side.

He then took a rawhide riata tether line from one of the now deserted sentry spots and gave one end of the rope to Ezekiel. Leaving their horses, the two each took an end to both corners of the remuda and caught a pony. Ezekiel and Colt tied the riata ends to the tail of a pony and then quickly returned to their mounts.

Ezekiel had the Henry repeater now and Colt pulled out one of his Peacemakers, gave the lad a wink, and fired into the air. Both of them started yelling and the pony herd stampeded directly toward the village. The two corner horses really panicked with the rope tied to their tails and they swept through the now alarmed village, the rope catching on the sides of lodges and spilling them over. Inside the collapsed lodges numerous screams could be heard and Colt laughed as they passed through the village with the herd, as he saw a half-naked Buffalo Horn clinging to the branch of the tree he had been under.

The herd rode into the night with only two shots following after them—attacks of complete desperation, with no chance of finding their marks. Colt rode forward and leaned down, Bowie knife in hand, and sliced through the rope binding the two panicked ponies from the herd. They each sprang free and kicked and galloped, dragging long lengths of rawhide rope behind them. Colt knew they would eventually work the ropes off. More importantly, the herd would make it to the Nez Perce with Ezekiel and him. Buffalo Horn and his warriors would not be pursuing them anytime soon.

Chapter 4

»»»»»»»»»»»»»»

Joseph

One week and two blizzards later, Chris Colt reported into Fort Lapwai, leaving the horses and Ezekiel tucked safely away in a hidden valley about twenty miles distant.

General O. O. Howard had a long, well-trimmed beard with a salt-and-pepper look to it from the graying. He wore a Napoleonic campaign hat and fancy double-breasted tunic with a red sash going across diagonally from his left shoulder to the right side of his gold belt. The right sleeve, with no arm in it, was tacked to the front of the tunic's pocket, near the gold braided epaulet on the shoulder.

His appearance was so flashy that it immediately reminded Colt of George Armstrong Custer, who Chris had not been able to respect or like. This appearance and first impression gave Colt a defensive attitude with the general immediately.

This was not the only thing that made Colt defensive. It was General Howard's words. Their first conversation put the scout off immediately.

Chris Colt believed in God. He didn't rise up on

Sunday morning and go to church, because he usually wasn't near a church, except the magnificent open-air cathedrals through which he scouted—lofty snow-capped mountains, blowing white clouds of powder off their windswept peaks. Sometimes, he would pass by a crystal-clear waterway teeming with brightly colored rainbow, brook, and brown trout. On other occasions, the cathedral turned out to be an evergreen wood, its needles providing a silent soft carpet for War Bonnet's hooves, the wind naturally creating new hymns as it worked its way through the myriad of thick branches and needles. At other times, the outdoor church was a panoramic painting of brilliant hues of gold and green covered by walls of blue and purple and red sky, filled with soft and puffy clouds of white cotton. This was the church that Christopher Colt attended and it had more majesty and beauty than Notre Dame itself, or St. Peter's Basilica.

Colt also was very attuned to the behavior and nature of people. He didn't need to listen to what they were saying to feel what was behind the words. He judged meaning by the look in their eyes and the language of their bodies when they spoke.

If a man told Colt over and over that he was brave, Colt, in his mind, then naturally questioned the man's courage. This was the case when Chris delivered his verbal report to the general, after giving a written report to the adjutant.

Colt and the general sat down over cups of tea on fine china and talked about the Nez Perce "problem."

At one point during the conversation, General Howard got up, left hand behind his back, and strolled over to the four-paned window and looked out. While he walked over to the window he hummed a hymn, and this struck Chris as strange.

The officer came back over and sat down across from Colt and leaned forward, a sincere expression on his stern face.

"Mr. Colt," he asked, "where will you go when you die?"

This caught the chief of scouts off guard, but he quickly replied, "I hope anywhere but Washington, General."

This did not bring a smile on the face of the general, or even a change in expression. He just went to another question.

"Tell me, Christopher," the general queried, "Have you been baptized in the Holy Spirit? Have you, Mr. Colt, taken the Lord Jesus Christ as your personal savior?"

"Well, General Howard," Colt said, growing a little irritated, "I think that's between me and Jesus Christ, isn't it?"

The commander did not like this answer at all, which was quite obvious as he made another hand-behind-the-back stroll over to the window. He returned to Colt and poured himself another cup of tea, sitting down.

"Mr. Colt," Howard went on, "when I am responsible for the lives of the men in my command, I also feel a responsibility for their souls. I am in command in a sense of the welfare of their spirituality. Do you understand what all that means?"

"Yes, sir," Colt answered. "It seems like being a general isn't satisfying enough for you."

Howard leaned forward and said, "What do you mean by that, young man?"

Colt gave the general a toothy smile and said, "Seems like you want to be God as well."

The general sat up stiffly but could not tell by the smile on Colt's face if he was joking or not. Uncomfortable, and not used to that feeling, the old soldier concluded it must have been a joke and laughed nervously.

Howard got up again and paced around the room, this time tucking his left hand into the pocket of his tunic.

Addressing the windowpanes, he spoke. "Mr. Colt, I want to bring these heathens to a personal relationship with Jesus Christ, the Messiah. I also have to move them onto reservation lands here on Lapwai Creek. You know when Old Chief Joseph died and his golden-tongued son took over, a lot of the bands started coming to Young Joseph. Oh, he's an orator that one. Would that I had him in front of my . . . in front of a congregation with a thorough biblical knowledge, he could save some souls. Aye, he certainly would. When Old Joseph died, he told his son to protect the land and never leave the Wallowa Valley. Defend it with your life, said he. But alas, Governor Lafayette Grover of Oregon wants the redskins out of there so more settlers can come in and make their homes."

Colt interrupted, "And let me guess, General. One of his friends who is pushing hardest for that is Colonel Rufus Potter, right?"

General Howard smiled. "Yes, that is true. You are a student, Mr. Colt, and upon a great deal of investigation, I find it difficult to verify the man's credentials as a retired or former colonel, but in any event, the Indian agent here wants all the Nez Perce close by so they can be better controlled. General Sherman told me as soon as spring has full arrived and troops can be mobilized more readily, I am to inform the chiefs of all the nontreaty and Lower Nez Perce bands that they are to move onto the Lapwai Reservation or else."

"Or else what?" Colt asked.

"Or else we will take their heathen lives and pray that the words of our missionaries have somehow gotten into their uneducated heads and hearts, Mr. Colt."

The general went on, "If we have no late spring snows, I will meet with the chiefs in May and give them a thirty-day deadline to move onto the reservation. I am concerned because the Nez Perce are starting to become a problem and they never have been before. They were one of the first tribes to become civilized."

"Civilized?" Colt said. "Are they civilized if they live the way we tell them to, General?"

The one-armed general didn't even sense Colt's sarcasm but answered the question with a serious expression on his face. "Essentially, yes. Mr. Colt, I had a good relationship with Cochise of the Apache," the general said.

Colt said, "I knew Cochise, General Howard."

Howard sighed and said, "Rest his wretched heathen soul. It's a shame he shall burn in the lake of fire for eternity, but he would not listen to the message of salvation."

Colt smiled and quietly said, "I'm sure he did, General. The Apaches call God, Usen, the Great Mystery, but he is still God."

Howard replied, "Aye, but that is not accepting Jesus of Nazareth as one's Lord and personal savior."

Colt smiled again and shocked the Bible-thumping officer with his words. "General Howard, didn't Jesus say, I have other sheep to tend in my flock?"

"Yes, I believe he did."

Chris replied, "Maybe they were Apache, Nez Perce, Sioux, Ottoman, Mongols. Who knows, but I bet Cochise knew God in his heart, but just with different words."

Howard stormed across the room and picked up a well-worn leather-backed copy of the Holy Bible and held it up, his face growing red. "But he did not accept this as his Holy Word, nor did he accept Jesus the Christ as his personal savior and that is the only way for him to get into paradise."

Colt took a sip of tea and said softly, "Excuse me, General, but isn't that God's decision and not ours?"

Again upset, the general let out a long sigh and said, "Well, listen, Mr. Colt, I understand that you have the respect of many of our red brethren."

"I treat them with respect, General. I think they appreciate it."

Howard went on. "From a logistical and statistical point of view, we would much rather have to rally our troops through sunshine instead of snow. We are really beginning, however, to have some problems with the Nez Perce, especially the nontreaty bands. They all seem to look up to Looking Glass, Too-Hool-Hool-Zote, Ollikut, and others, but the primary center of influence is Ollikut's younger brother Chief Joseph, as you already know. We are not going to issue our ultimatum until spring is well on its way, but I want you to make trips to Joseph's village, in the meantime, and work on him. Convince him to cooperate with the government. Let him know we will protect all the Nez Perce and tell him the government is aware of his political stature among the bands and would probably recognize him as the overall chief of the Nez Perce if he'd like."

Colt said, "From what I know, Joseph is interested only in the good of his people and not how many people our government wants him to have sovereignty over. I'll talk with him, General, but I have to have two assurances."

"What's that, Mr. Colt?"

Colt said, "That number one, my word is never broken by you or your command, and number two, that you never ask me to tell him a lie or even stretch the truth."

"That's certainly fair enough, Mr. Colt," said Howard. "I too am a man of honor and I respect those two conditions. You have my word that they will be met."

Chris went to the telegrapher's office after meeting with General Howard to see if there was a reply to the telegram he wired to Shirley Ebert upon arriving.

His telegram was short, simple, and to the point:

Arrived safely at Fort Lapwai STOP Miss you STOP Love you STOP Will you marry me STOP Love STOP Colt STOP Lots of babies STOP

Chris was anxious when he returned to the telegrapher's office, more anxious than he guessed he would have been. His anxiety turned to horror, though, when he read the telegraph waiting for him. It was from the city marshal of Bismarck and informed Colt that Shirley had left Bismarck weeks before, when she heard of Colt's blindness. He had received word that she was with four fur traders who were killed by hostiles in Montana, and it was thought that she was captured and taken away.

Chris Colt never felt true panic. He was always in control, one way or another, of any situation he found himself in. But this time a whimper escaped his lips. His heart pounded in his chest and he could barely breathe.

There were many bands of Lakotah and Cheyenne in Montana who would not care about Colt's relationship with Crazy Horse and the other Lakotah and Cheyenne. He pictured the mutilated bodies of his raped and murdered wife Chantapeta and daughter Winona, who had been killed by Crows, also found in Montana. Colt was about to befriend the Nez Perce and their biggest adversaries were the Blackfeet who inhabited Montana Territory.

It was midwinter and no group of Indians would capture her in Montana and then head toward Arizona or California. Of all the places Chris could think of where finding and rescuing Shirley would be most difficult in winter, Montana would just about head the list. Before anything, however, he had to return the herd of Appaloosas to Chief Joseph, then he would figure out what to do about Shirley.

Colt sent a telegraph back to Fort Lincoln to the chief of scouts there. He asked him to find out for him what the signs said about her capture. Chances were that it was investigated by a cavalry patrol out of either Fort Benton, Logan, Ellis, McKinney, or one of the new forts, Custer or Keogh. Colt knew, however, the chief of scouts who had replaced him at Lincoln and knew the man would know the story. It was a scout's job to know what was going on all over the territory.

The telegram Colt got back an hour later was not encouraging. A cavalry patrol out of Fort Benton had discovered the remains of the dead men, a rough lot of hide hunters. The attackers had been either Cheyenne or Sioux and were a small band. The village had been found nearby. Shirley had apparently been taken captive and the band headed north, probably making their way toward Canada to join Sitting Bull and Crazy Horse. That was one thing that lightened Colt's heart. Both men knew Shirley as did many of the people in the Minniconjou, Oglala, and Hunkpapa tribes of the Lakotah nation. There were also many more Lakotah, Cheyenne, and Arapaho who were in the Great Camp at the Little Big Horn who might spot Shirley and would know she was the woman of Wamble Uncha. If she had to be captured, Colt would prefer she be captured by the Lakotah or Cheyenne.

The problem was that there were so many small bands who were independent and may not have heard of him or her. They may not know other members of the Lakotah or Cheyenne nations, so there was no telling what happened to her. Shirley would have only her own ability to survive until he could locate and rescue her.

Colt sent a message back to the chief of scouts at Lincoln and asked him to find a couple of Lakotah who could be trusted. Tell them what happened and send them off to find Crazy Horse. Ask the chief about Shirley's capture and whereabouts.

Colt then went to the scouts' quarters and introduced himself. He told the newest scout to come to Chief Joseph's village with any telegrams that came in, as he was expecting one in a day or two. Chris picked up some supplies and rode away to rejoin Ezekiel.

Where he had left the Nez Perce boy was on the way to Joseph's village in the Wallowa Valley, so Colt figured they would spend the night and push on toward Joseph's the following day. It would take several days of hard pushing to get there.

Chris was happy to leave Fort Lapwai and ride among the seemingly disorganized but somehow symmetrical beauty of nature. Many dime novels illustrated cavalry forts as great-walled wooden stockades with pointed logs sticking straight up into the air and lashed or nailed side by side to ward off attacking, painted hostiles. In actuality, Lapwai, like other military forts, had a large parade ground that had a flagpole at one end. The entire fort was built around the parade ground with garrison buildings side by side and neat as a pin. Officer and enlisted barracks and housing, dispensary, mess, supply, livery, and all fort operations were laid out in a neat pattern and had the main entrances to each facing toward the fort parade ground, but there were no walls around the fort.

On the parade ground there was always activity during the day, whether it was drill and ceremony training, or classes on how to disassemble and clean weapons, or possibly the technique of tying and securing diamond hitches for pack mules.

The military had order but so did nature. Colt preferred the order of nature. A deer would be born and would never venture more than two miles from its birthplace. During its life span there would be a harsh winter and the browse line on the bushes and trees would grow to a height where only the tallest deer could stand on their hind legs and eat buds, bark, and vegetation. The smaller deer would die from overpopulation. The alternative to this starvation, however, was the mountain lion, which enjoys deer meat, with an occasional skunk or porcupine added to its diet. The average lion would eat two deer per week, as they were finicky eaters and would desert a deer before the meat got the least bit stale. This would leave a deer carcass for bears, coyotes, magpies, crows, and buzzards to feed on. The surviving deer would not only reproduce but would feed on grasses and plants, then move to a new area that may have been decimated by fire, avalanche, or some other calamity. They would then pass feces containing seeds from the plants and

grasses eaten elsewhere, and the deer feces would per-
petuate the grasses and vegetation.

Nature didn't lay out mountain peaks and trees in
neat rows like miilitary billets. Cloud formations constantly changed. Some days sunshine prevailed, while
on other days snow or rain fell. Still there was a subtle
but definite order to things and that was what Colt
liked.

He laughed at some of the do-gooder Easterners who
had spent their lives in big cities like New York and
Philadelphia and had already forgotten how their
grandfathers had fed their mothers and fathers as children with venison and wild turkey and other game.
These city-slickers were now putting down the practice
of hunting saying that the poor animals were innocent
victims of men with guns. Colt wondered what those
people would say if they went into the woods and saw
an entire herd of winter-killed deer that starved to
death because a bounty placed on wolves and cougars
had led to overpopulation.

Colt headed south toward the Wallowa Mountains
and took in the beauty of his surroundings. The sweep
of the angry winter sky was majestic in its blues and
other hues. Smoke coming out of the chimneys in the
billets and buildings behind him was curling and swirling parallel to the ground.

I better hurry, Colt thought, there's a big storm coming. Even before seeing the angry sky, Chris had sensed
a storm coming. Colt was paying the price for not being
an average man. He, because of his active and
adventure-filled life, had received numerous wounds

and scars. His body looked like an old target, and it felt like the carpet of a hotel lobby, walked over, stepped on, kicked, scraped, and soaked. When Colt awakened each morning, he felt and heard numerous bones cracking as he started to stir. He always awakened with aches and pains that had to be worked out after getting his blood going through his system. The pain was worse—much worse—if there was an impending storm. Chris would feel pain in several joints, and near mended bone breaks. Such was the case on this day, so Colt pushed his mighty paint into a lope and alternated between that and a fast trot, occasionally slowing to a walk, all the way to the valley some twenty miles distant.

When Colt arrived War Bonnet glistened with sweat between his legs, on his chest, on the sides of his neck, and in the saddle area. Colt unsaddled the big horse first, then rubbed him down with dry grass. The big horse rolled in a mud wallow and then cantered, proudly flipping his head from side to side, as he rejoined the horse herd. Colt saw him prancing and knew the big paint had smelled a mare or two in estrus. Chris decided that Joseph, with his selected breeding program, might not appreciate the scout's paint planting his seed in any of the Appaloosa mares, so Colt whistled like a red-tailed hawk and the big horse huffed once through his nostrils, probably in disgust, and loped back to the scout. Colt put a rawhide halter on War Bonnet and pegged a twenty-foot picket line to the ground.

After he finished taking care of his horse, Colt joined

his young red companion. He carried his saddle and the two canvas bags of supplies he had bought over to the fire. The small valley the two had picked out was just about perfect. There was graze, a moving stream running through it, a lot of trees and overhanging rock shelter, and tall cliffs all the way around the valley that pushed storms over and beyond the little canyon.

As soon as Chris sat down, Ezekiel handed him a steaming cup of coffee. Colt nodded, reached into one bag, and pulled out a piece of peppermint candy, tossing it to the young man. Ezekiel ate the candy with relish. This young man might one day be a brave and fearsome warrior, Colt thought, but he still *was* a boy.

Chris Colt had not been much older than Ezekiel when he left home to fight in the Civil War. He too had distinguished himself as a courageous and noble fighter, but like Ezekiel and most Indian boys he was robbed of part of his childhood.

Colt thought back to his childhood and how much he enjoyed candy himself. Like so many other boys, though, he was in such an all-fired hurry to grow up. He did grow up early, but he also didn't experience a lot of the fun times playing, working, learning, and growing like other boys. Consequently, Colt, who was now in his late twenties, had been somewhat immature in his early twenties. He had gotten in some gunfights that could have been avoided, some fistfights he could have talked his way out of. He had taken up the gauntlet on more than one occasion when a more mature man would have moved on and let the challenge die.

When he met Chantapeta and fell in love with the

Minniconjou Lakotah woman, he was ready to grow up some. His wild oats had been sown, but now Colt had an addiction. He was mature now, but he was also addicted to the rush of adrenaline through his blood. He still had to have that old feeling every now and then. It made him feel so alive.

He again thought back to his childhood and grinned. Colt reached into the bag and pulled out another piece of peppermint candy and popped it in his mouth. Ezekiel smiled at him while sucking his own, and Colt smiled back savoring the sweet taste of the striped candy. The two sat by the fire lost in thoughts of childhood and the past. The harsh winter of the Rocky Mountains went on around them, while they basked in the warmth of the innocence of youth and the wonderful taste and aroma of peppermint candy.

In the mansion of Rufus Birmingham Potter, the phony retiree paced back and forth across the library, a snifter of brandy in his left hand with a stick of peppermint melting in it. He took another swallow and thought about all the hired guns he had lost, all to a blind man. Maybe, he thought, he should have just ignored the legendary scout and let him alone. He hoped Colt didn't know of his involvement with the attempted killings. Indeed, Christopher Columbus Colt, he thought, lived up to the fame he had apparently earned. At this point, Potter had heard of the killing of most of his men but not the details. He did know that Rip, Clay, Moose, and many others were dead, and that they had been single-handedly defeated by Colt, with some help from a young Nez Perce boy. He decided that Colt must know of his involvement and would certainly be coming after him. The colonel concluded that he would have to hire the very best guns and killers that money could buy. He figured, if Chris Colt could kill those hardened men while blind, he would not be kept from getting to, and killing, Potter. The best hired killers in the country would be a worthy investment, Potter thought. Satisfied with his decision, the land-grabber took a long healthy sip of his peppermint-flavored brandy.

Chris Colt thought of the man who had hired so many killers to go after him and Ezekiel, and his blood boiled. He finished his candy and replaced it with a cigar, pouring himself another cup of coffee. He decided he couldn't do anything about Potter now, so he would put the cowardly conspirator out of his mind and take care of that horse when it was time to ride it.

Colt hadn't bathed in days, so standing by the fire he removed his weapons, he took a panful of water and a rag, and removed his buffalo coat and war shirt. Ezekiel for the first time looked at the scars crisscrossing Colt's body. Ezekiel admired the rock-hard sinew and muscles that rippled all over Colt's upper torso, but what amazed him more were the numerous scars on his body. They were like a written history of Colt's life, carved by time and experience into the flesh of a hero. Words didn't need to be spoken about Colt's past, for the scars on his body told an entire story like an

Indian's winter count painted on a tanned and stretched-out hide. On his pectoral muscles, right above the nipples there were telltale scars of the Sundance Ceremony, where a shaman had pierced his breasts with the talons of an eagle and placed wooden pegs through the holes. Then, staring up at the sun through the hole in the sundance lodge's roof, Colt had danced in circles with leather thongs attached to the wooden pegs and going up over a pole in the lodge's ceiling, then back down to a heavy bundle of buffalo skulls on the floor. He danced and danced until he almost fell in a faint and had a vision. The white brave was then lifted up by the thongs and spun in circles while the flesh and pectoral muscles stretched out grotesquely.

Right above the Sundance Ceremony scar on his left breast there was a bullet hole scar, with a larger exit hole in the back of his shoulder. There was another bullet hole scar low down on the right side of his abdomen, and a small slash scar going horizontally across his washboard stomach, just above the navel.

Finally, there were four long claw mark scars running down his very large right bicep. They had to have been made by either a bear or a mountain lion, but not the one that Colt tangled with early on the trip. This had been made by another monstrous creature.

Ezekiel had also noticed another slight scar under Colt's eye. It was a little line that puckered when Colt smiled or frowned and wasn't visible unless you really knew Colt well. Since the scout had become such a hero to Ezekiel, the boy had noticed it, just as Shirley had. He did not know that the scar had been made by a very sharp Comanche arrow. In fact, when Colt got his cheekbone laid open by the arrow and was facing certain death during the battle with the Comanche warriors who outnumbered Colt's men by five to one, Colt had rallied the men around him by joking about the incident. As the men wondered whether the big man would go down with the wound, Colt touched his cheek and looked at his hand covered with blood from the wound. "Men," he said, "when I said let's keep an eye out for the Comanches, this is not exactly what I meant." The simple joke was all that it took, at the time, to reinstill courage in the small group, and they ended up defeating the primitive cavalrymen.

Chris washed all over and replaced his clothing after drying by the fire. He rolled a cigarette and gave one to Ezekiel, and started making supper. He cooked hardtack biscuits, bison steaks, and canned tomatoes. Colt also opened a jar of apples he'd gotten from a sergeant's wife at Fort Lapwai. He fried the apples in grease and served them with the biscuits. Chris also made cups of hot tea for the pair. Ezekiel had never had tea; he enjoyed it with sugar added.

Chris enjoyed the apples and biscuits, but his mind labored over what to do about Shirley. He felt so torn between duty and love, what was right and what was wrong.

Ezekiel sensed a problem. "Great Scout, your mind fights with itself over something. Your face tells me so."

"Over other fires, little one," Colt said, "I have spoken of the woman who holds my heart."

Ezekiel smiled and said, "Yes, Shirley, the one with hair that came from the fire. You miss her and want *her* to eat apples with you. Not a Nez Perce boy."

Chris smiled and shook his head. "No, Zeke. She has been captured by the Lakotah or Chyela and has been killed or is prisoner."

"Your heart is torn. You want to find her, but you know the snows in the mountains are too deep."

Colt grinned. "You might be a kid, but you are damned smart."

Ezekiel remained solemn. "I have the answer. Tell Joseph. He will know what to do."

Colt said, "He has enough to think about."

"His job is to make decisions. He also does not have the feelings in his heart for this woman, like you. His decision will be smart. It will be from his head."

Colt was amazed by this simple but profound logic and decided that discussing it with Joseph would be the smartest answer. He was a center of influence among his people, because he did know how to make wise decisions and had helped many of his people.

Chris, normally smoking only rarely, pulled another two treasured cigars from his saddlebags and gave one to Ezekiel, lighting it. White parents would be appalled at their child smoking, or Colt helping him to do so, but Chris considered this lad beyond his years and smoking tobacco among most red nations was a real treat.

Enjoying the cigar and coffee, Chris realized that the

apples frying was what made him think so much right now about Shirley. He thought back to his first meeting with her. He had just reported into Fort Abraham Lincoln in North Dakota Territory, then went to the nearby town of Bismarck.

Walking down the street of the prairie town, he saw a restaurant called the Frontier Cafe, oddly enough, and it boasted a big sign in the front window advertising home cooking. That sounded like something Chris could appreciate as much as the sleep he had gotten.

He was feeling healthy already. His head no longer hurt from wounds he received while fighting his way to Fort Lincoln, and he felt rested. Well, he felt good until the auburn-haired waitress/restaurant owner/cook walked into the room to wait on him. He thought he was going to suffer a seizure. His breathing came out in pants. His heart pounded heavily in his chest.

The top of her full head of golden red hair would touch him right about the chin and the simple gingham dress she wore could do nothing to hide the curves of her body underneath it. Her lips were full and her cheekbones were high. She had a very proud lift to her chin, with a warm smile to make anyone feel welcome. The thing that caught Chris Colt's breath though, were her bright green eyes. They penetrated through his stare and went right inside his head, traveling all the way deep into his soul. He felt he could have closed his eyes tightly, and those green eyes would have still shot right through him.

"Coffee, sir?" she asked with a voice that sounded like crushed velvet.

"Thank you, ma'am," Chris said, nodding.

He wished he had taken a bath. He wished he had cleaned his teeth and combed his hair.

She poured him a cup and they stared at each other, smiling uneasily. She accidentally poured too much in the cup, hot liquid making Colt jump up and bump the table into her, spilling the entire pot of coffee over. She screamed and grabbed a napkin trying to clean up the spill, and Colt grabbed another one, also trying to wipe up the coffee.

"How clumsy of me," she cried, "I'm so sorry, sir."

Chris spoke softly. "You? It was my fault. *I'm* sorry, ma'am."

They stopped wiping and looked up at each other, first grinning, then both breaking into an embarrassed laugh. They ended up sitting down at the next table. Their laughing was infectious, and the more they giggled, the harder it made them laugh.

Finally stopping, Chris said, "This your place, ma'am?"

"Yes, it is," she said, offering her hand to shake. "My name's Shirley Ebert. Are you new in town? Are you staying?"

"Yes and no," he replied. "I'm the new chief of scouts for General Custer at Fort Lincoln. My name is Colt, ma'am, Christopher Columbus Colt, but folks call me Chris."

"Any relation to the famous Colonel Colt?" she asked.

"My uncle."

"Well, Mr. Colt."

"Chris, please," he said.

"Fine, call me Shirley, too," she responded. "Can I get you some breakfast, Chris?"

"Yes, ma'am," he said, "I am ready for some home cooking."

"What would you like?" she asked.

He looked into her eyes and didn't answer for a second and both of them blushed again.

Chris broke the silence by saying, "It's up to you, Shirley. You decide."

"Okay, I'll surprise you, and it's on the house," she said, "since I almost scalded you with hot coffee."

Chris laughed and blushed again. "Shirley, it would have been worth getting scalded just meeting you."

He shocked himself with the statement and felt like he shouldn't have said a word. He really blushed now, as did Shirley, but she also gave him a smile and a look that promised volumes of love poetry in just a glance. She quickly left the room, and Chris wondered if he had offended her.

Chris heard footsteps on the board sidewalk outside and the door opened suddenly. Three cowboys walked in, but each wore his gun low and looked more like a gunslinger punching cows than a cowboy who could handle a gun. They were followed by Goliath himself. The giant behemoth who walked in the door had to be Will Sawyer. He was every bit of seven feet in height and looked almost as broad in the shoulders as he was in length. He was filthy with a long unkempt beard and he wore a Colt .45 Peacemaker in a low-slung holster.

Colt imagined what would happen if this giant of a beast whose brothers were now dead partly because of Colt tried to egg him into a fight. Chris met the challenge, especially after Shirley Ebert stood up to the bully. The man could not believe that Colt would really fight him fist and foot, but Colt actually told him he would not only beat him but that, afterward, Sawyer would apologize to Shirley as well.

When Colt forced Will Sawyer and his friends outside at the point of a gun, so he and the brute could fight it out, Shirley begged him not to go and warned him that Sawyer had killed a man with his bare hands. He just smiled at Shirley, swept her into his arms, and kissed her passionately. When he stepped back, she had tears running down her cheeks, but she was smiling bravely. He removed his gunbelt and handed it to her, as well as handing her his Colt.

"If any of them go for a gun, shoot him," he said.

Shirley said, "If I can't talk you out of it, and you're bound and determined to do it, I want you to go out there and kick Will Sawyer's ass."

To everyone's but Shirley's amazement Colt, using his head and his fighting heart, soundly defeated the giant, then poured a hatful of water on him from a nearby watering trough. The unconscious man came to, shaking his head.

"Now, as I told you, you owe Miss Ebert an apology," Colt said.

Sawyer shook his head again and looked up at Chris, then at Shirley, a very blank and faraway look in his eyes. "Huh? Oh, I'm sorry, Shirley," he mumbled.

His eyes rolled back in his head, and he fell over backward, unconscious. Chris left him there and walked into the cafe. As he started back inside one of Sawyer's buddies challenged Colt to a gunfight and the scout did everything he could to avoid it, but the man wouldn't back down. They buried the man the next day.

After the killing, the marshal, who witnessed it, cleared Colt. He and Shirley went back into the Frontier Cafe. In the kitchen, she had him sit down on a stool. Shirley started preparing eggs and a large steak. She pulled a baked potato out of a pot covered with a towel and put it in the oven to heat it up.

She went to a cabinet in the corner and pulled out some towels, tape, and other items and went over to Chris.

"Take off your shirt," she commanded.

Moaning, Chris complied as she helped him with the tight leather war shirt.

She felt his ribs and secretly admired Chris's build. She also was amazed at the scars all over his torso. He winced when she pushed on his injured rib.

She felt all over it carefully. "It's broken. Do you want me to get the doctor or do you want me to mend it?"

"You don't have to worry about it. I'll have the regimental surgeon patch me up at the fort."

"Nonsense," she said, "I can bind it if you want, or I'll be happy to get Dr. Fedders. Now, what do you want?"

Chris raised his arms and folded his hands on top

of his head. Smiling, Shirley pulled out a rolled-up long cloth bandage and started wrapping it tightly, very tightly around Chris's chest and back. He smiled at her.

She smiled back and saw the question on his face. "My father was a regimental surgeon in the Civil War and was town doctor before and after that."

"Where?"

"Youngstown, Ohio."

Chris winced and said, "You're kidding. I grew up in Cuyahoga Falls and fought for the Ohio National Guard in the Civil War."

Shirley said, "Where's Cuyahoga Falls?"

"Right next to Akron on the Cuyahoga River," Chris answered.

Shirley said, "Aren't you too young to have fought in the war?"

"I lied about my age. I was young, too young."

She finished wrapping his rib cage and went back to her cooking right away.

Chris watched her as she was able to complete everything and not burn a thing besides wrapping his ribs. She put the steak, eggs, and potato on a plate and headed toward the door to the dining room.

She turned her head and said, "Follow me."

Chris started to follow her, and she turned at the door to the dining room, putting her back against the swinging batwing doors, and said, "You might put your shirt back on, Chris."

He sat at a table, and she was gone like a flash, returning with a steaming pot of coffee and two cups.

She set them down on the table and Chris poured out two cups, while she walked to the door and put the closed sign up, just as four people almost reached the door. She smiled politely and turned her back after having locked the door, then sat down with Colt.

"Aren't you going to eat?" he asked.

She smiled softly and said, "No thanks, I ate already. I'll just enjoy my coffee and watch you."

"Why did you close? You don't want to lose business."

She said, "I do right now. Maybe you could go through all that and not be affected, but I'd like to relax my brain."

Chris grinned and said, "You are a wonderful cook."

"Thank you," she said, "besides I want to spend some time with you alone right now."

Chris blushed again.

She went on, "You must think I am very forward. I just met you. We kissed already. I closed my restaurant and am sitting here alone with you. This has never ever happened to me in my life."

"Me neither," he said between bites, "and I don't think you're anything like forward."

"What do you think?" she asked.

"About you?"

Shirley nodded.

"I think you're absolutely wonderful, Shirley."

This time, she blushed, but Chris was familiar and confident about her now.

"In fact, you are the most beautiful woman I've met in my life."

That was their first meeting. Colt had fallen in love with her more, every day, since then. Now, for the second time in her life, she was a prisoner.

Colt's mind moved on to Joseph, a man who could end up being Shirley's savior. Chief Joseph had one quality that Colt really admired in a man or woman. He had seen this quality in Crazy Horse, Sitting Bull, Cochise, and Shirley Ebert. It was a penetrating honest gaze, a look that seemed to bore into all your secret thoughts. It was also a look that could put you at ease, knowing that whatever they were saying would be true.

Colt even sensed the same thing with General O. O. Howard, even though he was somewhat put off by him. Chris just felt that you could use a fly and entice a nice trout into biting it, but it would swim away if you tried to jam the fly down its throat. This was what Colt thought General Howard was trying to do with his religious beliefs. The scout figured that the bearded officer's practice had probably chased a lot more people away from Christianity than brought them to it. He did, though, believe the general's heart was in the right place. Colt had checked out the "Christian General's" background before even leaving for Lapwai.

In September of '74, Howard, then a brigadier or one-star general, had arrived in Portland, Oregon, and become the head of the Department of the Columbia. He had, by that time, already developed his nickname as the "Christian General," noted for his religious fervor and humanitarian efforts.

During the Civil War, he rose to command the Army of the Tennessee under Sherman. After the war, he helped elevate former slaves working as the director of the Freedmen's Bureau of the War Department. He also became the founder and first president of Howard University for black men in Washington, D.C. The assignment to make peace with Cochise and the Apaches in 1872 gave him an opportunity to apply his humanitarian instincts to the Indians. Unfortunately, he was not able to cram his Christian beliefs down Apache throats.

Sherman didn't approve of General Howard's outside activities, although Howard was sincere in trying to better the world around him and didn't seem to have any political motivations in what he did. Sherman simply felt an Army officer should stick to soldiering.

When unworthy subordinates coupled with the vicious crosscurrents of Reconstruction politics plunged Howard's administration of the Freedmen's Bureau into scandal, Sherman recommended Howard for the post vacated by the assassination of General Edward R. S. Canby—a post that had been held in the interim by Colonel Jefferson C. Davis. General Canby was the only U.S. Army general ever to be killed by Indians. He was shot during a supposed peace conference with the Modoc Indians in California.

Lavishing his humanitarianism and religion on the Indians of the Northwest, Howard pictured himself as their true friend and convinced himself that they viewed him in the exact same light. Actually his powerful brand of religion was his undoing with them, as it clouded his understanding of the equally strong spiritual motivation of the Indians. A cultural gap separated him from the chiefs with whom he dealt, although he was unaware of it. So, feeling he had a good relationship with the tribes, he decided he would solve the festering problem with the nontreaty Nez Perce. Joseph was the recognized leader of the Nez Perce bands that had not signed the treaty of 1863. Joseph's people had become General Howard's newest challenge.

When Colt and Ezekiel rode into the village of Chief Joseph at night, the chief strode out to greet them, wrapped in a multicolored wool blanket. His calm demeanor impressed Colt.

The chief spoke to Ezekiel. "You have returned the horses stolen from our people. This is a good thing. You are a good man, Man Killer."

Colt could tell that Ezekiel was doing everything he could to keep tears from his eyes as the chief turned from him and walked to Colt. No mention was made of the killing of Ezekiel's brother or Ezekiel failing to guard properly the herd that had been stolen. No mention had been made of how long Ezekiel had been gone, or his wounds and torture. Chief Joseph had called him a man and changed his name just like that, and the name, from a warrior's point of view, was an honorable one. Ezekiel would now be called Man Killer.

The chief walked over to Colt and shook hands with him. "You are Colt."

Chris nodded.

"Now is the time for dreaming," Joseph said. "The morning will be a good time to talk and smoke."

Colt knew he was now welcome in Joseph's village.

Chief Joseph turned and walked into the darkness, as Man Killer turned and grinned broadly at Colt.

A thirteen-year-old boy stood nearby in the night air. He had witnessed the words that passed between Joseph and Man Killer. The boy in the shadows stood taller than Ezekiel. He had picked two fights with Ezekiel, winning the first one. Ezekiel had trained himself, waiting for the bully to start the next fight. Ezekiel had pounded the bigger boy into submission the second time. Colt didn't know the story, but he could guess at the hatred between the two by the looks they had given each other when Colt and Ezekiel rode in.

Now the boy walked up to Man Killer to apparently make up to him. Ezekiel was no longer a boy, but a man—a full-fledged warrior. This much was obvious from Joseph's words.

Man Killer handed the lead to his war bridle to the bigger boy. "Put my horse with the herd."

Shamed and hurt, the boy said, "Yes, Man Killer," turning and disappearing into the darkness with the boy-turned-man's horse.

Colt smiled to himself as he followed Man Killer to his family's lodge. Man Killer's mother had witnessed the incident with Chief Joseph and was very excited and proud of her son. She already knew about the death of her youngest son and had grieved. Everyone had been hearing of Ezekiel's exploits with the great and powerful Wamble Uncha. Even though Colt was brother to the Lakotah and Cheyenne, enemies of the Nez Perce, he was highly respected by members of many nations. It was known already that he was a fair man and mighty warrior, as well as sympathetic to the plight and treatment of the red man.

Colt followed Man Killer into his lodge and watched the youngster strut proudly, being waited on hand and foot by his proud, doting mother. The lad would be treated by all now as a warrior, and he had earned it as far as Colt was concerned. Happy Magpie treated Colt with awe and respect, but it was obvious that her real pride and joy was treating her son with the dignity and respect of true manhood in the Nez Perce society.

Chris Colt lay in his buffalo robe and thought about his lover. Where was Shirley Ebert? Was she alive? Was she safe? Was she thinking of Colt? Nobody could see him now, and it was a time for private thinking, a time for longing, tears dropping silently on the buffalo hide and disappearing in the thick carpet of dark brown fur.

Shirley Ebert, in a hidden canyon in the valley of the Yellowstone, lay on her buffalo robe, tears falling from her cheeks as she thought about Chris Colt and wondered where he was. Was he still alive? How was his blindness affecting him? Was he hurt somewhere? Had he forgotten her? Would he find her and save her?

The next morning was a memorable one for Colt, as he got a full measure and insight into the man called Chief Joseph. He was a leader and an orator. It was no wonder that the perceptive Christian General wanted Colt to court the man. Other chiefs would certainly seek this man's counsel.

After eating and bathing in the stream that ran by the village, Colt went to the lodge of Joseph. He took coffee and plenty of sugar with him, as well as fresh tobacco.

Joseph wore a clean white broadcloth shirt and a green vest, both made in eastern textile mills and tailor shops. He had a high pompadour and long braids, which were wrapped in strips of beaver fur and hung low down the front of his chest. The ends were tied off with strips of white fur from a snowshoe hare. His ears both bore large earrings, brass hoops that ran through holes in large, round, decorated mussel shells.

He wore a white beaded necklace around his neck that was actually twelve necklaces, each one getting progressively larger and hanging lower on his chest. He also wore a single strand of brass beads tightly around the base of his neck. He had a dark green breechcloth and Hudson's Bay blanket leggings, like Colt's, along with quill-decorated soft-soled moccasins. An Army blanket fell around his shoulders. His lips were thin and pressed together and his cheekbones were very high. He had a stocky frame, well muscled with a dark copper complexion.

Chief Joseph exuded a quiet strength. So did Colt.

Colt brought his coffeepot, and he placed it on the cooking fire to brew. Chief Joseph broke out a long-stemmed pipe and lit up, after filling and tamping the baked-clay bowl with the tobacco Colt brought.

The first words out of Chief Joseph's mouth after

handing the lighted pipe to Colt were, "One-Arm sends you to become my friend and tell me to move my people to Fort Lapwai."

Colt grinned and took a puff of the pipe, offering smoke to the four corners of the compass. "Joseph is indeed the wise leader all people say he is."

Joseph went on. "One-Arm and the other white chiefs have thought that it is hard to fight when the snows and angry winds come in the wintertime, but in the spring, there is grass for the ponies of the horse soldiers. There is much water and you can ride many miles in one day. It is easier to fight, and without snow, it is easier to make men and women and children walk to a reservation when your soldiers push them along with the ends of their rifles. If the Great Scout Colt can make friends with Young Joseph, he can tell him to move to Fort Lapwai maybe. If Joseph doesn't listen to the wisdom of Colt there will be two or three more months for them to talk. If Joseph still doesn't listen, there are many horse soldiers and their guns. They will make him listen."

Colt laughed. "Joseph, were you there hiding in a corner when General Howard spoke with me?"

Joseph poured himself a cup of coffee and dropped in a liberal amount of sugar.

"When an owl flies through the door of your tepee, and it flies around your head, Great Scout, do you have to catch him and look closely at his wings, and head, and body to see that it is an owl and not another bird?"

Colt took a sip of coffee. "You mean it is very obvious?"

"If you first think of those things that your enemy will think of, your enemy will not defeat you."

The two spoke for about an hour about the differences between the Nez Perce, Sioux, Cheyenne, Apache, Crow, and Comanche.

Colt pulled two cigars out of his pocket and handed one to Joseph. The chief smiled and stuck the cigar between his lips after smelling it, biting the top off, and licking the entire tobacco stick. Joseph seemed quite accustomed to smoking cigars. Colt lit Joseph's, then his own. They blew big clouds of smoke toward the air hole in the center of the lodge.

It was time to speak about Shirley and find out what Joseph thought he should do.

"Chief Joseph," Colt began, "I have a woman who makes my heart beat hard and steals my sleep from me many nights."

Joseph smiled.

"She has been taken captive by a band of the Chyela or the Lakotah, but I do not know where to find her or what to do."

Joseph poured himself another cup of coffee, sweetened it, and started drinking. He kept sipping the coffee and enjoying his cigar, and it was as if he had not heard a word Colt said.

After ten minutes Joseph spoke, "You have work with the cavalry. You felt you had to bring Ezekiel and our ponies to us. You have worry that the horse soldiers may start war with the Nez Perce. You think of all these things that weigh heavy on your heart, but your heart is also sad because the woman you dream of each night is somewhere. She is captive and your mind sees the many things you do not want for her. Should you just ride toward the lands of the Lakotah, or should you do your work for the cavalry first?"

Colt nodded and took a sip of coffee.

"Where were you born?" Joseph asked.

Colt said, "Back east in a place called Ohio."

"I learned about it at mission school," the chief said. "If my wife was taken from me by your people, and she was taken on the iron horse, and she was taken in the wagon. If your people took her and hid her somewhere in Ohio," Joseph said, "would I go to Ohio and find where she has been hidden?"

Colt said, "No. It would be impossible for you to do."

Chief Joseph said, "But does not Ohio have trees and rocks and dirt and clouds like here?"

"It doesn't look like this land, but it has all those things."

Joseph went on. "I grew up hunting and fighting and fishing as a Nez Perce. I have fought the bear and taken many scalps. I have counted coups. Am I not a good tracker, do you think, Colt?"

"Of course," Chris said. "You would have to be a good tracker. You are chief."

"Then," Joseph said, "could I not go to Ohio and look for sign and find my wife?"

Colt said, "No, it would still be impossible."

"Then who would I ask to go find her for me?"

Colt said, "You could ask me. I am white. I am from

Ohio. It would be easy for me to find a Nez Perce woman there."

Joseph poured another cup of coffee and spent another two minutes drinking it and enjoying the taste. Finally, he spoke. "Wasn't she taken by someone who was Sioux or Cheyenne?"

"Yes."

Joseph said, "Are not the Sioux brothers to the Cheyenne?"

"Yes."

"Are you not brother to Crazy Horse, who is Oglala Sioux?"

"Yes, I have sent word for him to find her."

"Then you have done the right thing," Joseph said. "Crazy Horse will look because he is your brother. He will find her because he is Sioux, and the Sioux and Cheyenne are like the left hand and the right hand. You must now do your work and trust to your brother."

There it was; pure, simple, the answer to Colt's problem. It was brilliant because it was so simple, as is the way with most good answers.

Chief Joseph went on, "Do you believe in the God spoken of in your Bible?"

"Yes, yes I do."

"This is a good thing, indeed," the chief said. "A true warrior lives for his Spirit Leader. And your God teaches you to believe He will solve your problem if it is too big."

"How about you, Joseph? Do you believe in my God?" Colt asked.

Joseph smiled warmly. "I did when I was a boy. My

father got angry at your Catholic missionaries and tore up his Bible. Like my father, I believe our ways, but I think maybe your God and my God are one and the same. Are you not called Colt?"

Colt nodded.

Joseph said, "Are you not also called Wamble Uncha?"

"Yes."

"Can your God have many names?"

Chris Colt took a long sip of coffee himself. "That is for God to decide, not me."

Chief Joseph laughed and said, "You cannot even make a decision to go see your woman. You must ask a savage heathen."

This joke sounded so unusual and out of place coming from the lips of the wise Nez Perce chief, it was even funnier to Colt than Joseph expected. Chris literally held his sides laughing, as did Joseph's wife across the lodge.

The matter was now settled in Colt's mind, though. He would constantly think and worry about Shirley, but he would have to wait for Crazy Horse to get the word and hope the Oglala war hero could find her. In the meantime, Colt would be friends with Joseph. Even if General Howard hadn't asked him to make friends, he would become one. He liked Joseph and respected him. But he did not know how close he and the Nez Perce chieftain would become in the months ahead.

Chapter 5

>>>>>>>>>>>>>>>>>>

A Flight and Fight for Justice

By the time the spring rains came and the rivers started flooding from snowmelt, Chris Colt and Chief Joseph had become fast friends. Colt had spent much more time at Joseph's village and on hunting treks with the chief than he did at Fort Lapwai. Man Killer had gone out on two hunting parties as a warrior, no longer a wide-eyed boy. He spent as much time as possible around his big friend and hero Colt and seemed to get wiser, bigger, and stronger with each passing day.

There still was no word from Crazy Horse about Shirley, and Chris was getting restless, especially since the white blanket covering the mountain land had melted away and was being replaced by a carpet of green. Travel would be easier, and if she was being held by some Plains band, it would be traveling soon to different hunting grounds.

Although Sitting Bull had been saying for some time

he was taking all his people to Canada, he still spent much time in Montana and North Dakota.

In September, Sitting Bull had the remaining tribes from the Great Encampment split up so they could hunt buffalo more effectively. Sitting Bull and the Hunkpapas, his tribe, were encamped on Grand River near the Black Hills about thirty miles from Slim Buttes, North Dakota Territory.

In all, forty families of Oglala, Brule, and Minniconjou—all Lakotah tribes—were encamped at Slim Buttes, to hunt buffalo, when troops from General George Crook's command attacked. A young boy had been sent to get Sitting Bull to reinforce them. When Sitting Bull and his warriors arrived, they found nothing but dead Sioux—men, women, children, old people. Many of the dead Lakotah had been scalped by the cavalry soldiers and many of the bodies had been stripped. These people had all taken part in the Battle of the Little Big Horn and had taken many trophies from the Seventh Cavalry, including Custer's guidon. The American "horse soldiers" were infuriated at this and killed the assembled Sioux completely and with relish. Sitting Bull's heart was very sad.

A month later the cavalry got a shock themselves. A cavalry commander, Lieutenant Colonel E. S. Otis, was escorting supply wagons along the Yellowstone River. One of the scouts, a young Crow warrior, excited and heart pounding, rode up to the officer. The young man was fortunate to have his scalp, as he related a story about running into a Sioux war party led by Sitting Bull himself. Several of the Hunkpapas had learned to read and write from Christian missionaries and Sitting Bull gave the Crow scout a note to give to Colonel Otis. It read:

I want to know what you are doing on this road. You scare all the buffalo away. I want to hunt in this place. I want you to turn back from here. If you don't, I will fight you again.

When Colonel Otis returned to the fort, he gave the note and a report to his commanding officer, then Colonel Nelson Miles, who would soon figure heavily in Colt's and Joseph's future. Miles would eventually become a famous general. Already he was known as a great Indian fighter.

Miles sent scouts out and located Sitting Bull. They told the Hunkpapa chief that Miles wanted to parley with him. Sitting Bull agreed to meet and a place was arranged near the border of Montana and North Dakota.

The two men met and Miles tried to convince Sitting Bull to surrender his people to the cavalry.

Sitting Bull, according to the official military transcription of the meeting, said angrily, "No Indian that ever lived loved the white man, and no white man that ever lived loved the Indian."

The chief of the Hunkpapa flatly refused to surrender and the peace treaty broke up. As Sitting Bull and his small contingent returned to his people and the cavalry contingent with Colonel Miles returned to the

parent unit, some of the troopers angry at the message
fired at the distant Sioux. A battle began.

The cavalry greatly outnumbered the Indians, so the
Sioux took flight. On several occasions, the Lakotah
stopped and fought, but they largely fought in retreat
for over forty-eight hours. At one point, Sitting Bull
tricked Miles into pursuing a small group of Hunkpapa
braves waving blankets and whooping at the soldiers.
The soldiers chased the small war party into a hollow
and the main body surrounded the hollow, setting fire
to the grass and guarding the entrance. Miles's troops
were pinned down by gunfire. Fortunately for the cavalry, Colonel Miles had artillery that he fired at the
blocking force of Sioux and escaped before all his
troops were consumed by the flames. Sitting Bull and
his followers finally got away but left behind most of
their possessions to do so.

Disheartened, just days later, two thousand Minniconjou and Sans Arc tribal members surrendered to
Miles and his men. They were sent to the Powder River
Agency. The rest of the Lakotah from the Great Encampment joined Crazy Horse's or Sitting Bull's
groups, who kept venturing farther north.

In early March, two Minniconjou braves, who had
been relatives of Chantapeta and were contacted by
scouts from Fort Lincoln, finally made contact with
Crazy Horse and got Colt's message to him. The Oglala
warrior sent runners to every band of Cheyenne and
Lakotah he could think of. The runners were instructed to tell the chief of each band that Shirley

Ebert was the woman of Colt and was under Crazy Horse's protection. That was message enough.

Finally, the last runner returned in early May with a message for Crazy Horse, telling him of her whereabouts.

A group of Bannock scouts came from Fort Lapwai to Chief Joseph's camp in late April and summoned Colt to see General Howard.

When Colt arrived at Lapwai, he was summoned immediately to the general's office. Arriving there, Colt learned he was to notify all the nontreaty Nez Perce that Howard wanted a meeting with them at Lapwai. Colt sent scouts and went himself back to Joseph's village and notified all the chiefs. Chris Colt then accompanied Chief Joseph back to Fort Lapwai.

In early May the last of the nontreaty bands arrived and a meeting was set up right away. General Howard arrived with a contingent of troops and essentially got right to the point. He told the leaders of each band to select a place for their bands on Lapwai Reservation and move there within thirty days. If not, he said that he would consider that they wanted to fight and would send soldiers after them to make them obey.

Chief Too-Hool-Hool-Zote jumped up, furious, and screamed at General Howard. "I am not going on the reservation!"

Chief Joseph stood and everyone became quiet, all eyes fixing on him, all men in the meeting waiting to hear the words of wisdom that would surely come from his mouth.

Joseph spoke, "Hear me my brothers. My father, Old

Joseph, spoke to me before he left on the spirit trail.
Some of you heard him speak. He spoke of the Wallowa Land and said that it was our home. He told me
never sell it to the whites, because it is not ours to
sell. It belongs to Mother Earth, and she lets us live
there and use the land. We are warriors and all of us
have counted coups many times. We are not afraid to
fight, but we have seen the power of the big guns of
the horse soldiers, and we know that every time a red
man kills a white man, ten more white men come to
take his place. One-Arm says he wants to be our friend,
but we have seen he has been bringing many Sioux
here to be scouts against us. They bring the great Colt,
Wamble Uncha, to be chief of scouts. The horse soldiers would like for the Nez Perce not to come to Lapwai, so they can fight with us and kill many. If they
do, we will not want to say that the beautiful land is
ours, because we will all be living with our grandfathers. General One-Arm Howard, I will bring my band
here to Lapwai before one moon has passed. When I
do, your horse soldiers will not have a reason to kill
my people. I have spoken."

With that, Joseph rose and walked away, hopped up
on the back of his pony, and started toward the Wallowa Mountains. This gesture moved everyone there to
follow his lead. Those who were with his contingent
quickly packed Chief Joseph's belongings in an effort
to catch up to him.

As the assembled chiefs left the meeting to pack and
head for their camps, a Lakotah scout staying back
because of the hard feelings between the Sioux and

Nez Perce waved at Colt. He let Colt know in universal sign language that he had to speak with him.

General Howard walked over to the chief of scouts. "Oh, yes, I meant to tell you, Mr. Colt. That young scout yonder has been telling everyone that he needs to speak with you badly."

Sarcastically Colt said, "Thanks for getting word to me so quickly, General."

Not waiting for a reply or reprimand, Colt walked away and joined the Lakotah warrior. Colt handed him a cigarette he had just rolled and rolled another for himself, lighting both.

The man spoke, "Wamble Uncha, I bring a message from the mighty Crazy Horse. I am Three Ponies of the Oglala. Crazy Horse sent runners to every Chyela and Lakotah band. He told the runners to tell the chiefs that he was looking for your woman with the hair that is from fire and she is to be protected. He learned she was captive of Screaming Horse's band of Chyela and were in the Land of Many Smokes for winter. Screaming Horse says she is good woman and five ponies is good price for her."

"Will she be okay there?" Colt asked.

Three Ponies said, "Yes. Crazy Horse will kill any man who harms this woman."

Colt felt relieved. He shook hands with Three Ponies and patted him on the back. The brave, however, wore a somber look.

"What's wrong?" Colt asked.

The brave said, "Crazy Horse wanted the mighty Colt to learn of this fast. He put on best clothes and best paint and led his people. He surrendered to the Long Knives, so he could send message to you."

Colt looked at the ground. As much as he was elated about Shirley, he was upset about Crazy Horse.

"How is my brother?" Colt asked.

"He is dead," Three Ponies responded, "in his heart. His eyes are open, and he walks, but inside, he is dead. The *wasicun* want to kill him, as they fear he will soon escape the reservation and follow the warpath once more."

"I must go and find my woman," Colt said. "Do you know where this Screaming Horse's village is?"

"He goes to seek out Sitting Bull who has taken his people, and those who follow him from other tribes, to the Land of the Great Mother." Chris knew he meant Canada.

"You must go," Colt said, "and find my brother Crazy Horse. Tell him to leave and be free like the eagle. Tell him I have received his message and he truly has been my brother, but now he must go and be free."

Three Ponies said, "But if I leave, One-Arm will have me followed. I will be shot. They will call me a deserter."

"No, I will tell them I gave you a job to do. I did. Go home to your people and live for Wakan Tanka. Hunt the mighty herds of *pte*. Do not come back here for I have also become brothers with the Nez Perce and they too are noble warriors. It makes my heart sad to see the Lakotah scout against the Pierced Noses, for the two peoples should surely be brothers instead."

"The Pierced Noses and the Lakotah were enemies

before I was born," Three Ponies replied, "but I see what is in the heart of Wamble Uncha. I shall go, and I shall carry your words to the ears of your brother, the great one, Crazy Horse. The words shall also be taken to Screaming Horse that Wamble Uncha will come for his woman."

Colt escorted the Sioux brave to the livery and called for the NCOIC—the noncommissioned officer in charge. A big burly sergeant came out and played with the ends of his handlebar mustache. The man was mixed race, maybe black and white, Colt couldn't tell for sure, but he had a twinkle in his eyes and certainly knew how to take care of horses.

"Sergeant," Colt said, clapping the man on his beefy shoulder, "I have given this lad a hard and dangerous assignment that will take him many miles over hard and dangerous territory. Do you have a mount to suit his needs?"

"Aye, Mr. Colt," the sergeant said, "I have an ugly bay Appaloosa that will serve him well. The horse looks to have a bit of the Arab in it and has slender but well-muscled legs. It might stand fourteen-two hands but will run our best mounts into the ground, even the mules on the forced march. Wait here."

The man disappeared into the depths of the livery and reappeared a few minutes later, leading the Appaloosa with a good head and straight back and cannons. It was saddled with a standard cavalry blue blanket with gold trim and McLellan saddle and a leather bridle with a good curved bit.

He handed the reins to the Sioux warrior, saying, "Do ya speak our tongue, young buck?"

Three Ponies nodded his head.

"Do rein him with a gentle hand, lad. He will move like the wind and remember: He's Appaloosa. He might be ugly, but he's stupid."

The big strange sergeant started laughing powerfully at his own joke and disappeared into the dark cavernous bowels of the livery, leaving Colt and the Sioux wondering where the man came from and what his background was.

Colt wouldn't dwell on it though, because that was the way of the West. Only about one third of the cowboys in the West were white. The rest were black, Indian, Mexican, or half-breeds. Some cavalry privates had been generals in the Civil War. Others had fought in battles as officers in foreign lands across the seas. Some men had different names before and had a price on their heads. Some were doctors or teachers from back east, maybe with a broken heart, who wanted to journey west, become a cavalry trooper and fight Indians, or a cowboy and eat a lot of dust. Colt knew you didn't ask a man about his background, and you didn't spend much time worrying about it either.

Three Ponies grabbed Colt's forearm in the Sioux style of handshake. They shook and Colt gave him two cigars out of his pocket. He did not thank him, for that was not the way of the American Indian. It was understood. The brave grabbed the girth strap on the McLellan rig and untied it. The girth strap fell away under the horse, and he pulled the saddle off, setting it on the ground. He took the canteen off and removed the rifle scabbard and admired it. He held it up proudly and showed it to Colt, who smiled. The scout stuck the Henry repeater he had been carrying into the scabbard and swung up on the horse's back and rode off for the scouts' billets to retrieve his belongings.

Colt grabbed another new scout, not far away. A Bannock. "Speak English?"

The scout nodded. "Yes, sir."

Colt said, "Take a message to One-Arm's office. Tell him I am going to Joseph's village and will come in with his band."

"Yes, sir," the Bannock said, and ran off toward the commanding officer's office centered in front of the flagpole and facing the parade ground.

Colt mounted War Bonnet and galloped off into the night.

Chief Joseph and his band, joined by several others, arrived in several weeks and made an encampment just outside the reservation with the other nontreaty bands.

They had left some of their cattle behind, so having complied with Howard's orders, Joseph and his giant brother Ollikut led a small party back to the Wallowa Mountains to butcher some of the cattle for the people. Colt had explained his situation about Shirley to Chief Joseph and the chief asked Colt to please remain with him for now. Joseph explained that Howard would let Colt go to find his woman once he was sure that Joseph and his people were safely on the reservation, but Howard would be cautious right now. Joseph told

Colt that he would not want to leave without permission, because he would be arrested and then could never save her. Joseph also promised a contingent of warriors to escort Colt most of the way there, although he did not want his men to engage any Sioux or Cheyenne unless they had to.

Colt felt trapped. Howard had encouraged him to escort Joseph on the trip to butcher cattle. Howard was not happy about Joseph and Ollikut leaving to butcher the cattle in their homelands, as the chief had been the voice of reason among the five bands of nontreaty Nez Perce. He was also scared of Joseph's power and leadership, though, and decided to go out of his way to keep the chief happy for now. Although Howard did not respect the Nez Perce's ability to fight, he had originally underestimated the military genius of Cochise and the fighting ability of the Chiricahua Apache, so he did not want to make the same mistake twice. His religious convictions kept him from wanting to kill anyone, unless he was forced to.

While Joseph and Colt were in the Wallowas, certain horrible incidents occurred that played into the hands of people like Colonel Potter, and those members of the Indian Ring out of Washington who wanted the decimation of the red tribes. Of the four other Nez Perce bands, the least powerful chief was the oldest, Chief White Bird, who was seventy. One of his young braves, named Wallaitits, took two friends and went to the nearby farming community wanting to exact revenge against whites, because of his father's death at the hands of whites years before. They killed four white men.

The next week, twenty-one more warriors, all young bucks, killed fourteen white men, women, and children.

Joseph was upset when he returned and heard of this and Colt immediately reported to General Howard that Joseph's band had nothing to do with the killings. Howard didn't care. In his eyes, the Nez Perce had defied the government and would pay.

Colt did not wait for the general to forbid him from returning to Joseph's camp, which he knew Howard would surely do. He left immediately.

When he arrived, there were murmurs among the people, as the leaders of the other bands had assembled at Joseph's council fire. Bad feelings were running high and Colt sensed it, as did Joseph.

The chief spoke, "Let all my words fight their way through your angry heads now and travel into your hearts. This man has become my brother and is not our enemy. If your heart is black at him, it is black at me."

Colt was touched by these words. Man Killer, who had accompanied his older friend to the council fire, sat up a little straighter, a little prouder.

Chief Joseph went on. "We must now fight if the horse soldiers attack us, but hear me now brothers. We must take no scalps. We must kill no women or children. We must kill no white eyes unless they are soldiers. We will let the horse soldiers take scalps if they want. The people will be angry at them. Some white eyes are now angry at their own people because they know our lands have been stolen. We must not make those white eyes angry at us. Let them stay angry at their own people. Let them think the horse soldiers are the enemy, and not the Nez Perce. If we must fight, we will, but we will only fight and kill bluecoat warriors. There can be no more killing of farmers or women or children, like some of our people have done. If we do, all the white eyes will cry for the Nez Perce to be no more. You must go on, for One-Arm will send horse soldiers after us. One of my wives is with child. When she gives birth, I will join you."

Colonel Potter, meanwhile, was excited and upset. His men who had survived the Bannock massacre made it to civilization and sent him telegrams, all quitting, to the last man. He also got reports from cavalry units who found the bodies of the other shootists he had sent after Colt. Colt's sight had returned and this frightened Potter very much.

Potter thought back to Hans Bermeister, near Wichita. Rufus had decided that he wanted Bermeister's wife in the worst way. He decided the best way to get her would be to run the man off his homestead property, which was easier said than done. Bermeister was a German who had immigrated to the United States some years before. He had a sod-roof log cabin and some acreage he farmed outside Wichita.

Potter had two gunfighters riding with him then and boldly rode out from town to Bermeister's place after bragging around town that he had bought the property back east and held a deed. He also bragged that Bermeister would be leaving the land. Those who knew the crusty German thought better of that idea.

When Potter arrived, he held up a printed piece of paper and said that he had the deed to the property and told Bermeister that he had five minutes to be off the place. Potter then informed the man that his wife could remain behind and pack their belongings. Potter said he would provide her with a buggy and an escort to Wichita, as he couldn't find it in his heart to pick on a poor woman. He stated that he was a businessman but he certainly wasn't heartless.

The problem was that Hans wasn't the type to waste time arguing. While he listened to the ultimatum from the phony colonel, he was standing in the doorway of his sod cabin. When Potter finished, Bermeister gave him his answer. He yanked up a ten-gauge double barrel shotgun and unloaded both barrels, hitting Potter in the shin with one pellet and killing both gunfighters and one horse. The suddenness of the attack probably saved Potter's life. Hans was nervously trying to reload, and the colonel was so frightened he fell out of the saddle, jumped up, and limped toward Hans as quickly as he could hobble forward. A lucky bullet at close range hit its mark and caught the German between the eyes just as he was raising the scattergun again.

So much for the idea of convincing the wife that she needed to be with Potter—a man tougher than her husband. Potter raped her and then strangled her. He buried Hans, his wife, and the two gunfighters out on the prairie about a half a mile from the cabin, carefully cutting away blocks of sod to cover the graves. Potter stayed there for about six months for appearance's sake before moving on. He told anybody that inquired that Hans knew he was trespassing and had gladly taken his wife and moved west. He said his cohorts had left for greener pastures.

The funny thing was that Potter could not forget how he was so frightened when Bermeister stood up to his bullying that he was almost paralyzed by fear. He started having nightmares after that in which he could not move while Hans was reloading the shotgun.

Colonel Potter was alone in his massive library, his heart pounding. He started breathing heavily and was sure he was having a heart attack. Some of his men came into the mansion to talk with him and knocked on the double doors to the mahogany-walled library.

"Go away!" he shouted and the high pitch of his voice scared him.

This episode recurred seven different times in April and May, but finally stopped. It stopped happening when Colonel Potter decided that he would spare no expense to get rid of Chris Colt. He would also put his mansion and Oregon holdings up for sale and move to Denver, Colorado, where he could oversee his burgeoning mining empire. The decision to make a change of scenery and to make absolutely sure that Colt would be eliminated from the face of the earth were all that was needed to end the episodes of panic.

Chris Colt returned to Fort Lapwai and got an immediate meeting with General Howard.

"General," Colt pleaded, "I know I can talk Chief Joseph and his band into coming back to the reservation if you will just let me try to talk him into it. Let me go after him and talk with him."

Howard said, "Go ahead, Mr. Colt. Talk to him, but be careful. They've killed innocent civilians, and they won't hesitate to kill you, too, if it suits their needs."

"General," Colt went on, "Joseph would not allow anyone to kill me. There's another matter I have to discuss."

"What's that?" Howard said.

Colt continued, "My fiancée was captured by the Cheyenne earlier this winter. She was kept in winter camp in Yellowstone, but they are on their way north to Canada to join Sitting Bull. I have to rescue her, sir."

Howard was amazed. "This is incredulous. Wasn't your fiancée kidnapped once before and held captive by the Sioux and you had to rescue her?"

"Yes she was," Colt replied, "but it's not so unusual. She left Bismarck alone in a wagon and tried to make it here when she heard I was blind."

"She must love you very much to try a stunt like that," Howard said. "I thought you were close with the Cheyenne. Why would they kidnap her?"

"It was a small band who never met me. She should be safe for a while though. Crazy Horse guaranteed her safety."

"Oh, yes, Crazy Horse," Howard said. "Your blood brother. Frankly, Mr. Colt, I do not understand how you feel you can trust that cutthroat, but when I was in Arizona, Cochise and Tom Jeffords were as close as two men could be. They were like brothers, and supposedly Jeffords is the only man who knows where Cochise is buried, but I just don't understand it. Pour yourself some tea."

"Thanks, no."

Howard poured a cup of tea and walked across the room drinking it, staring out the window. He walked back to the couch and sat down.

"Mr. Colt," he said, "I can certainly sympathize with you, and I will send dispatches to all the forts in Montana to rescue her, but I need you here right now. As soon as this Nez Perce issue is settled, and we push the hostiles back to the reservation, I will give you leave to go search for your loved one. Until then, I need you here to help with the Nez Perce. I want you to know that I have my orders, and Indian Affairs and my superiors are not happy about the killings of innocent civilians. They want retribution. They want the Nez Perce to know that they won't get away with this. I'll let you see if you can get them to come in, but I have sent for troops and am getting them, and I cannot guarantee that there will be no killing if they do come in. I have cavalry troops on their way here from San Francisco, artillery on its way from Alaska, and even infantry on its way all the way from Atlanta, Georgia. I also have every available troop in my department on its way here. We have tried everything we can to be good Samaritans to the Nez Perce, but I feel we will end up having to smite down these heathens. I also don't believe, Mr. Colt, that it's going to take very long either."

"General," Colt said, "the Nez Perce have gotten along well with the white man ever since the Lewis and Clark Expedition three quarters of a century ago. They are tough and smart, but they can be good allies if we only treat them fairly. I think that's all they ask."

Howard said, "Colt, the simple fact is five bands of Nez Perce refused to sign the treaty with the government, years ago, and the rest did. We have been patient long enough. They will now sign it and live on the reservation, or else."

"Or else, Colonel Rufus B. Potter and others won't be able to grab up and make millions on the beautiful land in the Wallowa Valley and the other lands the Nez Perce occupy," Colt rejoined.

"You're out of order, mister!" the general said.

Colt replied, "I am not one of your soldiers, General Howard. I am a civilian employee under your hire and an American citizen with the right to think and speak about whatever I choose. You are my boss and might not like what I think or say and may fire me for thinking it, but I have the right to think it."

"Mr. Colt, you are absolutely right on that count, and I am sworn to uphold the Constitution, which includes your freedom of expression. I apologize for my remark."

"I respect that, General," Colt said, then chuckled. "Boy, I bet that was hard to say."

Howard turned and grinned for the first time ever in Colt's presence and replied, "Amen."

Chris started for the door.

"Mr. Colt," the general said as Colt stopped and turned, "I want to tell you something off the record."

Chris said, "What's that, General?"

"Your blood brother Crazy Horse."

"What about him?"

The general went on, "He has a tremendous amount of influence with the Sioux and Cheyenne both."

"What you're trying to tell me is he's a marked man. Right, General?" the chief of scouts asked.

The commander replied, "Yes, I'm afraid for your sake that he is."

Chris Colt chuckled and opened the door, starting to walk out again.

The general said, "Wait. Why do you laugh?"

"Hell's bells, General Howard. Crazy Horse knew that when he turned himself in, so he could warn me."

"What?" Howard replied. "What do you mean so he could warn you?"

"General, Crazy Horse surrendered so he would be able to send me an accurate message that he had located my fiancée. He knew that he would be killed by our people if he was ever captured or surrendered. So will Sitting Bull."

General Howard seemed perplexed. He stroked his beard with his hand for a few seconds and again walked to the window, looking out.

"Why did they figure they'd be killed?" the general asked.

"They are both leaders and have vision. They are too dangerous to the white man to continue to live."

"You mean to tell me that knowing he would be killed, Crazy Horse turned himself in just to get a message to you? Out of friendship?" the one-armed officer asked.

"No," Colt replied, "not friendship, brotherhood."

General Howard turned around and stared at Colt with a look of astonishment on his normally controlled expression. "Just how close to these hostiles are you, Mr. Colt?"

"Very close, General. Very close."

The chief of scouts turned and walked out the door.

Chief Joseph wanted the information from Colt badly. He knew that Chris would not sugarcoat it in any way.

Colt also knew that the truth was what the chief wanted to hear, and the general wanted delivered. The scout gave Joseph a briefing on what he was told by General Howard.

Joseph thought a few seconds. "Many will want to kill us for the whites who have died?"

"I believe that General Howard is a fair man, but I do not think he understands the red man. I believe there are other white chiefs who care more about killing the red man, selling good farmland, and winning battle honors than they care about the plight of the Nez Perce."

"If our bands go to reservation land and live in peace under the rule of the white grandfather, will they make war against my people?" Joseph asked.

Colt said, "I think that General Howard would try

to treat you respectfully, but there may be others who will want your people killed. There may not, too."

"You speak true and straight, as you always do, my brother," the leader said. "The white grandfather and other leaders look at the Nez Perce as children, not men and women. If a child gets angry and runs away to the distant mountain, what should a good father do?"

"I don't know," Colt said. "I suppose let him run away and wait for him to come back."

Joseph said, "And when he comes back, a good father should first ask him if he is hungry or thirsty."

"That tells him he is loved and cared for," Colt added.

Joseph went on. "Then shouldn't a good father ask the boy why he ran away?"

Colt thought for a moment. "Yes, that makes good sense."

"The white grandfather and his men do not want to ask the child why he ran away. They want to cut the muscles in the back of his legs, so he cannot ever run away again. Such an important choice should be made after rest."

He got up from the council fire and left Colt and the other seven men sitting there. The wise chief walked to his buffalo robe, lay down, covered himself up, and seemed to go to sleep, his back turned toward the group. All the people in the council looked at each other, some shaking their heads, then stood and left the tepee. Chris Colt sat by the fire and finished his coffee.

When the last one exited the lodge, Colt spoke to the back of the snoring red leader. "Good night, Chief. You sure know how to make people hear your words."

The snoring stopped and Joseph said, "Too bad the horse soldiers won't listen to them."

He sat up and turned around, smiling at Chris Colt.

Colt started to step out of the tepee but stopped at the round hole that was the door and tossed a cigar to the older man. "Now you can smoke this while you sit by the fire drinking your coffee and thinking about your decision."

Joseph gave Colt a knowing look, and the scout winked, turned, and went out into the night. Man Killer met him and they walked to the tepee provided for the scout. Chris noticed that the young man was fitting into his role ever since being declared a man by Joseph. He held his shoulders back proudly and they already seemed a little larger and the former boy Ezekiel seemed to be filling out all over. They entered the lodge and sat by the fire when Chris finally brought up the side arm Man Killer was now wearing.

Man Killer said, "It was a gift from Ollikut, the giant who is brother of Joseph."

"Most Indians prefer long guns. Why did he give you a .45, young brother?"

Colt made no more references to Man Killer in childlike terms, such as "little one," ever since Joseph gave Man Killer his new name.

Man Killer poured a cup of coffee from the pot on the fire and stirred in sugar. He sipped it, burning his upper lip without showing any emotion. "I speak all the time about you and the speed and accuracy of you shooting your guns. Some men in our band have even been joking with me about it. They say I want to be a white man."

Colt smiled. "Well, do you?"

Man Killer's chest puffed out and said, "No. I am Nez Perce and am proud to be Nez Perce. I will always be Nez Perce."

"You are Nez Perce, my friend."

Man Killer smiled, realizing Colt had only been giving him a hard time. He went on. "I want to learn from you how to draw and shoot. As I get older many of our ways will die, only because there are so many of you and your weapons are better and stronger. I must learn to live in the world of the white man and walk as a chief among men, but I will always be Nez Perce, no matter where I walk."

Colt whistled and said, "How old are you?"

Man Killer took a long sip of coffee.

Chris said, "If you already think like that at your young age, you will be a chief among all men. Man Killer, I will be happy to teach you to shoot, but you must make a promise."

"What?"

"You must only shoot your gun under three conditions. One is to practice; two is to kill food; three, and the most important, is to defend yourself only when you are attacked."

"You have my word," the man-boy replied.

The sun heated up the morning sky quickly the next

day and Colt could virtually see the snowmelt going on in the far-off mountain range.

The scout and Man Killer went off from the village and stood at the edge of the campside stream, down-river from the village. They faced a steep, high cut-back, where Colt had placed some old pieces of pottery. He asked for Man Killer's pistol and looked at it more closely. He had spent two hours already just speaking about gun safety and showing the youngster how to clean and load his Smith & Wesson American .44, a cheap copy of the scroll-engraved Colt Peacemaker. The man who had owned the new gun had filed the sight off to make for easier draw. The oiled leather holster was well worn and fit Man Killer very well. Whoever donated the gunbelt to the Nez Perce had also unwillingly contributed a large cloth bag of .44 rounds and all the loops in the holster were also filled with bullets.

Chris loaded the gun, reviewing with the brave how to do so. Man Killer had been dry-firing with no bullets until his right arm felt like it couldn't be raised an inch. He also had a blister on the inside base of his right thumb from earing the hammer back over and over again.

Colt faced the cut-bank and pointed at the second cracked pot from the left.

"That one. Draw and fire," Colt said.

Man Killer drew his gun and the hammer came up under his thumb, his finger closed around the trigger and snapped the shot. The bullet kicked up a big puff of dirt about five feet to the upper right of the vase.

Man Killer was frustrated inside but showed no emotion. He was smart enough to realize he was just starting to learn.

Colt drew his gun slowly, the hammer being cocked by the forward action of his arm coming up and pointing at the target. Colt stopped and froze his hand and arm in place.

"Here," Colt said, "is the important part of shooting. Right here, you have to bring the trigger back fast, but you have to squeeze it, not jerk it. The reason your bullet hit high and right was because you jerked the trigger, like this. It pulled your hand up and to the right when your right index finger jerked."

The warrior had a troubled look, so Colt reached into a basket and pulled out a freshly picked spring berry.

Colt took one and smashed another berry under his palm on a log nearby. Man Killer imitated the action.

Colt said, "Here," as he tossed a second berry to the young man.

Colt took another and held it up between his forefinger and thumb. Man Killer did the same.

Chris said, "This is squeezing the trigger."

He squeezed the berry quickly, and it exploded with berry pulp and blue juice running over his fingers and hand.

Man Killer did the same and licked his fingers.

He said, "I understand, but can you shoot fast 'squeezing' the trigger?"

Colt walked over to the stream and rinsed off his fingers and palm. He wiped his hand on his yellow-striped pant leg while he walked back to Man Killer's side. Without saying a word, Colt's hands dropped down to his side and both came up with a mother-of-pearl-handled .45 Peacemaker in them, which then boomed simultaneously. The pot Man Killer had fired at disappeared in two explosive puffs of smoke and dust. This coordinated violence occurred in milliseconds, and Man Killer just stared in awe. He had seen Colt fire and shoot multiple opponents; but at that time, Man Killer's own adrenaline was coursing through his veins. He hadn't really had the opportunity to closely watch and study the absolute speed and accuracy that Colt had in his hands.

Man Killer said, "Your hands have lightning in them both, Wamble Uncha. How fast can you shoot? Show me again."

Colt walked over to the cut-bank and picked up a small clay cup they had placed there as a more difficult target. He returned to Man Killer's side and faced the cut-bank again. Colt pointed at the third pot from the left and held out his right hand in front of him, palm down. He placed the little cup on the back of his hand. Man Killer stared in wonder and noticed a lot of the boys and some of the young maidens from the village had gathered at the watercourse's edge and were watching intently.

Suddenly Colt's hand dropped down to his gun and came up while the cup was still falling. The pistol exploded and so did the small cup, right in front of the barrel, as well as the distant pot on the cut-bank.

Colt had actually dropped the cup, drawn, and fired,

hitting the cup before it had dropped more than an inch or two.

Man Killer was dumbfounded. He stared at the smoke coming out of the end of Colt's Peacemaker, then at the pieces of clay cup on the ground, then at the shattered pot on the cut-bank. "Great Scout, I have never seen such handling of any weapon. I want to shoot like that."

"Man Killer, bullets cost much money. You must practice drawing and firing all day and all night with no bullets in your gun. Every once in a while, you load it up and practice shooting at targets. It would even be better to practice while hunting. If you miss a lot, you will go hungry. Now, let's try that next pot. Remember what I told you. Point at the pot with your gun barrel, like pointing your finger. Don't worry about speed now. Lots of men have been killed who got their gun out of their holster much faster, but they missed the first shot. For now, take your time and hit the target."

Man Killer faced the pot, bent his knees in a gunfighter's crouch. He drew fairly smoothly and fired. The bullet kicked up dirt two inches to the right of the pot. He smiled, cocked the gun, and fired again, and the pot shattered into a thousand pieces. He smiled briefly again, then got serious, facing his hero.

"It is good, Chris Colt. I have to pull out my gun and fire many times, as much as rocks in that stream, but someday I will shoot like you."

"That might be good, Man Killer, but why do you

want to be that fast? Do you want to live up to your name?"

"What do you mean?"

"I mean," Chris replied, "do you want to be able to kill many men?"

"No, I want to learn to shoot like you, because others, red or white, cannot do the same. I want to kill no men, unless they are my enemy and first want to kill me. Besides, I would like to count coup on an enemy more than shoot one."

"Spoken like a true Nez Perce warrior," Colt said.

The next day Colt returned to Fort Lapwai to inform General Howard about his meeting with Joseph.

Having reported that Red Echo had already taken his band to the reservation and that Chief Joseph was going to lead the other bands back as well, Colt was greeted with a different attitude from the Christian General—one that he didn't like.

Howard fumed. "Mr. Colt, that is indeed good news. I have received orders from my superiors and we will strike the scoundrels down with a carefully laid ambush and teach them about killing white settlers once and for all."

Colt was shocked. "What! What are you talking about, General?"

Howard said, "Well, first of all. The bands are not on their way back. Chief Too-Hool-Hool-Zote and Chief White Bird have their bands camped on White Bird Creek and Chief Looking Glass has his camp on Clear Creek. They are in direct disobedience of government orders. If Joseph does indeed convince them to

return, we will lay a good tactical ambush with suffi-
cient blocking forces and I guarantee you, sir, that we
will have no more Nez Perce problems. I am a Christian, but I am not losing a star because I have been
too lenient with a group of heathens who don't even
appreciate what they've been offered."

"So that's it," Colt said angrily. "General Howard,
you know that there are plenty of women and children
in those bands, yet you are willing to risk their murders
just to save yourself a damned star on your epaulets."

"Who do you think you are talking to, young man?"
the general replied, fuming.

Colt started to reply but stopped himself and pulled
out a cigar and chomped down on it. He knew that he
must warn Joseph and he also had to save his love. He
remembered how he had to save Shirley once before,
and he ended up blowing his top with General Custer.
It was almost like history repeating itself, except Colt
learned from his mistakes. Also, he had at least liked
Howard, but he hated Custer and everything he stood
for. Colt now felt that Howard was clearly showing his
colors. Chris was always suspicious of anybody who
thumped too hard on their own chest bragging about
what an outstanding and caring Christian they were,
instead of simply showing it with their actions. Howard
had just reinforced Colt's feelings by risking the deaths
of innocent women and children, let alone men, just
to help his career. Chris, however, decided he would
watch his step because Custer had had him seized and
cuffed and shackled when he blew his top with him.

Colt would show his displeasure, even anger, but he would carefully choose his words.

"General," Colt said, "how do you know where the bands are located?"

"Although I don't believe in or advocate gambling at all, Mr. Colt," the commander said. "I will use a cliché and state that we should lay our cards on the table. Buffalo Horn, the Bannock scout you mentioned in your report, told me what actually happened to you in your fight. He has successfully scouted for me in the past and has been honest and loyal, and quite frankly, his story has a great deal of plausibility. He told me that he and his band were quietly camped and you raided his camp, along with a large group of Nez Perce, including Joseph and Ollikut. He took some scouts out and found the Nez Perce camps straightaway."

Colt was bubbling inside but remained calm and quietly said, "General, I cannot believe that you would take the word of a cutthroat and scoundrel like Buffalo Horn over mine, but if that's how you feel, maybe you should make him your chief of scouts."

General Howard said, "Maybe I should, Mr. Colt. Maybe I should. You can pick up your pay voucher from my adjutant and final pay from the paymaster. I want you off this fort before sunset."

Colt smiled now. "General Howard, if you can be so ignorant as to trust someone like Buffalo Horn, instead of trusting me, then you probably deserve whatever happens to you. I also will not stand here and defend myself with you, if you are that foolish. Whatever I say will fall on deaf ears. But I want to tell you something right now. If you make war on the Nez Perce who have had their lands stolen away by us after being loyal allies all these years, this country will turn against you and the Army."

Howard laughed. "You must be joking, you pompous ass. Have you read previous newspaper stories about other Indian campaigns? If we wipe out the entire tribe of Nez Perce, we would all be heroes in the eyes of the citizens of this country. People are sick of all the scalpings and killings and raping."

"I am sure they are, so why don't you and other leaders get your soldiers to stop doing it?" Colt said, trying hard to hold his tongue with little avail. "You know it was our Army, back east, that taught the red man how to take scalps. A lot of your buddies, who are probably in the Indian Ring, are paying bounties for Apache scalps down in Arizona Territory right now."

"That's enough insubordination. Leave now," General Howard said firmly.

Colt walked to the door, stopping and turning, hand on the knob. "Remember my warning, General, and give my warning to both Colonel Potter and Buffalo Horn. Tell them I'll be paying each of them a visit when I'm ready. They won't know when, but I will."

"You murder one of my scouts or a civilian under my department," Howard said firmly, "I'll hang you from the nearest oak tree."

Chris said, "Be kind of hard to do that, wouldn't it, General?"

The commanding general said, "Why?"

"Can't pull a rope very well if your only good arm's

been shot off," Colt said. "I'm sure I'll be seeing you real soon."

He walked out the door and left the Christian General standing in his office staring after him and silently praying a prayer of intercession to keep him protected from this dangerous man, Christopher Columbus Colt.

Chief Joseph did not doubt Chris Colt's words at all. His second daughter safely delivered, he packed up the remnants of his band and headed toward a rendezvous with Too-Hool-Hool-Zote and White Bird at their camp. He had sent Man Killer and two older warriors ahead to give the other bands a warning and tell them not to go to the reservation.

Word had already gone around Idaho, northern Utah, and eastern Oregon, and hundreds of volunteers, looking for action and a shot at possible free farmlands, traveled to Fort Lapwai to help join in the rumored upcoming fight against the Nez Perce. A large group of reservation Sioux were shipped in boxcars to help out as scouts. Chief Joseph started getting regular messages from sympathetic whites, living at and near Fort Lapwai to keep him abreast of General Howard's plan and activities.

With all the support that Howard received, and with his constant habit of underestimating the fighting ability, intelligence, and ingenuity of the American Indian, he knew that he would simply go out on a few patrols, whip the Nez Perce back into shape, and decimate the troublemakers.

The first officer in Howard's command to help Colt's dire prediction come true was Captain David Perry. He led the first operation against the Nez Perce, leaving Fort Lapwai on June 16 with a last-minute caution from General O. O. Howard, "You must not get whipped."

His reply, taken down by a stenographer, would come back to haunt him, when he said, "There is no danger of that, sir."

Howard had told him to try to avoid engagement with hostiles. His primary mission was to provide protection and set up a security perimeter for the town of Grangeville, some fifty miles distant. Grangeville was a small settlement of farmers. With the column of one hundred plus men approaching the town, several Bannock scouts sent along by Buffalo Horn rode up and reported to Captain Perry that White Bird's band, along with Too-Hool-Hool-Zote's band and even Chief Joseph's, were still camped at White Bird Creek.

At the same time, Chris Colt, scant days after the scout's firing by the Army, sat in Chief Joseph's lodge, smoking and speaking with the leader over hot cocoa. Chris was glad he had been fired, because he sensed an upcoming bloodbath and also had to get away to save Shirley. He could not leave Joseph right now, however, because the chief and his people would need Colt's help. Chris knew that there would be an all-out effort to nail Joseph's hide to the wall, along with a lot of his people. It wasn't hard for Colt to read between the lines. The Nez Perce were to be killed—many of them—as an example to prevent another Battle of the Little Big Horn.

Chief Joseph said, "Tell me, Wamble Uncha, now that the One-Arm has told you to leave, where will you go?"

"Right here," Colt said. "There will be war, and I do not want you and your people to be killed, and I do not want your people to kill more of my people. If the cavalry makes war against you now, I want to help you to escape them and make my people all over the country angry about your plight."

Joseph thought about this and puffed on the cigarette he had rolled. He watched the smoke curl lazily toward the ceiling.

Finally, he spoke, "If we are attacked, what do you think we should do?"

"Run, fast and far," Colt said.

At first, Joseph's temper flared but his face belied his inner emotions. He remembered the courage, attitude, and friendship of the man called Colt. The great scout would not suggest that the Nez Perce were cowards to run like dogs away from the pursuit of the horse soldiers of One-Arm Howard.

He took another puff, slowly. "Why do you say this?"

"The only protection your people will truly have is if *my* people become very angry about the way your nation is treated. If you run away, but fight and win only when you are attacked, that will help."

"What else will help?" Joseph asked.

"If you must kill, only kill soldiers. Take no scalps, kill no civilians, take no prisoners, unless they are soldiers and treat them well. Be very good to women and children," Colt said. "Feed them and give them blankets for sleeping. Do not attack towns, and even treat white farmers and miners you run into like they are neighbors. While we run, my people will talk about the noble Nez Perce, who only want peace, and are being hunted down like coyotes by the U.S. Army. The newspapers will hear of it and soon the whole country will speak of it. Telegrams and letters will be sent to the white grandfather in Washington."

Chief Joseph said, "But will he listen?"

"I do not know," Chris said. "Do you hear your people when they say they are angry?"

Joseph said, "Does the marmot run into his hole when the great bear walks toward him?"

There was a scratching on the outside of Chief Joseph's tepee and he said, "Who is there?"

"Man Killer," came the voice.

"The cocoa is good in here and the fire is warm," Joseph said. "Join your older brother and me."

Man Killer entered the lodge and looked five years older to Colt, especially with the entire upper half of his face painted completely black with war paint. He smiled and nodded at Chris Colt, but looked to his chief with a serious gaze.

"Joseph," the young brave said, "there were twelve handfuls of horse soldiers headed toward Grangeville. Three Bannocks came out and scouted us, not seeing me and the others. We followed them and now the horse soldiers from Lapwai follow the Bannocks to our camp."

Joseph stood, as did Colt.

"Where are the others?"

Man Killer replied, "They are watching the horse soldiers and wait for your orders."

"Quick, young man, summon the other chiefs and the elders," commanded the chief.

Man Killer ran out of the tepee and Chief Joseph added earrings and a necklace to what he was already wearing. He got out his best pipe and wrapped a Hudson's Bay blanket around his shoulders, sitting by the fire and asking Colt to do the same. He packed the pipe with tobacco and lit it, while Colt rolled himself a cigarette, tobacco playing such an important part in discussions and ceremonies among the American Indians.

Within minutes, the rest of the chiefs and the elders were assembled in Joseph's lodge.

Joseph told them that over one hundred soldiers were within fifteen miles of their camp and headed their way.

Joseph spoke in the Nez Perce tongue. "My brother Colt has told me that they will wait until daybreak to attack, because they can control their warriors better. They will put a group of warriors across the stream and maybe at the head of the canyon to block us if we flee. They will probably want to parley and ask us to return first. If they do, we will talk, but if they trick us and start shooting, we will have warriors pointing our rifles at their men. We will not rush at them. Our best shooters will have our best rifles and will first shoot the men with the horns that tell the soldiers

what to do. Then our shooters will kill the chiefs who
wear gold and silver sticks on their shoulders and those
who wear stripes on their sleeves. Our people will be
hiding behind the rocks and trees and will then shoot
the horse soldiers until they run. We will not take
scalps. We will not take trophies off dead soldiers. We
will not kill their wounded. We will beat them, then
leave quickly. If scalps are taken, if fingers and heads
are cut off, let it be the horse soldiers' bloods that cut
our flesh. We will make them start battles, but we will
win them, and the white eyes will all speak of the
mighty Nez Perce who are being slaughtered like the
buffalo. When we travel, we will be good to white eyes
who are not soldiers and will kill only blue coats, in
battle. First, we will speak of peace. We will only do
all these things if they want to fight."

The chiefs murmured and arued about his words
and Joseph raised his hand. "Listen to my words, my
brothers. Are you with me on this?"

Ollikut stood and said, "I follow my brother."

The rest did the same.

Chief Joseph stood again. "Hear me now, for we
must make ready through the night. First, we make
ourselves ready for the spirit walk, then we must take
the old and weak ponies and keep them with our camp.
The good ones we will keep will be hidden along the
stream toward Clear Creek. If we are attacked, and the
Great Mystery favors us, we will rendezvous there with
Looking Glass. One man will go to his lodges tonight
with our plan. We will make ready to move the camp
quickly, but we must make the eyes of the horse sol-

diers and their scouts see us and think that we sleep.
Five men from the band of White Bird should go tonight, and be our eyes and watch the horse soldiers.
This is a good day to die, my brothers. Let us go now
and make ready for war but know that we will first ask
for peace."

As Chris Colt predicted, the cavalry appeared right
at daybreak from the long hill overlooking the camp.

Captain Perry had divided his men into three different groups, but unlike Colt's warning, he didn't even
take the Nez Perce seriously enough to establish
blocking forces. He was just going to attack on line
with his three groups coming off the ridge.

The tactic was a simple spearhead campaign, with
his best lieutenant, a man named Edward Theller,
commanding the lead element of the spearhead. They
would attack through the village and kill anybody who
fought, including any women and children who looked
like they might have weapons.

Lieutenant Theller ran into an unexpected event
halfway down the slope, however, when six Nez Perce
warriors, carrying no weapons, suddenly rode out of
the trees by the camp. All six wore bright war paint,
and their Appaloosa ponies were covered with coup
stripes and other decorations. The man in the middle
carried a white flag of truce and side by side the six
rode bravely toward the lieutenant and his guidon.

Halfway up the ridge, one of Theller's soldiers, in a
panic, raised his repeater and fired, the bullet skim-
ming over the shoulder of the brave carrying the truce
flag. The six wheeled their horses through a hail of

gunfire, while their rifles barked. Both of the buglers
with the cavalry patrol toppled backward out of their
saddles and two more bullets made their lifeless bodies
jump on the ground.

Suddenly Nez Perce arrows, bullets, shotgun blasts,
and war whoops poured out from behind every conceiv-
able hiding place on the ridge line. Two of the Bannock
scouts, out in front of Theller's column, decided to
charge down into the village instead of retreating, as
it was closer and looked to be safer. Maybe, they each
thought, they could even count some coups in the
camp.

The two inadvertently rode directly at the lodge of
Chief Joseph. When they were almost upon it, Chris
Colt stepped out, drew both Colt Peacemakers, and
fired. Both riders toppled backward over the rumps of
their horses.

Joseph had asked Colt to stay hidden, so the soldiers
wouldn't think Colt had betrayed his people, but he
wanted to protect the innocent women and children
hiding in tepees in the village.

Joseph gave sign language hand signals to his braves
fighting on the ridge line as they pushed the cavalry
back up the ridge in a near-panic retreat. In the meantime, he walked to and fro around the camp, a Henry
repeater in his left hand, giving orders to Nez Perce
men, women, and children emerging from their lodges.
In no time, the tepees were struck and travois loaded,
the united bands ready to move. Joseph kept moving,
giving more commands, and kept an eye on his fighting
men on the ridge above them. The cavalry was now in

a full rout and this encouraged the warriors to pursue faster and more aggressively.

The third of Perry's command to the north dismounted and tried to make a stand on a small hillock covered with boulders, hiding behind the large rocks. The mounted Nez Perce warriors swept around the knoll and the defenders panicked, feeling they were cut off, and fled back toward the rest of the command. Joseph gave the command to let them flee and chase them. He wisely figured this would help encourage the others in the rest of the command to panic and retreat.

Spotting this weakness now on Perry's left side, Joseph signaled for the warriors on that side to take the place of the soldiers in the rocks and pour aimed fire in on Perry's left flank. This caused many of the soldiers there to flee or fall in place.

Perry was frustrated and frightened, wondering how these Indians learned military tactics and were fighting differently from any other tribe he had ever confronted or heard of. This Chief Joseph not only knew tactics, but was actually a brilliant strategist, he thought. Somehow, he would have to figure out how to survive this battle. The hostiles had a much smaller fighting force, and within sight of the battle, laughing men, women, and children were striking their camp and preparing a move. The soldiers had been totally outfoxed. He didn't fear death: he feared disgrace and humiliation, and he was feeling both right now.

He spotted Chief Joseph, who he had seen before at Lapwai, down in the circle of tepee skeletons giving a hand signal to someone off of his right flank, not knowing it was Ollikut, Joseph's six-foot six-inch brother and a group of warriors. The chief's brother attacked the right flank, and it quickly gave way, while Captain Perry and his command post, in the center behind where Theller had been, started retreating, leaving small elements to provide covering fire.

In the meantime, Theller and nineteen men had been cut off by the first countercharge, since it was one of these men who had first fired at the men with the flag of truce. They were now surrounded on another hilltop. Warriors rode around the hilltop in circles, yelling and shooting under the necks of their spotted horses. While Theller's men were occupied with the mounted braves, other marksmen picked them off one at a time. After less than thirty minutes, the mounted warriors swept over the top of the hill wiping out Lieutenant Theller and all nineteen of the men.

There was a temporary lull in the fighting while the Nez Perce warriors picked up only the rifles of dead and wounded soldiers. True to Joseph's suggestion, they did not collect scalps, trophies, or strip and mutilate bodies.

While the lull occurred, Captain Perry took advantage and assembled the remaining two thirds of his command and headed to the rear as quickly as possible. Two hills away he finally started to breathe easier, when suddenly a horde of pursuing Nez Perce warriors swept over the ridge line and attacked him again, knocking two men from the saddles with rifle fire and another with a blow from a war club.

Leaving a small covering force behind, the captain

retreated again. The Nez Perce kept shocking him by continuing the attack. This just did not happen in Indian fighting and Perry didn't know what to expect next. He kept choosing different men to leave behind as a covering fire to hold off the determined Nez Perce warriors, but like a swarm of angry hornets, the excited and determined warriors kept pursuing the retreating unit.

By noontime, Captain Perry's unit was in full rout, the trailing Nez Perce force attacking over and over again. They reached the town of Mount Idaho and rode into the town at full gallop and full panic, with the horde of angry braves chasing them all the way to the outskirts of the town. Remembering the words and caution of all the chiefs, the warriors were careful not to shoot any innocent civilians. They actually rode by several townspeople outside of town without even looking at them. The citizens just stared in shock and disbelief. The Nez Perce turned and headed back to join the camp, which was now eighteen miles behind them.

Captain Perry rode to the telegraph office immediately and sent a telegram to General Howard. He could not believe the report he had to send. He was at least an honest man. One third of his command was gone. Four had been severely wounded and thirty-four were dead along with four scouts. He didn't think any Nez Perce had been killed, and in actuality only two had been wounded in the battle. There were no widows or orphans among the Nez Perce lodges that night, just much celebration.

The word about the Nez Perce beating the cavalry

and sparing townspeople started spreading among the citizenry more rapidly than the telegram could be sent. Many gunfighters, settlers, drifters, miners, farmers, soldiers, and cowboys rode into and out of that town in the next few days, and each one carried the incredible story with them. Newspaper reporters sent the story to each other and each found it exciting and fresh.

Howard was furious and totally humiliated. He had, once again, underestimated the resolve and intelligence of the Nez Perce.

A week later the one-armed commander personally led a much larger force of over five hundred men to White Bird Creek where the battle took place. They had the mission to recover what was left of the scalped and mutilated bodies and were shocked when they arrived, especially the two reporters who accompanied them. The bodies were decaying but intact and fully clothed and untouched after death. The soldiers were buried at the battlefield and Howard prayed over their graves, his mind worried over Colt's incredible prediction coming true.

By the time the general's patrol left Fort Lapwai, Shirley Ebert, in northern Montana, heard about the battle. She had been learning Cheyenne and had befriended several women. Her treatment had gotten much better ever since word came to the band that she was truly the woman of Wamble Uncha and was under the protection of Crazy Horse. Screaming Horse was a hardheaded, independent old cuss, but he was smart enough to become chief. He might be hard about giving up his slave, but he was sure going to protect her and certainly not do anything to incur the wrath of Crazy Horse, who all thought had a direct line to Wakan Tanka, the Great Spirit.

Shirley had still heard nothing of Chris. Did he still live?

Chris Colt and Man Killer sat on the banks of the Salmon River with two poles and fishing lines in the water, the early summer sun beating down on their naked torsos.

Colt had won great favor with Chief Joseph for his words of wisdom and the military strategy he had taught the chief. So far, it was working wonderfully, and the chief was well pleased.

Chris had been teaching Joseph a great many things about military tactics because he knew that the man had to do the best he could to protect his women and children from the U.S. military forces, some of whom were quite angry from previous skirmishes with the Nez Perce and other nations. Chief Joseph actually figured out his own battle plan and tactics after the battle, but he had learned much with Colt. The chief of scouts knew that Joseph was a wise leader and would not follow victories over the whites with atrocities. Traveling along the Salmon, the assembled bands, along with Looking Glass's, encountered several groups of white men and treated them with indifference. They even left an old Appaloosa for an old miner they found weeping over the carcass of his dead mule. These actions were soon being told all over the West and stories started circulating back east. Several papers picked it up and sent ace reporters on the nearest train out to the wild frontier. Many civilians, frightened to death by the power and ferocity of the normally tranquil Nez Perce, scurried for the nearest towns.

Going by word of mouth from the whites who had encountered Joseph and his people, General Howard's scouts led the giant column to the Salmon. When the main body arrived at the river, they couldn't cross because the snowmelt was swelling all watercourses throughout the Rockies. What made matters worse was that a large war party rode up out of a gully across the river and shouted and waved blankets over their heads. They whooped and hollered and finally disappeared to the south. Howard left his rear elements behind and took off along the river, looking for a fording point.

Finally, Howard forded the river on July 1. By this time, Chief Joseph had a twenty-five-mile head start, but he turned and backtracked almost. The assembled bands with women and children walking and dogs and horses pulling heavy travois covered over twenty-five miles in less than thirty-six hours and recrossed the river not far from their original crossing. By the time Howard finally made it to the river crossing point, the snowmelt and recent rainstorms had made the river uncrossable. Howard finally had to return to his original crossing point and ford back across the river almost a week later.

While this was happening two Nez Perce chiefs with small war parties attacked Howard's rear guards. The two war parties combined at one point and surrounded an eleven-man security patrol for the wagon train and killed all the soldiers, again respecting Joseph's orders to take only weapons and leave the bodies untouched.

In the meantime, Joseph established a camp on the south fork of the Clearwater River. Runners had come to the bands and let him know that others were on their way to join him. Now out of his defeatist frame of mind, Red Echo had abandoned the reservation and joined up with Joseph and the others. That strengthened the resolve of the Nez Perce. An hour later the lead party of Chief Looking Glass's band showed up and the entire group was soon within sight.

The Nez Perce totaled now about seven hundred strong, but only one hundred and fifty of those were warriors. The mighty herd of carefully bred Appaloosas numbered over two thousand, and the intelligent warriors also pushed a herd of over one thousand range cattle with them to feed their people.

In his meetings with Chief Joseph, Colt had made several things perfectly clear. Number one, he felt that the red man was a citizen of the country as much as the white man was, and he wanted to protect and preserve the rights and way of life of each. Number two, Colt explained that stronger tribes and nations among the red man had taken over lands of weaker or smaller tribes. No matter what, the white man was not going to go away. Right or wrong, they had come to America and planned to settle it and nothing would stop them. Number three, he would give Chief Joseph advice on tactics and strategy, but he would take no part in making plans to kill white men. He would, however, do whatever had to be done to protect any Nez Perce women, children, or old people if someone attacked the village or assembled band. He would fight and kill Lakotah and Bannock scouts who came against them, because the Sioux would understand that he had chosen one side, and they had chosen another for this war, but he was still their brother, too. Number four, he would stay with the bands as long as he could help keep innocent villagers alive and provide advice on how to manipulate public opinion and the newspapers. He explained that, at some point, he must leave to seek out and rescue Shirley. Chris wanted to go immediately, but he knew that Shirley would understand that the safety and welfare of hundreds of men, women, and children were more important than her own. Besides, the word from Crazy Horse's tribe was that Shirley would be kept unharmed.

When Chris was laying down his understanding with Chief Joseph, the wise man also told Colt something that he felt was very important and was to be respected.

Joseph said, "As you were with Sitting Bull at the big Battle at the Greasy Grass, you had to keep your tongue in your mouth about it, because many of your people would think you had betrayed them and fought for the Sioux and Cheyenne against your own people. It is the same here, my brother. Hear my words. When the horse soldiers come and fight, you must hide and protect my family. You must not be seen, for it will be the same if it is known you have been with us. If you are spotted by any white eyes, we must kill them or make them think you are our prisoner."

Colt nodded. "What you say makes sense, and I do not want to kill my people anyway. They would not believe I am prisoner, because you have been taking no prisoners. You are right. It will be done."

With the cavalry far behind them, Chief Joseph declared that the group would rest and let the animals graze awhile along the Clearwater River. They stayed there five days letting the animals fatten up and the people regain their own strength.

Colt and Man Killer were once again trying some fishing, while Colt gave the brave more instructions on the use of the short gun. Again, they were next to the river and firing at a steep cut-back, simply sticking little branches in the ground to use as targets.

Suddenly Colt heard a far-off distant booming sound, followed by another and another.

He sprinted toward War Bonnet and vaulted over the paint horse's rump, yelling, "Come on! Cannon fire!"

He leaned over the big horse's neck and grabbed the reins, tapping War Bonnet in the ribs and sending the horse scampering for the nearby village. Man Killer also vaulted on his horse and was just a few strides behind Colt.

General Howard, up on the bluffs, looking through his binoculars, saw the two Indians running their horses full-out from the river and thought that the big one looked sort of familiar but couldn't place him at the great distance. He saw the rounds from his cannon explode. One seemed to make a direct hit on a tepee and another splintered a treetop. The rest hit along the riverbank. The dust cloud from the first round cleared and Howard saw that the ball had actually hit ten feet in front of the lodge.

He had received reinforcements and now had six hundred soldiers with him. Chris, as per agreement with Joseph, jumped off War Bonnet and sprinted to the chief's tepee, running inside to give the red general tactical advice.

Colt said, "Chief Joseph, I looked up on those bluffs and can tell, he has lots of men."

Suddenly there were cracks and tearing sounds, and Colt dived into Chief Joseph's midsection, the two men flying across the cooking fire and into a pile of buffalo robes along the edge of the lodge. Colt held the chief down as the top of the tepee was ripped to shreds and screams could be heard outside.

Colt said, "Gatling gun."

The firing stopped and Colt could hear the far-off muffled sounds of the Gatling being fired up on the bluffs.

"He could not have cannon and Gatling guns without lots of men," Colt breathed. "You must attack on several fronts and make him think you have many more warriors than you have."

Chief Joseph said, "Stay, my brother," and ran out of the tepee.

Colt heard him giving orders outside and he heard people scurrying around. Chris sneaked out of the tepee and into the nearby trees. He couldn't just stay in a lodge while there was a battle going on. Besides that, in the trees, he would be close to Chief Joseph's wives who had been washing at the river and would have taken cover there. He also would be near his horse in case he had to ride.

Joseph summoned Too-Hool-Hool-Zote, who was already painted and ready to fight. The other chief assembled twenty-four of his warriors and headed up the valley to the east. There had been a dust cloud from a column of cavalry troops galloping down a long ravine, and the chieftain set his men up in fighting positions on the cliff sides overlooking the ravine, pouring deadly volley after deadly volley down on the soldiers, halting them in mid-attack.

The lieutenant in charge of that group sent a sergeant and ten men out to threaten a flanking movement on Too-Hool-Hool-Zote from the north. The soldiers poured fire from the side on the Nez Perce warriors, so the chief led them downhill where there was more cover.

Man Killer, instead of thinking of himself and his own battle honors, thought of his tribe and grabbed several young warriors, pushing the big herd of horses and cattle far down the valley and out in the middle, where they could not be surprised and stampeded by the cavalry troopers.

The troopers in the ravine and the flanking unit poured a fusillade of small-arms fire in on the small band of twenty-five warriors, but soon Ollikut, Five Wounds, and Rainbow, all war chiefs, attacked the cavalry and pushed them back into a defensive posture.

New warriors joined the ones who had been pinned down.

Colt saw Chief Joseph and signaled the chief over to him in the woods.

Colt said, "An Army cannot fight without its stomach."

Joseph smiled and whipped his big bay Appaloosa around and headed toward Chief White Bird.

Minutes later a group of warriors from the band of White Bird headed up the valley and over a ridge in search of General Howard's supply train. Fifty minutes later a courier galloped up to Howard still up on the bluffs, in the center and rear of his command.

"General," the courier said, eyes bulging and words spewing out like steam out of a whistling teapot, "the supply train is under attack by a horde of them damn red devils. We alriddy got two wagons afire and thay're shootin' flamin' damn arrows at the rest a the wagons."

General Howard looked at all the activity at the camp in the valley below and the men down at the east end of the valley out of sight. The dust cloud from just the three-thousand strong horse and cattle herd made it look like there were even more warriors to contend with. He told his bugler to summon his nearest commanders for instructions.

"Captain Perry," the general said hurriedly, "the supply wagons are under attack. We will assemble all the troops and head east down the valley and form a defensive perimeter. You take a platoon and reinforce the wagon train. We'll be along straightaway. There are hundreds and hundreds of hostiles, and we aren't going to have another Custer debacle here."

A voice came out of the small group of officers saying, "Or a White Bird Creek debacle."

The officers chuckled and Howard's face reddened.

Captain Perry's didn't redden. It turned into a bright tomato.

He mounted his horse and looked at the group. "The hell with the lot of you."

He took off and assembled a platoon of troopers who followed him toward the black columns of smoke appearing to the north.

"Quickly," Howard said, "go assemble your men and prepare to move out on my command."

The soldiers got up and ran to their respective units. Within an hour, the wagon train and the entire command of General Howard was circled in a defensive posture at the east end of the valley. Howard's command post was set up in the center of the large circle and the units were deployed around him in every direction. Apparently underestimating the ability of the Nez Perce earlier on the White Bird Creek operation, he developed a tremendous respect for Chief Joseph's tactical ability.

The Nez Perce warriors attacked the assembled troopers and ran around the giant circle, leaning under the necks of their spotted horses, while they fired rifles at the soldiers. This continued well into the afternoon, with the attack finally stopping just before dark.

Joseph had a group of warriors go out and build fires outside the cavalry's perimeter, just to make them think they were totally surrounded by hostiles all night. Then Chief Joseph instructed the warriors to dig trenches and build rock piles all around the soldiers' positions to be utilized the next day.

The following morning the cavalry troops and General Howard were greeted with something unseen in the experiences of any men who had been involved in Indian warfare.

They were completely surrounded by piles of rocks and military foxholes with rock walls around the lips, dug and constructed during the night by Nez Perce warriors, one hundred of them, who now had the force of six hundred surrounded and pinned down by a constant barrage of well-aimed shots. Chief Joseph led another three dozen Nez Perce men on horseback and rode around the positions of Howard, again firing under the necks of their ponies. This was done to get the cavalry troopers to expose themselves more to the sniper fire of the braves in the fortified rifle pits.

By late afternoon Howard's troops were completely out of water, pinned down by gunfire, sweltering in one-hundred-degree heat, and totally demoralized.

When it got close to dark, Joseph had the Nez Perce start pulling back, as it did not take that many braves to keep the soldiers pinned down.

Howard and his officers got together during the night and made plans to try a frontal assault at daybreak, heading right at the distant camp. They could not keep going without water, and the general knew that his men could not make it another day.

Daybreak came and the bugler sounded the charge. The desperate soldiers attacked straight at the western positions surrounding them. With prearranged strategy, the Nez Perce warriors set up lines of braves who held the advancing troops in check while the rest retreated to the camp. The women and children in the camp, in the meantime, hastily packed up, leaving anything that was unimportant.

While the small force stayed behind to slowly retreat and hold the attacking cavalry at bay, the rest of the bands, and the herd of three thousand, headed north. Finally, the small group of defenders broke off contact and withdrew, rushing to catch up with their families who were nearing the white settlement of Kamiah.

Cheering his men on, Howard watched them overrun the remnants of the now deserted camp. They captured everything that was old, worn, or broken, which included a few beat-up tepees, some utensils, and clothing. Howard started making his report that would end up on General Sherman's desk. He reported numerous enemy casualties and the capture of Chief Joseph's entire encampment.

Unfortunately, there were several things that were going to go against Howard and the entire Army for that matter. One, Tom Sutherland was a newspaper reporter traveling with the cavalry. His report of the so-called capture of Joseph's camp differed greatly from Howard's account.

One of the items he wrote was: *"For my part, I found a much worn pair of small moccasins and an absurd little rag doll under a tree."*

Chief Joseph had four men killed during the fighting and a few more were wounded. The general, however, had thirteen soldiers killed in action and numerous wounded. That fact was hard to hide from superiors.

Howard was also plagued by the fact that many of his officers had also written accounts of the campaign thus far, and a totally different picture was painted of the operation than the one by General Howard.

One troop commanding officer wrote in his report: *"The Indians were not defeated. Their loss must have been insignificant and their retreat to Kamiah was masterly, deliberate, and unmolested, leaving us with a victory barren of results."*

Up to this point, the assembled bands had followed the leadership of Chief Joseph simply because he was a natural leader. He had proven his ability to not only motivate the people but figure out intricate and successful battle strategies as well.

Because of the nature of all people and the politics that goes on with any group of people, the elders and war chiefs asked for a council and stated that the decisions should now be made by the joint council of chiefs of the five bands.

During the council session, which took place in the hills north of the town of Kamiah, Chief Joseph stood and said, "We have shown One-Arm and his horse soldiers that we are not like the cattle to be driven into corrals. Let us go, my brothers, back to the land of our grandfathers in the Wallowa Mountains. It is the land given to us by the Great Spirit to teach our children to hunt and fish and live the ways of the Nez Perce. I do not want to venture farther. I do not want to die in a strange land."

White Bird stood and said, "We have been friends with the Crows before. We should leave here, because the horse soldiers will be like the angry hornets stinging us on our rumps. Let us go to the Great Plains and make an alliance with the Crows like the Lakotah Sitting Bull did with the Cheyenne and Arapahoes. There is great strength in large numbers of people. If the Crows will not take us, maybe Wamble Uncha will talk to his brothers and we can join the mighty Sitting Bull in the land of the Great Mother, where the Army will not chase us anymore."

Chief Joseph said, "White Bird speaks with the wisdom of his years. We have indeed made the Long Knives to look like fools and One-Arm to look more like a young child than a mighty soldier chief. What say you, great chiefs?"

Rainbow stood and said, "Chief Looking Glass has made the trip along the Lolo Trail to the lands of the Crow as many times as the fingers on my hands. We should be governed by the council of chiefs, but he should be the chief for this part of our journey. We also must ask our white brother, Wamble Uncha, to lead us through the treacherous mountains if we make this journey. Some of our old people, our women, and our children will die, but if we go back to Wallowa and fight, we will die, too."

Chief Joseph stood again. "There is much wisdom in this council. Colt has been right. The white eyes are angry with their own horse soldiers for attacking us and stealing our lands. One of our women got a newspaper and there have been some killings and scalpings by whites back at Lapwai. The talking papers, the newspapers, of the white eyes speak much about us and our plight. Let us give them more words to put down, not just for us, but for our grandchildren and the grandchildren of even our enemies who are also red."

Everyone stood and raised their hands in unity and enthusiasm. The pipe was passed around. Colt made several pots of hot coffee to be shared. He and Joseph then shared a pair of cigarettes with their cups of hot brew.

The next day, July 16, with Colt in charge of picking out the way through the rough mountains and Chief Looking Glass in charge of the assembled tribes, the Nez Perce began the treacherous journey up the Lolo Trail. Colt knew that people would be lost, and animals. But he also knew that every step was bringing him three feet closer to Shirley Ebert.

Respectful now of the power of the Nez Perce, General Howard ordered his men to bivouac on the Clearwater. He waited fourteen days to regroup, rest up, and wait for fresh supplies. The general who had gotten peace with Cochise, the mighty Apache leader, had lost the respect of many superiors, subordinates, civilians, and more importantly himself. He also had sent off dispatches to other military commanders to let them know the gravity of the Nez Perce problem. The newspapers were also starting to make it harder on the military as they were stirring public opinion in the favor of the Nez Perce. General Howard decided that something had to be done to stop Chief Joseph fast. He would not pursue the tribes again without blocking forces waiting.

The route that Colt chose was rough. Feet were cut open, legs were broken, and horses fell off cliffs. The assembled bands had to follow Colt up an immediate incline for seven thousand feet, and it got worse.

Several days out, Colt and Man Killer, followed by two other braves, rode at the head of the long column, scouting for the best way up over one granite-loaded ridge line. They were making their way up a narrow, rock-walled, boulder-strewn gulch.

High above them, between treetops, Chris Colt could occasionally see the bright, snow-covered, rocky peaks that they would soon be crossing. He also saw angry black storm clouds hovering over the peaks and pushing up against them, wanting to cross over the lofty heights themselves, so they could spill their contents in the next valley. Riding along one stretch bare of trees, Chris could clearly see the peaks and watched tendrils of snow blowing off them, looking like wisps of downy blond hair blowing in a summer breeze. In actuality, Chris knew, from many days spent up in the high lonesome, that the white wisps of snow were actually very strong winds blowing so hard that icy crystals of snow and ice were being whipped off the slopes with incredible power.

They rode on for another hour and the walls of the gulch got higher and the trail at the bottom of the ravine much steeper. Chris could no longer see the peaks, but he threw his hand up at more explosive sounds in the distance and up above him.

Man Killer got a concerned look and said, "Cannon fire?"

Colt said, "No! Quick, we must get everyone up the sides of the ridges!"

Man Killer was an Indian of the mountains and now knew what was happening. He had seen whites come from cities back east and see this phenomenon for the first time. They could not believe it. If he and the others could not get the people and animals up the sides of the ridges immediately, many would die.

Colt, Man Killer, and the other two scouts rode back among the bands and shouted warnings at everyone to get up as high as possible on the rocky cliffsides. Horses and cattle were pushed up and many travois were quickly unloaded, their bulky tepee covers and bundles of supplies carried up as high as possible.

The chief of scouts couldn't believe it, but within minutes, the entire group of Nez Perce and all the animals were high up above the floor of the gulch looking down from their steep perches.

Colt heard a rumbling sound up above him, high up in the gulch. It was getting louder. That was when Colt spotted her, the little girl from Too-Hool-Hool-Zote's band. She had apparently gotten lost in the rush and stood crying at the gulch bottom, a small bundle on the ground at her side.

Having dismounted, Chris Colt ran and jumped on a boulder and leapt onto the back of his trusty horse, just as the girl's mother and grandmother started to scream. Scraping his rump on the rocks and stones on the steep-sided canyon and seeing the girl and almost sensing what had to be done, War Bonnet went straight down the side of the cliff. Most horses would have started tumbling to their death within the first twenty bounds, but not War Bonnet. He used his front legs, braced out in front to guide him down while his hind legs bent fully, and he carried Colt down safely to the gulch's bottom.

His work was only half-done, however. The big Appaloosa swept down on the little girl as Colt heard a great roar right behind him and muffled screams from the cliffside. Chris ignored the roar and leaned down low and scooped the girl up in his powerful right arm, placing her in the saddle in front of him.

Only then did Colt feel he could afford the luxury of turning his head to assess his situation, while War Bonnet bounded across and down the gulch bottom. Colt gulped as he looked at the giant thirty-foot-high wall of water sweeping down on him and his little charge. He bent forward forcing the little girl to bend over the muscled black and white neck, too.

Colt yelled, "Go, War Bonnet. Fly!"

The emotion of Colt's words seemed to strike a chord somewhere deep in the horse's heart. The mighty stallion seemed to pull up an extra reserve of power from somewhere and they were almost to the beginning of the far cliffside in seconds. They made it and War Bonnet didn't slow down one bit, although he was going almost vertically up the cliff and had to pick his way among giant rocks. Chris looked back and the wall of water was ten feet away, logs, boulders, and up-rooted trees churning in it like mighty vegetable parts being stirred in a giant stew.

The giant flash flood's killing wave of water struck the horse's hind legs and rump with a roar, and his rear end was swept sideways, but he still found footing and made one more lunge that brought them safely out of reach of the horrible, wet death. They kept climbing until they perched twenty feet above the churning torrent.

Across the canyon, Colt could see masses of warriors, women, and children blowing eagle bone whistles, waving blankets, and cheering. The roar of the water was too loud to hear anything. He watched the wall of water strike down giant trees in its path as it roared down the mountain. Colt could also now see the peaks and the sky above them was pure blue. Almost as quickly as it started, the flash flood ended, and they could continue their climb, a little stream of water still running down the middle of the gulch.

On July 27, almost two weeks after starting the treacherous journey across the Bitterroot Mountains, Chris Colt led the combined bands of "renegade Nez Perce" out of that chain of homicidal mountains and into the western boundary of Montana Territory, only to run into a blocking force called for on the "singing wires" by General Howard, who was finally in pursuit.

Shortly after first light, their first day on the eastern side of the sharp ridge line, they headed down the Bitterroot Valley and soon came to an area called "the Narrows." The entire canyon had been blocked off by a giant wall of logs and manned by thirty-five soldiers, over two hundred civilians, mainly miners, and a group of Flathead Indians, also traditional enemies of the Nez Perce. The soldiers were out of Fort Missoula, only twelve miles distant, and commanded by Captain Charles Rawn.

Chiefs Joseph, White Bird, and Looking Glass took Man Killer and five other braves forward with them carrying a flag of truce, electing to try trusting the horse soldiers once more.

Being an outstanding leader, Chief Joseph deferred to Looking Glass to parley with the "soldier chief," but Looking Glass also knew his limitations and asked Joseph to be spokesman for the bands. Captain Rawn rode forward with a small contingent of soldiers and civilians, his guidon bearer having attached a white flag to the staff just below the unit guidon flag.

As the two small groups halted facing each other, Chief Joseph raised his hand, as did Captain Rawn.

"I am called Hin-Mut-Too-Yah-Lat-Kekht. Your people call me Chief Joseph of the Nez Perce," the leader said.

"Greetings, Chief Joseph. My name is Captain Charles Rawn of the U.S. Army."

Joseph went on. "Captain Rawn, you have come here to stop us because you were told on the singing wire that we have been fighting One-Arm Howard who pursues us and makes us fight. We do not want this. We want to journey across the land you call Montana to join our brothers the Crow. My brothers and their families have just passed across these mountains and are tired and sore. If you will let us pass in peace, Captain Rawn, I give my word that we will not harm the people of Montana and will start no fights with the horse soldiers or farmers we see along the way. We come in peace."

Captain Rawn straightened his back and threw back his shoulders. "Chief Joseph, I have my orders. You cannot pass but will turn back and head to Fort Lapwai. You may bivouac, ah, you may make camp where you are for the night, but in the morning, you must turn back or we will drive you back."

"Bull manure!" a wealthy-looking rancher said from the group. "The dad-burned Army! Everyone knows that Chief Joseph here don't ever break his word. Any man who keeps his word is all right in my book, no matter the color. I'll not take arms agin you or your people, Joseph. You're an honorable man who has been wronged by the greedy bastards that lead my people."

Joseph bowed his head at the rancher as the man wheeled his horse, after spitting a big stream of tobacco juice on the forelegs of Rawn's horse.

The rancher started to ride away, but stopped and said, "Cap'n, you can forget the men from my spread fightin' with ya. We're goin' home. Good luck, Nez Perces."

He rode off to rejoin the waiting group of civilians and cavalry while both parties watched. He hollered something but couldn't be heard by the truce parties and rode away with a large group of cowboys following. Rawn saw other civilians, one after another, ride off after the cowboys, too. His face was red when he turned back around but the Nez Perce faces showed no emotion.

"We ride away in peace," Chief Joseph said. "You have spoken."

This last little sentence made Rawn throw his shoulders back and puff his chest out a little more.

The Nez Perce turned and rode off toward their waiting tribes, while the contingent from white America watched. An old mountain man named Grizzly Potter, who was no relation to Colonel Rufus Potter, spat out some tobacco juice and laughed with an almost toothless chuckle. Rawn turned his horse and led the group away, wondering why Grizzly was laughing so. He was self-satisfied and said so as they returned to the giant blockade. This caused Grizzly to laugh even more. The Army officer was especially irritated because Grizzly had spent so much time with the Indians and seemed to know so much about them. He had worked for the cavalry as both a scout and interpreter, and always seemed to have a different Indian "wife" with him.

The laughing irritated Captain Rawn so much that he halted the patrol and said, "Mr. Potter, would you mind, sir, sharing with us what's so damned funny?"

Potter spit out another mouthful of brown juice and said, "Wal, wal, wal, Cap'n, ef'n you think thet Young Joseph is jest gwine ta tuck his tail betwixt his legs an' ride off back into Idaho Territory, ya got a lot ta learn 'bout redskins. He's the wisest chief they is. He's smarter than old Sittin' Bull, brainier than Ouray of the Utes, and smarter than Cochise was of tha A-pach. He's got somethin' up his sleeve, but he's smart enough to not to buck a stacked deck."

The next day Rawn had his men up and ready for battle at daybreak. Almost all the civilians were gone and the captain was nervous about being attacked after the words of Grizzly Potter.

One of the soldiers on the skirmish line in front of the giant barricade heard some voices. It was Indians singing.

"Sir, Captain Rawn," he hollered, "look."

The officer looked up on the vertical cliff hundreds of feet above them and there was a long line of Nez Perce singing as they walked along a narrow ledge. It was barely wide enough for a mountain goat but here were seven hundred Nez Perce men, women, and children, one thousand cows, and two thousand Appaloosas walking along with the people *singing,* no less. He could not order any troops up there because they could not possibly make it on that trail without falling to their deaths. Amazed, the soldiers watched as the Nez Perce passed beyond the giant barricade and went farther down the Bitterroot Valley, finally dropping down to the valley floor. If Rawn overtook them then, he would have a great running battle on his hands with the people who had not only defeated but also humiliated the Army on the Clearwater and at White Bird Creek. His orders were to set up the barricade and man it, but the Nez Perce had bypassed it, so he decided he had done all he could do. He would keep a watch on the Indians for a while, then return to Fort Missoula.

Out of sight of the soldiers, the Indians stopped and at Chris Colt's urging, the council of chiefs reminded the people to treat the white people with friendliness and courtesy.

First, they came to a ranch whose hands were all out on a big drive from Kansas. They went into the ranch house and removed several hundred pounds of provisions. In their place, they went to the barn and got one of the ranch's branding irons, heating it in a fire. They hobbled up the hind leg on seven good Appaloosa geldings and mares from their herd and branded them with the ranch's brand and left them in the pasture, where there was graze and water.

From there Chris Colt went alone into the town of Stevensville. He went into the saloon and ordered a cold beer. Saloons in the Old West were the gossip centers and the best place to get the most current information about what was happening in the area. It was also the best place for Colt to put his finger on the pulse of the community.

He said, "Heard Chief Joseph and the Nez Perce are coming down the valley right now and are planning on coming into town and buying provisions."

There was a man at the end of the bar drinking a cup of coffee and talking to the bartender.

"Yeah, a runner that was at Fort Fizzle just came in here and said they were headed this way," the man said, "but how could they pay for it?"

Colt said, "Well, those people have been raising cattle and horses for years. They sell them just like anybody else would. What do you mean Fort Fizzle?"

The man said, "Oh, did you hear what happened

about them walking on a ledge two inches wide and going around the blockade the soldiers had?"

"Yeah, I was crossing the big range and saw it after daybreak this morning. Two inches wide, huh?"

"Yeah," the man said. "Incredible, ain't it? Some of the citizens that were out there named the barricade Fort Fizzle and just about laughed the cavalry out of the valley. So the Nez Perce have money, huh? Well, they'll sure be welcome here. Chief Joseph gave his solemn word that he wouldn't harm civilians."

"Do you trust him?"

"A hell of a lot more than I'd trust that Bible-thumper Otis 'You're-all-going-to-hell' Howard," the man said. "That Joseph grew up getting along with whites and was trained by Christian missionaries. I got to go, mister, and open my mercantile store back up."

The man ran out the door and Colt waited a few minutes, then left himself. He jumped over the hitching rail and onto the back of the big paint. War Bonnet proudly pranced and danced in a slow trot leaving the town, sensing the several groups of woman staring, but not knowing that their stares were directed at his master atop his back.

Out of town, Colt touched his calves to War Bonnet's flanks and said, "Canter," and the big horse took off at a fast lope.

In less than a half hour, he came to the group of Nez Perce and rode directly to Joseph, who nodded toward Looking Glass. Colt rode over to the other chief.

"Looking Glass, you can take your people into Stevensville. I will ride around the town and meet you a couple miles south of there."

The tribe went down the road paralleling the Bitterroots and went right into the town. Herdsmen carefully pushed the giant herd on through the town, while the tribal members went into stores. Educated by Christian missionaries, most of the Nez Perce spoke English and knew how to spend money. They were not shocked when the white shopkeepers charged them hellacious prices, but they paid them anyway. The public relations coup Joseph's people were counting was much greater than any they had counted on the battlefield. Now resupplied with new provisions, they happily traveled south out of the town, leaving several storekeepers a little richer and the townspeople much happier.

Colt met up with them and rode by the side of Chief Joseph.

"I cannot believe that your people have acted so stupidly," Colt said. "You led them so well against Howard's forces. Nobody could have done better, yet they want Looking Glass to lead them now, because he has been this way so much."

Joseph offered one of his rare grins and said, "Do not worry. If shooting happens, they will look back to me. All people would like to be the leader, red or white. We all want everyone to think what we say is very important. A good leader cannot be so unless he has also learned how to be a good follower. I do not mind, my friend."

Looking Glass felt that the horse soldiers of Howard

had either given up pursuit or were weeks behind the tribe, so he sent out less patrols each day. Everything seemed so peaceful as they moved south, because they followed Joseph's advice and treated settlers in a friendly manner they were treated the same. Whites seemed so relieved that these Nez Perce were not on the warpath that they even went to extra lengths being friendly, bringing food and gifts for the people. Looking Glass became more and more lax in his security.

The bands had to cross the Continental Divide—not as bad as the trip across the Lolo Pass. They went down into a valley called the Big Hole.

One of the commanders that General Howard had telegraphed was Colonel John Gibbon from Fort Shaw, about 250 miles due north of the Big Hole Valley. They were almost a week ahead of General Howard and Colonel Gibbon moved his men at a very rapid pace. He had two hundred men, including a wagon train, left Fort Shaw on August the second, and still caught up within scouting distance of the fleeing bands on August 7.

They watched the Nez Perce all through the next day and planned to attack the unsecured camp at daybreak the next morning.

Colt slept in Man Killer's tepee that was located two tepees away from Chief Joseph's. It was right at daybreak when Colt opened his eyes and sat up wide-awake.

"Man Killer," Colt said, "something's wrong."

Looking Glass had allowed the people to remain in

the Big Hole Valley, which was full of streams, good graze, and big trees with rolling hills. The camp was located where Trail Creek and Ruby Creek came together. There were plenty of fish, wood, and meat animals, and the Nez Perce warriors had been hunting antelope for several days. Joseph and Colt were both upset about the lax security, but the wise chief kept quiet and let Looking Glass run the camp.

When Colt whispered his warning, Man Killer quietly but quickly exploded out of his buffalo robe, grabbing his rifle on the way up. His other hand grabbed his gunbelt and six-shooter and strapped it on, while walking to the tepee door. Colt also had his weapons ready by then, too.

The pair went out the tepee door and spotted something not often seen, cavalry without horses. Colonel Gibbon had them leave their mounts behind with the reserve force and the soldiers were wading across Ruby Creek on line.

Colt fired both guns in the air and shouted, "Horse soldiers! Horse solders!"

The cry was picked up by others and the cavalry were soon at the edge of the village firing into the bodies of women, children, and men who were trying to run into the nearby trees for cover, get to horses, or run to tepees to save children and family members.

The bluecoats poured into the village and the fighting was hand-to-hand. Many of those being killed and wounded were women and children, falling to the butts and barrels of rifles. Colt saw a large sergeant viciously swing his rifle up, the butt smashing a woman under the jaw. She had dropped her baby's hand when the man hit her and the baby fell on the ground. Before Colt could even react, the NCO's size-twelve foot went up in the air and his heavy boot came down, smashing the toddler's head.

Colt screamed, "No-o-o-o!"

His hands flashed down to his pistols and came up, the right gun bucking in Chris's palm. A big spot of red started spreading on the big sergeant's chest. He looked down at it as Colt, in a seething rage, walked forward and his left gun exploded, another bullet slamming into the soldier's chest. The big man dropped to his knees and Colt's right gun boomed again and the man's head exploded.

Colt looked around and women and children were being killed everywhere. Two privates were standing next to the body of a dead woman about eighteen years old. Both were laughing and had their knives out trying to scalp her.

Colt, teeth clenched tightly, yelled, "Try me. I'm not a woman."

Both men clawed for their rifles and Chris let them grab them before firing both guns at once. The one on his right flew backward into the wall of a tepee, while the other dropped his rifle and clutched at a nasty shoulder wound. His face was white and he looked at Chris with eyes open wide. Colt's hand went up inside the back of his shirt and came forward in a whipping action. The big Bowie knife turned over twice and buried itself into the right side of the soldier's rib cage, breaking a rib, puncturing the right lung, and slicing the edge of the aorta artery.

The soldier's eyes bulged out as he looked down at his own bright red blood spurting out next to the handle of the knife protruding from his chest. The blood shot out, every second, for four or five feet and stained the ground to his right front. Colt walked forward and roughly yanked the knife out of the man while he stared at the scout in shock.

Chris ran to Joseph's tepee because he had given the chief his word that he would protect his family in case of attack. He ran inside and soon Joseph appeared carrying his infant daughter and followed by his youngest wife. Joseph smiled at Colt, which struck the scout odd, and disappeared into the melee. There were screams and shouts everywhere and Colt could hear Joseph's calm voice giving firm commands in the Nez Perce language.

Chris huddled the women and children in the far corner and Joseph's oldest wife smiled and grabbed Chris's cup, pouring him a cup of coffee. Suddenly a soldier burst through the door and Colt drew, but the woman was in his line of fire. She screamed and the soldier shot her through the side. Colt dived literally into the fire, his gun going off a millisecond before he hit. The soldier's head exploded and he died, his neck across the bottom of the round bull-hide door. Colt hit the fire and rolled, shaking hot coals off his left hand, and crawled to the wounded woman. He put his hand over the wound and pushed on it until it stopped bleeding. He saw a soldier outside aiming at the woman, and shoved her aside and drew again. The soldier's shot came through the door and tore into Colt's right thigh. He fired and rolled to his left firing again and again. The man took five steps backward, a bullet tearing into him with each step.

Colt limped outside and stood near the door to keep any soldiers away from the chief's tepee. He hollered at Man Killer's mother in their tepee, and her terrified face appeared in the doorway. He signaled her to join him, and she dashed for Joseph's lodge. He helped her through the door and noticed she was carrying's someone's infant child, shielding it with her body.

He watched Joseph who had moved to the far end of the camp with Looking Glass, and White Bird emulating the calm chief barking directions and orders. The Nez Perce may have been surprised, but Colt saw Joseph developing a counterattack.

Joseph summoned Rainbow and the man ran to him, but flew sideways, a bullet tearing through his heart when he was just two steps from Chief Joseph. Colt had seen another war leader, Red Echo, go down earlier and didn't know that Five Wounds lay dying from a fatal wound behind the tepee Colt was now protecting.

Joseph now had a skirmish line formed, and the Nez Perce poured deadly fire on the cavalry and advanced forward shooting with each step or two. They didn't panic and shoot blindly or wildly either. They aimed and fired, bullets whistling by their ears, with the discipline and precision of any well-trained military unit.

Colt saw Joseph say something to Looking Glass who jumped on a pony and raced to the Nez Perce hiding in the trees along the river and firing into the troops. Chris watched as Looking Glass rode around pointing at certain trees and placed them in good positions to pour carefully aimed sniper fire at the soldiers, who now started pulling back under the deadly Nez Perce guns.

Colt looked around the village and saw dead babies and women everywhere. Occasionally he spotted a dead warrior, but they were few and far between. Chris estimated over five dozen dead women and children that he spotted and not even a half-dozen men. Many babies had their heads bashed in, and so did some of the women who were wounded first, then kicked and riflebutted. Colt felt tears start streaming down his cheeks. He couldn't help himself. He had just seen the bloody corpse of a ten-year-old girl who had flirted with him every time he was near. Colt had thought she was cute, but now her mutilated face and scalped little head were anything but cute.

"Why?" he asked himself out loud, but already knowing that nobody had the answer to the gross stupidity and hate of such atrocities.

The day before the battle, one of the Nez Perce shamans, Pile of Clouds, warned everyone, "Death is on our trail," but Looking Glass hadn't listened.

The soldiers were now caught in a deadly cross fire between Looking Glass's snipers and Chief Joseph's fast-advancing skirmish line. They pushed the cavalry farther up the hill. Colt saw Colonel Gibbon fall, a bullet collapsing his leg. A medic ran to the officer and wrapped his own scarf around the thigh.

This made Chris remember his own wound, and he grabbed a scarf off the dead trooper in the door of the tepee and tied it around his thigh. It was aching like a pounding toothache, but the blood was just oozing out and seemed to be clotting.

The bugle call came for the troops to withdraw and the Nez Perce seemed to pour even more fire into their positions. Colonel Gibbon, limping badly, mounted a bloodred sorrel horse and led his men into the woods on the hill he had been on. There they formed defensive positions and the Nez Perce kept sniping at the soldiers, leaving them pinned down.

The tribal members now started moving around the village and found their family members, quickly burying them in shallow graves. The wailing and crying was a sound that would haunt Chris Colt the rest of his life.

Chief Joseph summoned his brother Ollikut and had him take a force to replace those on the hillside. In the meantime, Colt treated Joseph's wounded wife as best he could. Ollikut was to hold the Army as long as possible while the Nez Perce buried their dead, made travois, and tried to escape. They would have to move slowly because so many were wounded. Colt put on one of Joseph's war bonnets, so he would not be recognized as a white man by any of Gibbon's men, who were now busy just trying to stay alive. They were also one third of a mile away and above the encampment. Chris knew that some soldiers saw him in the first part of the fighting, but he didn't care, nor did he worry about it. There were so few still alive who did see him, they probably wouldn't be believed, if they even mentioned it at all. Besides that, right then, Chris Colt was proud to have been with the Nez Perce and ashamed to be a white man. He could not believe that professional soldiers could have killed babies and innocent children, and even scalped women.

With Ollikut's force holding the horse soldiers at bay, Joseph and Chris Colt led the Nez Perce away as rapidly as they could move for over twenty-four hours before Ollikut finally broke contact and raced after his brother and his people.

While the Nez Perce fled, Joseph suggested that White Bird tally up the dead. Seventy-seven women and children had been killed and only twelve men. Gibbon had lost twenty-nine troopers. Not all the Nez Perce had been buried and the cavalry of Gibbon went through what was left of the village and some men and scouts scalped more of the Nez Perce bodies, including children and women. General Howard arrived the next day, and his scouts even dug up graves and scalped the Nez Perce.

When the tribes finally made camp, they immediately held a tribal council. Many men were angry and complained about Looking Glass's failure to provide security and speed for their movement. They also complained to both Joseph and Colt for saying that they should only kill soldiers and not scalp or mutilate bodies or fight against civilians. They talked about the numerous atrocities committed by the white men. Most people complained about Looking Glass, however, and he seemed to be very depressed.

Chief Joseph stood and all eyes centered on him as he spoke. "You complain of our brother Wamble Uncha, yet many of you saw him have to shoot his own people. How many of you had to shoot bullets into the flesh of your brothers or your uncles?"

Colt stood. "My red brothers, my heart is sad, not because I killed white men, but because of what they did to your people. If I was with you and saw your people shooting babies and women, I would kill them, also. It is important that you know that most of my people would not do to your people what those soldiers did."

Chief Joseph stood again and said, "We do know that, Colt. You have also been angry at Looking Glass, but you wanted decisions to be made by council of chiefs. You should also be angry at me and the other chiefs who also make decisions."

Again, the stoic Nez Perce commander endeared his people to him and commanded more respect through his words and deeds. It was an everyday event with Chief Joseph. He could not help himself. No word was made about dissolving the council of chiefs but Colt knew that Chief Joseph was clearly the leader of these people, intertribal politics or not.

On August 18 the assembled bands made camp on the Camas Prairie less than fifty miles from the Yellowstone. Howard had been pursuing them again for half a week, and many of the Nez Perce wanted to stop and fight. Colt had gone into a small mining tent town that had sprung up near someone's strike. He learned about the bodies of the Nez Perce being scalped by Howard's scouts, without the Christian General intervening and preventing the hideous event from taking place. Apparently his Christian principles were taking hind tit now, as he had lots of egg on his bearded face, thanks to Chief Joseph and his followers.

When the bands stopped on Camas Prairie, General Howard and his troops were less than a day behind them. Colt and Joseph conferred and Chris suggested that Joseph take some kind of action to hold the general for a while, while the group tried to make it over Targhee Pass and head into Yellowstone in Wyoming Territory.

While the tribes started the climb toward Targhee Pass, Ollikut and a small force of warriors went back to Camas Creek where Howard was bivouacked. The raiders tore into the cavalry camp and drove his two hundred pack mules off, pushing them for miles and scattering them into the foothills of the nearby mountains. The small party of Ollikut again took off after the main band that had crossed into the Yellowstone. In the meantime, Howard dropped back another half a week behind the Nez Perce and ended up buying and commandeering many pack mules from the local civilians within a fifty-mile radius of his moving headquarters.

In the Yellowstone, two of the scouting parties Joseph sent out stole supplies from white prospectors and miners but didn't kill them. Another group killed some tourists and captured several more, holding them until

Joseph found out and ordered them to let the white men go. The warriors were just too frustrated over what happened to their family members in the Big Hole Valley.

Chapter 6

》》》》》》》》》》》》》》

Montana

Shirley was picking berries when the Crows attacked the village. She had been the subject of much jealousy among the women, because in the months since her captivity, she had proven herself capable of outworking any woman or girl in the village. She also became a cook of great renown, teaching the Cheyenne women who did like her how to become great cooks themselves. Many men were turning their looks and attention to this strange *wasicun* woman. She might have started out as a slave, but she had really gained stature among everyone in the tribe.

The Crows who attacked were a small war party and wanted to take some more coups after a successful two weeks out from their western Montana village. They had taken some scalps from some hapless teamsters and some more and one woman at a Flathead village. The Flathead woman was young, but the warriors wanted mobility, so they took their turns with her and then clubbed her head in.

Shirley had no chance really. The raiding Crows came right through the berry patch to the southeast of the village. The white woman had been with a middle-aged woman named Yellow Moons and her little daughter. The Crows swept down on the three and grabbed Shirley and Yellow Moons, the two kidnappers flinging them up across their horses' shoulders in front of them. For some reason, the one with Yellow Moons clubbed her head over and over and dumped her as they splashed across the stream and entered the village. The other was going to keep the white woman.

In the village, the first warrior who mounted and was ready to meet the attackers was a large well-built man named Death Yell. He ran his pony forward right into the face of the oncoming Crow warriors. He had had his eyes on Shirley Ebert for a long time and felt she would be good medicine and great in his buffalo robe. On top of that, he had tasted her berry pies. His pinto war horse slammed into the shoulder of the Crow's horse and sent the man and the screaming Shirley, along with the red dun Crow pony, flying backward over the lip of the stream and crashing into the water. Death Yell lifted the dazed Shirley up behind him and ran down the Crow, diving off the horse onto the other warrior. The battle was short-lived as he first cut the man's tendons with a slash across the arm holding the war club. He then stuck him in the stomach lightly, and quickly brought the knife up and slashed across the Crow's throat. He took the dying brave's scalp and returned to the pony and raced back to camp with Shirley behind him, dropping her off at Screaming Horse's lodge. He then wheeled his horse and charged at the other attacking Crows.

The camp defenders effectively mounted a counter-charge and killed all but three of the attackers who made good their escape. One old warrior had a leg wound and another young one had a knife slash across the forehead. Still another had a broken collarbone from a Crow war club, but other than that, Yellow Moons was the only casualty. The woman's daughter had ducked down into the berries when her mother and Shirley were grabbed, and she now sat on the ground crying and wailing, rocking with her mother's body in her arms. The little girl grabbed her mother's skinning knife and cut five slashes on her arms as a sign of mourning.

As Shirley looked at the big Cheyenne who had saved her riding back into the camp, she noticed that he tried to look straight ahead and act very proud, but she caught his glance at her several times. He had not rescued her as a favor to Screaming Horse.

Two days later Death Yell rode up to the tepee of Screaming Horse with three fine horses in tow. He swung his leg over his horse's neck and tried to hand the lead ropes on the horses to Screaming Horse, along with a clay pipe and a new Hudson's Bay blanket. He looked at Shirley and nodded toward her with his head, making a noise she didn't really hear. She did know what was happening, though. Death Yell was offering these gifts in exchange for her. He wanted Shirley Ebert for a wife.

She could not understand the words between the two men, but Screaming Horse was very expressive, and she knew what it meant when he held up five, then six fingers. That's how many ponies he wanted for her.

Once the Nez Perce made it through the Yellowstone and were trying to climb the eastern ridges of the Absarokas, Looking Glass and a small party went ahead to meet with the Crow and seek refuge. He came back with bad news, the Crows did not want to make the white men angry, especially the military because they provided the cavalry with a great many of their scouts.

In the council, Chief Joseph said, "My brothers, we have one good hope left. We have journeyed many steps (over a thousand miles) and are tired, but we should try to make it to the land of the Great Mother and rendezvous with Sitting Bull."

Speaking in English, he went on, "Great Scout Colt, you are brother to the Sioux. Our friends tell us that One-Arm is still behind us, and like the winds, horse soldiers come from four corners to catch us. Can you help the Nez Perce and Sioux become brothers?"

"Can the Nez Perce forget old battles and old raids?" Colt asked.

Chief Joseph said, "Well spoken, my friend. Yes, we can do that."

Colt said, "Then I can help the Nez Perce and Lakotah become brothers. Like Joseph, Sitting Bull is very wise and will see the good in this. Besides, like the Nez Perce, he wishes many friends right now. And because of what you all have done, you now have many friends who are white. They have read about you in the newspapers and are angry about your lands being stolen and your people killed. You won't get your lands back, but your people are respected by many whites."

"When a warrior dies and walks the spirit trail, he cannot carry land on his back," Joseph said, "He cannot ride his horse. But he can take respect with him, not much more."

The council of chiefs voted and agreed to try to meet up with Sitting Bull in Canada, although they would have more than seven hundred miles of travel.

Joseph said, "How should we go, Colt?"

Chris replied, "The Absarokas are too hard for your people to cross. We should go to the east along the Shoshone River or take the Clark's Fork of the Yellowstone River. When we get out of the mountains, we turn north and head for Canada."

Joseph looked at the others and saw heads nod affirmatively and he said, "So it shall be."

Looking Glass stood and said, "Wamble Uncha, our scouts have come back and said many horse soldiers block the Yellowstone."

Colt said, "Good, that's the way we'll go."

The bands left the next day, but that night Chris Colt's mind was on the woman he loved. She was somewhere in Montana Territory he thought or was with Sitting Bull now if the band she was with went to Canada. In any event, she was not far. He would find her, and she would never be in harm's way again.

Hundreds of miles northeast of Colt, Shirley lay in her buffalo robe and prayed. She saw how Death Yell, and other warriors for that matter, looked at her. What if one of them brought five or six ponies to Screaming Horse.

Howard was excited. He was pushing the Nez Perce hard, and he had lost some respect for Chief Joseph's intelligence as a strategist after the Big Hole fight. He didn't know that Looking Glass had been in charge. He had wired more units and right now he had word that Colonel Sturgis with remnants of the Seventh, Custer's old outfit, had blocked off the valley where the Clark's Fork of the Yellowstone flowed. The Nez Perce would surely have to take that route or the Shoshone River and the former was more likely.

When the Nez Perce arrived at the Shoshone River, they pretended to be cautious, but Colt made sure that several tepee fires added some green wood to their cooking fires. He wanted to make sure that the scouts from Colonel Sturgis didn't miss them. He pictured the Crow, Shoshone, or Sioux scouts laughing at the stupidity of the Nez Perce—using wood that gave off so much smoke. That was indeed what happened.

Sturgis was excited when he received the report from his scouts that the Nez Perce had made camp on the Shoshone River, which they had started up.

"By God," he exclaimed, "we've got those red devils now! They figured that they would take the river that's farther south and throw us off. Ha."

The normally staid officer was like a little boy who had just received a new wagon filled with licorice whips. He had lost any respect he had had for General

Howard and could not understand how the man had been foiled and outfought so many times by a savage. Now he had them.

Colt and the five tribes of Nez Perce had prepared a nice surprise for the good colonel. Man Killer and four other volunteers drove a small herd of injured cattle and horses dragging empty makeshift travois. This was to create tracks for the scouts of Sturgis, thinking they were following the Nez Perce up the Shoshone. Right after dark, the rest of the people backtracked up through the wooded slopes. They made it to the confluence of the Clark's Fork of the Yellowstone and headed east. By the time they reached the place where Colonel Sturgis had tactically placed his blocking force, the cavalry had just moved out after the Nez Perce on the Shoshone.

Man Killer and the four braves with him pushed the herd far out to the east, took a one-hour break to rest the animals, then stampeded them. They took off cross-country on a course to intercept their families.

They caught up with the Nez Perce about the same time that Colonel Sturgis and almost four hundred very angry troops caught up with the old and injured cows and horses. Furious, Sturgis turned his column and force-marched his men after the fleeing hostiles. General Howard was even angrier.

He pushed his men to the very limit. They were pursuing worn-out men, women, and children with many animals and dragging travois. The cavalry finally caught up with the Nez Perce several days later. Colt had turned them north up Canyon Creek, which was really an intermittent stream that only had water in it after big rains. Because of cutting floods though, most of the streambed had thirty-foot-high walls on both sides of it and rough country around. The decision to go this way was made after consulting with Joseph first, because travois might have to be abandoned this time in case of another flash flood. The chief decided that it was well worth the calculated risk and the relatively easy going up the soft ground of the dry streambed.

It was late September and the rear patrols put out by Joseph reported that the horse soldiers had caught up and were only an hour behind the column. Again, Joseph called on his brother and sent Ollikut and others back to hold off the cavalry. Ollikut took twenty-seven braves and set up good shooting positions from which to snipe at the cavalry.

The covering force of braves pinned down the cavalry that could not advance around the creek bed at that point, and they slowly and carefully retreated, having followed Colt's advice. Ollikut divided his force into three nine-man groups. As two groups laid down a heavy volume of covering fire, the other one would beat a retreat up the ravine and set up a new position. The other two would then do the same thing leap-frogging each other backward. This strategy continued for seven miles while the rest of the Nez Perce beat a hasty retreat. The country all around was very rocky and the three groups then started using tepee lodges left by the main group as levers and they pried big boulders loose from the banks of the wash and rolled them into the

streambed to impede the progress of the cavalry. Ollikut finally came to one place that was already partially
filled with boulders from the tribe. He and his men
pried more loose and blocked the entire arroyo with
giant rocks, then rejoined the rest of the tribes. Colonel
Sturgis and the Seventh Cavalry were thoroughly
blocked from any more pursuit. They had to turn and
backtrack.

Colonel Nelson A. Miles, called "Bear's Coat" by the
Lakotah and Cheyenne Indians, was an ego-driven
Army officer, but he was also skillful and full of energy.
When he received a summons for help from General
Howard, that was all he needed. The man was almost
as fanatical as Custer had been about publicity and
advancement, and he saw the defeat of the legendary
Chief Joseph and the Nez Perce as the ultimate feather
for his campaign hat—worth at least one star on his
epaulet.

On September 25 the tribes reached the Missouri
and crossed to the Cow Island Army Depot, which they
attacked. The members of the combined bands had
been starving, sore, tired, and wounded. They overran
the supply depot and replenished their depleted stores
of supplies, crossing over the Missouri River. Colt
would not take part in that raid or the planning of it.
He had agreed to meet them on the other side of the
Missouri.

A day later they reached the camp area Colt had
picked for them north of the Missouri. The Bear Paws
lay in front of them in the distance. While the people

made camp, Joseph asked Colt to ride out and speak with him.

They looked at the distant range and Joseph accepted a cigarette from Colt, while Chris lit one himself.

Joseph offered puffs to the four winds, then started smoking with purpose. "You have been a good and loyal friend, a brother to the Nez Perce, and our people will speak of you to their grandchildren. I will miss your tobacco, too," he said, offering up another of his rare smiles.

"What do you mean?"

Joseph smiled again. "You have sensed that your woman is near. It is in your eyes and your heart has told your face to show how it feels."

"No, Joseph," Colt said. "I have looked sad because so many of your old people have left us to die along the trail and not slow you down. It is very sad what has happened to your people, but you are almost to Canada. You will not need me to speak with Sitting Bull. He is a very wise and reasonable man. I have to find her. She is near. I feel it."

Chief Joseph said, "You will take Man Killer with you. He wants to follow your trail, and it is a good thing."

Colt said, "You need every fighting man here."

"No, too many have died. We might make it to Sitting Bull and we might not, but the fighting is almost over. If we win a war to save our people, but all our people die, what does the war matter? Your brother is called Tashunca-Uitco?"

Chris Colt's heart leapt into his throat. "That is the Lakotah name for Crazy Horse. What have you heard?"

"There was a Cheyenne at Cow Island who spoke the tongue of the white man. He became a friend to the Nez Perce. It was a smart thing to do at the time."

Colt didn't want to hear the news.

"He rides the spirit trail now, your brother, and is happy."

"Bullets?"

Joseph shook his head. "Rifle-knife," he said, meaning a bayonet. "They said he was trying to escape when they were going to put him into a cage. He was stabbed in the belly."

Colt smiled and said, "They didn't put him in a jail cell, though?"

"No, he died first."

"Good. Now he is free."

Chris had bittersweet feelings. He knew that Crazy Horse would be killed. It had only been a matter of when, and he knew that he would be miserable every minute that he felt trapped by the white men. He would miss his blood brother, but Colt had already known this would happen. He also knew that Crazy Horse had known it would happen when he turned himself in.

He wanted to shed tears, but it was not the way with the Indian or with men in those days, so he hid his emotions.

"I have good news," Joseph said. "Your woman is named Shir-ley and has hair stolen right from the hottest part of the cooking fire?"

Chris started. "Yes, you heard something?"

Joseph, for the first time Colt had seen in the months since they met, smiled broadly. "She is with the Cheyenne village of Screaming Horse. A man named Death Yell tried to buy her with three horses and Screaming Horse told him no, he wanted more, five or six. Death Yell is a mighty warrior and went out and stole more ponies. It is rumored that he will go to Screaming Horse with six ponies soon."

Colt jumped up. "No, he can't."

Joseph put out his hand and they clasped forearms in a handshake.

With his other hand, Joseph pointed at the far-off blue mountains in the dusk and said, "The village of Screaming Horse is in the Bear Paw Mountains, yonder."

Colt looked at Chief Joseph and the gaze made the wise chief smile broadly once more. Colt didn't know what to say, so he wheeled War Bonnet around and was about to ride when Joseph raised his hand.

"Wait!"

Chris waited and suddenly Man Killer trotted out of the camp leading eight outstanding Appaloosas. Man Killer rode up to Colt. Each horse had a lead line tied with the tail of the horse to its front by a square knot. The young man grinned from ear to ear.

"What's this?" Colt asked.

"A gift from Joseph," the chief said, "a friend I hope you think of sometimes when you have a smoke."

Colt could not refuse the gift. He choked back his emotions and drew his left-hand eagle/snake grip Colt

Peacemaker from his holster and handed it to Joseph, then reached back into his saddlebags and pulled out a box of shells and handed them to the chief. "Thank you" was not spoken among the red nations. The gesture said it.

"What if eight horses is not enough?" Colt said. "I do not want to fight the Cheyenne."

Joseph smiled once more and added, "You will figure out what to do. Farewell, my brother."

He raised his hand and suddenly kicked his spotted horse into a lope toward the camp.

Colt winked at Man Killer and took off toward the Bear Paw Mountains. The wind was chilly in Colt's face, and it made his eyes sting and water. They watered a lot.

Shirley made her very best crabapple and rhubarb pie and rabbit stew for Screaming Horse's dinner. She could only pray that he would value her cooking too much to let Death Yell trade for her the next day. If it wasn't the next day, it would be soon. The talk was all over the camp. No woman had ever been sold for six horses in their band before, and she was a white woman and a slave. She figured her hair was such a novelty that it caused it, not realizing that her figure, face, work habits, cooking ability, and spirit all were cause for the buck's passion. If only Chris would come and save her. She felt like he was near. She wondered where he was, and whether he had heard about the death of Crazy Horse.

*   *   *

Chris Colt and Man Killer traveled long into the night and were in the foothills of the Bear Paws when they saw the fires of Colonel Nelson Miles.

Miles had taken off from Fort Keogh with seven infantry companies and one troop of cavalry on September 18 and was sure that the Nez Perce were on their way to Canada to join up with Sitting Bull. He would stop them, because he knew he was better than all the other military commanders. It was the end of September, and it was cold, very cold.

Seeing the fires of the Fifth Infantry, Chris Colt got an idea. He slid to a stop with Man Killer following suit.

Chris said, "Young brother, I am going down there. It is night, so you can wait here, or go around and meet me on that ridge line later."

"Mighty scout, you forget that I am a Christian. I do not fear fighting at night, for whenever I die, I shall go to heaven. I have been there already—Wallowa Valley. What will we do?"

"Something that will make me feel very good right now," Colt replied with a wink.

Two hours later Chris Colt, wearing moccasins, and Man Killer sneaked away from the camp of Colonel Miles with their considerable booty. They had left their horses in the pines on the hills north of the encampment, and they now returned to them and then headed into the mountains in their search for Shirley Ebert.

It was right after daybreak on the last day of September when the Cheyenne scouts of Colonel Nelson

Miles discovered Chief Joseph's camp and alerted their commander. At eight o'clock in the morning, they crept in on the camp hiding behind the natural terrain. Joseph's original seven hundred men, women, and children had been considerably whittled down. General Miles had six hundred hardened fighting men.

Most of the village was already packed up on travois and the bands were ready to move on. It was only forty miles to the border of Canada from this spot in the Bear Paw range.

The cavalry troop of the Fifth Infantry topped out on a bluff north of the camp and were immediately spotted by the Nez Perce. Looking Glass and Too-Hool-Hool-Zote organized a line of skirmishes in front of the camp as the cavalry charged down the hill, followed by some of the infantry.

Too-Hool-Hool-Zote said in their tongue, "Aim well, brothers, but do not shoot until I yell!"

The line of Nez Perce warriors held their rifles at the ready. Some waited to aim until the advancing troops were a little closer. The fact that the seasoned warriors held their fire and didn't run under the initial charge unnerved the soldiers. Looking Glass rode up to the best marksmen and pointed out officers and sergeants to aim at. The soldiers kept on, the bugle blaring the charge over and over. The warriors held their fire. One hundred fifteen soldiers were attacking. One hundred yards from the village, Too-Hool-Hool-Zote yelled to the braves, and they opened fire. Many soldiers toppled backward out of their saddles. The survivors ran into the arroyos and gulches around them and hid from the deadly fire. The initial fire by the Nez Perce left fifty-three soldiers, almost half of the attack force, lying dead on the battlefield, with numerous wounded.

The adjutant with Nelson Miles recorded the colonel's official statement, upon seeing the decimation of his point force. "They are the best marksmen of any Indians I have ever encountered."

The colonel was upset that so many of his cavalry mounts had been stolen by these Indians right out from under his very nose two nights earlier and decided a few extra horses would have meant more dead soldiers. It seemed like every one who charged could be shot out of the saddle.

Unfortunately for Joseph and his followers, the colonel had already surrounded the camp and the attack was ordered all the way around.

When the attack started, Joseph was with the pony herd with other warriors and family members. They were catching ponies to ride and use for travois in the move.

He yelled to some braves, "Save the horses! Save the horses!"

The braves jumped on some ponies and took off racing north toward Canada. Joseph boosted his daughter up on his best mount and told her to overtake them and bring them back. The twelve-year-old girl, Sarah, raced after the warriors and caught them before they could even reach the cordon of soldiers around the camp. They would have been killed otherwise.

One group of infantry was between Joseph and the

camp, but he charged right through their line, ducked down flat on the spotted pony's back. He made it through the infantry—bullets whistling all around him—without injury.

When Joseph reached the camp, his tepee had not been struck yet and his oldest wife appeared in the door, handing him his eagle-feather-decorated and brass-stud-covered Winchester carbine. His gift from Colt had already been tucked into his waistband.

She said simply, "Here is your gun. Fight!"

He wheeled his horse and started assisting the other chiefs in organizing the camp's defenses.

A second charge by the infantry took place at midday, but it was repelled by the Nez Perce, being led personally on horseback by Chief Joseph. Too-Hool-Hool-Zote had been killed in the first charge and many were upset about that. Joseph also learned that his brother Ollikut, called the "Gentle Giant" by everyone, had also been struck down dead under a hail of gunfire. The leadership of the Nez Perce was down to Joseph, Looking Glass, and old White Bird.

That night, Joseph and Looking Glass sent for three good warriors from each of their bands. The men reported to them in Joseph's lodge, where the council of chiefs met.

Joseph spoke. "You must ride to the country of the Great Mother. Find Sitting Bull and tell him how close we are. Ask him to come and help our people with many warriors. Can you do this for your people?"

All six nodded proudly and left the tepee in a hurry.

Joseph reached for his pipe and said, "Let us rest and enjoy a smoke, brothers."

When he grabbed the small parfleche that held his favorite pipe, he found a leather bag with Lakotah decorations on it. He opened it and found a note inside.

It read: *"I know I will be leaving this night, old friend. I will always remember the Nez Perce with a smile on my face. Enjoy the tobacco and think of me when you smoke this."*

Joseph looked in the bag and saw that it was filled with Colt's good tobacco and cigarette papers. He kept the note's words to himself but he rolled cigarettes for each of the chiefs and elders.

Joseph lit his own. "A gift from our brother Colt."

Chris Colt looked down into the valley and saw the light coming out of the smoke holes of each of Screaming Horse's tepees. It was snowing, and Chris wondered if Joseph had made it into Canada. He and Man Killer retreated back behind the hill and made a fire where they found shelter. The next day he would try to find and save Shirley, even if she was in her bridal tepee.

Shirley cried herself to sleep again. It was cold and snowing hard. How could Chris Colt find her with another winter starting? She wondered if she could make it through another winter. Tears ran down her cheeks and then she decided she was being a fool. She was acting like one of the women she could not stand—a whiny, wispy woman who always worried about what would happen next. She would survive. She would be rescued by Chris Colt, or rescue herself and find him somewhere, somehow, some way. She was worried though, despite her bravado. She had seen the way Death Yell had looked at her that day, and she knew that he would ask for her hand in the morning and she knew that Screaming Horse would not turn down six ponies. Crazy Horse was dead and no Cheyenne warrior would fear a white man, even if it was Chris Colt. How could they know the value he placed on her? Tears dropped onto her buffalo robe, and she dreamed of being held safe and sound in Chris Colt's massive arms.

It was daybreak when the six Nez Perce galloped their horses down the steep gulch and ran into an Assiniboin ambush. The fight didn't last long. The Nez Perce were surprised and outnumbered five to one. The Assiniboin Sioux war party took off down the gulch a half hour later with six bloody scalps attached to their belts and coup staffs.

The village of Screaming Horse was already active at about eight o'clock when Death Yell, dressed in his finest porcupine quill headdress with five eagle feathers decorating it and porcupine-quilled buckskin shirt and leggings, walked his pony toward the tepee of Screaming Horse. His brother walked forward carrying a large buffalo robe, the Hudson's Bay blanket turned into a pair of leggings, the clay pipe, and a bone hair pipe breastplate. Death Yell led six fine ponies. He stopped in front of the chief's tepee and the chief came out, followed by his old wife and Shirley Ebert.

The warrior asked the old man for the *wasicun* woman and showed what he offered. He reached out with the reins toward the chief, and the man looked at the many fine presents. He had only to grasp the offered bridles of the ponies, and the woman would be betrothed to Death Yell. He thought of the taste of her pies and food and the warning of Crazy Horse. But Crazy Horse was dead, he thought, and how rich would he be with all these gifts. His hand went forward and started to take the bridle ropes.

"*Hokahey!*" came the yell in the distance.

All eyes turned to identify the drumming sound, and Shirley's heart leapt up into her throat. A herd of U.S. Cavalry horses galloped into camp.

A woman cried, "*Wasicun!*"

Screaming Horse, however, held up his hand and all watched. Behind the fifteen cavalry horses were eight beautiful Appaloosas, and behind them rode Chris Colt and his young companion Man Killer. One warrior leaving to shoot buffalo raised his bow with an arrow, but Screaming Horse raised his hand.

Colt slid to a stop in front of Screaming Horse and jumped off War Bonnet.

A warrior said, "Wamble Uncha."

Shirley said, "Chris! Oh, Chris!"

But he would not look at her, for he had to do things the Cheyenne way. Colt spoke in a combination of Lakotah and sign language.

His hand went up in friendship, and he barely glanced at Death Yell.

Colt said, "I am Wamble Uncha, brother to Tashunca-Uitco, who now walks the spirit trail. This was my woman, but she was taken fairly in battle by a warrior who must be blessed with great powers by Wakan Tanka. I offer, for her, fifteen horses that I stole from the bluecoats and eight of the finest spotted mountain horses from the herd of Chief Joseph of the Pierced Noses."

By this time, several warriors and Man Killer had rounded up the herd of horses that Colt galloped into the camp. They brought them back to the chief and the horses milled around in the pale morning sun. Man Killer handed the tether rope of the lead Appaloosa to Colt, and the scout, in turn, offered the lead line to the chief.

Tears streamed down Shirley's cheeks, and she could hardly contain herself.

Screaming Horse took the lead line from Colt's hand and nodded affirmatively.

A sob escaped Shirley's lips and she ran into Colt's arms, but he threw her aside, knowing what to expect. Death Yell gave out a bloodcurdling scream and slashed at Colt with a bone-handled knife. Colt's right foot came up in an arc and the inside of his boot instep caught the Cheyenne brave's wrist and it broke with a loud snap. Death Yell's knife flew to the side, but he showed no emotion but anger.

Shirley spoke quickly and said, "Chris, he saved my life!"

Colt jumped back, palm up, and reached behind his back with one hand and pulled out his own magnificent spare Bowie. The other was in a sheath behind his right holster. He flipped the big knife, handle first, to the warrior, who caught it with his left hand, his right hand hanging limply at his side.

Colt, in Lakotah and sign language, spoke again. "You saved my woman and are a brave warrior. I give you a gift. I am brother to the Lakotah and Chyela and will not fight a fine Chyela warrior. Your tribe needs you to help protect the pony herd and women and children. There has been too much killing between the white man and the red man. I have spoken."

Death Yell, now able to save face, looked at the knife and nodded. He stuck it into his sheath and walked forward offering his hurt hand in friendship. Chris gripped it firmly, knowing the pain would have made a normal man faint. They stepped back, eyeing each other, a twinkle in both men's eyes. The warrior and his brother took their gifts and walked away. Screaming Horse walked to his new horses and started checking teeth and cannon bones, admiring them all.

Chris grabbed Shirley and kissed her like it would be his last chance to ever kiss her again. They hugged so hard that they looked like one being. The Chyela women and girls giggled.

Colt, Shirley, and Man Killer left immediately, with Shirley riding on the extra cavalry horse that Colt had saved for her. She did not look back.

Colt and Shirley headed due south escorted by his little adopted brother and friend. Colt would try to get to a train and take Shirley back to her own civilization, and to a big city where she would feel safer.

Colonel Miles had the second of a number of parleys. Chief Joseph wanted assurances that his people would be protected and returned to Idaho. Miles could not promise that, but he kept trying to negotiate.

Colonel Miles kept the camp surrounded, but talked with Joseph several times each day until the fourth of October. The chiefs were again meeting in Joseph's tent. Hearing the approaching cavalry, Looking Glass said that hopefully the six were coming back with Sitting Bull. He stepped out of the door of the tepee and took a long-range cavalry bullet in the forehead from General Howard's approaching column. He was the last casualty of the Nez Perce War. Joseph and White Bird were left, and Joseph sent word to Miles and Howard that he would meet with them the next day. He purposely did not say that White Bird would be there.

That night, White Bird, fourteen warriors, and seven women sneaked their way through the soldiers' lines and made off to the north. They were in Canada before daybreak.

Only Chief Joseph remained to take care of his people. After eating, he dressed in good clothes and sent two men to fetch Howard, Miles, and their staff into the camp. It was there that he made his famous surrender speech that touched people's hearts all over America.

Chief Joseph said, "It is cold and we have no blan-

kets. The little children are freezing to death. My people, some of them, have run away to the hills and
have no blankets, no food; no one knows where they
are—perhaps freezing to death. I want time to look for
my children and see how many of them I can find. Maybe
I shall find them among the dead. Hear me, my chiefs.
I am tired; my heart is sick and sad. From where the
sun now stands, I will fight no more forever."

The 700 nontreaty Nez Perce now numbered 431.
Joseph and the rest were given some blankets and the
Army helped look for the sick children. They were
bound for Fort Lincoln in North Dakota Territory,
Colt's old post with Custer. They did not know that
they would be marched through the main street of
Shirley's former home, Bismarck, and there would be
throngs of cheering citizens applauding them and
handing them food and clothing while a band played
"The Star-Spangled Banner."

Denver was a big city and bustling with activity. The
buildings and people amazed Man Killer and everyone
stared at the young Nez Perce warrior. The trio walked
down the sidewalk and Chris finally stopped in front
of a brick building. The sign read Justice of the Peace.

Colt grabbed Shirley's hand and said, "Shirley, I love
you with all my heart. I will never let you be exposed
to so much danger again. Will you marry me right here,
right now, and have lots of children with me? We'll get
a ranch in southern Colorado, but I will have to leave
and scout for long periods of time. I want—"

She put her fingers on his lips and said, "Are you

going to shut up and let me answer, Chris Colt? Of course I'll marry you and live with you anywhere you want. I love you with all my heart."

Colt swept her up in his arms and lifted her off the ground, kissing her.

Laughing, Man Killer looked at the kissing couple and the many, staring passersby. "The ways of the white man are very strange, I think," he said.

In the back of the crowd, ironically, was Colonel Rufus Birmingham Potter and his foreman. He turned quickly and walked away, as if Colt knew what he looked like.

He turned to his foreman and said, "He must have followed me here. We'll follow him and ambush him when they leave Denver. We'll finally be shut of Mr. Colt."

When the two finished kissing, Man Killer grabbed Colt by the arm and said, "We must talk."

"Right now?" Chris asked.

Man Killer said, "In those people who were watching you and Shirley, there was Potter from Oregon. He snuck away."

"You know what he looks like?"

"Yes, I saw him at Fort Lapwai when he had powwow with General Howard and the agent before you and I met."

Colt squeezed Shirley's hand and smiled.

"Problem?" she asked.

"Problem? Heck no, honey. It is wonderful. He is an enemy, and I guarantee you he will try to ambush us when we leave Denver."

"Aren't you worried?" she asked.

"Worried?"

Colt started laughing, as did Man Killer.

Christopher Columbus Colt looked into the eyes of the woman he loved and said, "Honey, we have him right where we want him. Let's go get hitched."

The trio turned and walked into the door of the office of the Justice of the Peace.

Inside, Chris turned to his betrothed. "If our first child is a boy, can I name him?"

Shirley stood on her tiptoes and pulled him down and kissed him.

"Of course, Chris," she said. "What will we name him?"

Colt smiled and said, "Joseph."